EVERYONE ... EVI
TEDDY L

THE THINGS THAT ARE NOT THERE ... Introduces Teddy London, P.I., on the trail of unearthly winged creatures who stalk a terrified young woman.

SOME THINGS NEVER DIE ... Teddy London's second supernatural case takes him into the ultimate criminal underground—of vampires.

THE THING THAT DARKNESS HIDES ... Monsters and vampires are child's play compared to Teddy London's newest foe—the Prince of Darkness.

ALL THINGS UNDER THE MOON ... A client wants Teddy London to track the butcher of his entire family. There's just one problem: the tracks belong to a wolf.

THE ONLY THING TO FEAR ... Teddy London is lured to Shanghai for an unknown purpose ... until his assistants discover a massive supernatural force that could trigger the Apocalypse.

And now, Teddy London's most horrifying case yet ...
SOME THINGS COME BACK

MORE MYSTERIES FROM THE
BERKLEY PUBLISHING GROUP ...

GARTH RYLAND MYSTERIES: Newsman Garth Ryland digs up the dirt in a serene small town—that isn't as peaceful as it looks ... "A writer with real imagination!" —*The New York Times*

by John R. Riggs

PETER BRICHTER MYSTERIES: A midwestern police detective stars in "a highly unusual, exceptionally erudite mystery series!" —*Minneapolis Star Tribune*

by Mary Monica Pulver

JACK HAGEE, P.I., MYSTERIES: Classic detective fiction with "raw vitality ... Henderson is a born storyteller." —*Armchair Detective*

by C. J. Henderson

TEDDY LONDON MYSTERIES: A P.I. solves mysteries with a touch of the supernatural ...

by Robert Morgan

SOME THINGS COME BACK

ROBERT MORGAN

BERKLEY PRIME CRIME, NEW YORK

SOME THINGS COME BACK

A Berkley Prime Crime Book / published by arrangement
with the author

PRINTING HISTORY
Berkley Prime Crime edition / April 1995

ISBN: 0-425-14690-1

Berkley Prime Crime Books are published by
The Berkley Publishing Group,
200 Madison Avenue, New York, NY 10016.
The name BERKLEY PRIME CRIME and the BERKLEY PRIME CRIME
design are trademarks belonging to Berkley Publishing Corporation.

PRINTED IN THE UNITED STATES OF AMERICA

10 9 8 7 6 5 4 3 2 1

Every author is influenced by those they themselves read for pleasure in their youth. I am no different. I ate from a thousand different tables, but only certain chefs could satisfy me time and time again. They took me to other worlds on a regular basis, filled me with a passion for the written word and, to put it simply, made my life special . . . for all that they showed me—for all that they taught in the showing.

There is no doubt that my style is firmly rooted in theirs, blended from bits and pieces of all of them. My best is their best, there is no doubt. And thus I would, with the greatest respect, like to dedicate the Teddy London series . . .

To Colin Wilson;

To H. P. Lovecraft, James Clavell, and Lester Dent;

To Clifford D. Simak, Jonathan Swift,
Edgar Rice Burroughs, John Brunner, C. J. Cherryh, and
Sax Rhomer;

To Poul Anderson;

To Stan Lee;

To Rex Stout, Jack Vance, Brett Halliday, C. L. Moore,
Jack London, and Percy Bysshe Shelley;

And to
Robert E. Howard.

Writing the Teddy London series has been very special for me. If you, the reader, have enjoyed it, you can now see that I cannot take all the credit.

And, if you have not, please do not blame those listed above. They are all terrific teachers. Perhaps I might have been a better student.

We have left undone those things which we ought to have done; and we have done those things we ought not to have done; and there is no health in us.

—**Book of Common Prayer**

"Know thyself" is indeed a weighty admonition. But in this, as in any science, the difficulties are discovered only by those who set their hands to it. We must push against a door to find out whether it is bolted or not.

—**Montaigne**

It is the confession, not the priest, that gives us absolution.

—**Oscar Wilde**

Prologue

"EEyyyyyyyyaaaaaahhheeehhhaa!"

The piercing shout was loud and echoing and not a good idea, but none of those assembled cared. They . . . had . . . *done it*! Done what no one had thought possible. Done what no one had believed could be done. After all, it was common knowledge: the Confessor had been alive for centuries—millennia. He had escaped every death trap ever set for him—including the knuckle-stiffening touch of time herself. It simply was not possible, and yet they all had seen it.

The Confessor was dead.

"I congratulate you, sir," said one of the dark-cloaked figures, her voice filled with warm admiration despite the dropping temperature setting in around them.

"And I, you . . . madame," answered the man, silvered breath flowing out of his mouth and nose. "This hand has been played far better than I might have hoped. Far better. A thousand times better. We wanted to send a message. By my dancing feet, we've done that now."

With smug cheer turning the thin line of his mouth into a smile that filled his face, the man picked up the binoculars hanging against his chest, having to see it all for himself once again. Running the powerful glasses over the side of the frozen mountain in the distance, he stopped and zeroed in on the figure hanging awkwardly in the limbs of the long-dead tree. Old broken branches pierced the body that had been lifeless even before the force of its impact had shattered it against the spearing, frost-covered limbs.

The man stared, but even seeing the blood on the deeply packed snow below the corpse, even seeing the cracked bones and flesh and strips of lung flapping in the wind—proof positive that the mangled body would never breathe again—still, it was so hard to believe.

So many before them had planned the Confessor's death, thought the woman. So many had built their plans for conquest on the death of that one humble man. So many had tried. Attempts that had only left so many failures. Centuries of failure.

The smile she had allowed herself—the bit of self-indulgence stolen from the attention she should have been paying to her surroundings—had stayed with her, warming her immensely. Looking at the man next to her, watching him as he stared out through his binoculars, she thought of the circumstances that had brought them together.

They had had nothing in common when they were first introduced. She had found him shallow, arrogant, snide, and defensive. And she knew he had found her to be pushy, vulgar, and mercenary. Under any other circumstances, neither would have borne the other's company for more that a few polite moments. But theirs had not been normal circumstances. For, despite all their differences, the pair had found that they did have one thing in common: their shared need to rid the world of the Confessor.

"So," asked the man, dropping the binoculars, their strap pulling taut behind his neck, "how does it feel to have helped kill a legend?"

"Very calming," she answered, putting her hand on his chest, pushing down through the layers of clothing beneath his cloak. "I hadn't realized until just this moment how little chance I thought we had of pulling it off."

"Oh," he agreed, his voice bouncing out from under the weight of his own disintegrating doubts, "don't I understand. Don't I understand exactly what you're saying there. When this . . . this, what would you call it? Assignment, perhaps? Or maybe better . . . *opportunity*. Yes, when this opportunity came my way . . . I mean, first, who could believe such a person even existed. Did you?" When the woman only stared, the man asked her,

"I'm serious. Did you believe in the Confessor when first they told you about him?"

"What? A man who's supposed to be thousands of years old . . . wise as Solomon and Confucius? Who travels around hearing the sins of the world, who knows everything and can't be killed? Sure. What's not to believe?" The man looked deep into the woman's eyes, knowing instantly that she was teasing him. She understood the depth of his gaze, admitting,

"No, of course not. I'm not sure I believe any of it now."

"Especially not the part about no one being able to kill him, eh?"

"Yeah," she agreed, growing surprisingly quiet. "Especially that part, I guess."

Although he heard the sudden shift in the woman's voice, the man did not ask what the matter was. He knew. Almost enemies when he had first found her, they had come to respect each other's abilities, and then . . . even each other.

She had thought for some time that if their search had bound them together much longer, they would certainly have become lovers. She had felt the attraction for some time, was certain he did, too. Now regret flooded the space between them as she realized their time together was over and that it was too late to act upon what she was positive they mutually desired.

Suddenly the air around them was stiff, quiet and awkward. Before either of them could say anything, one of the other dark-cloaked figures approached the pair, carrying a freshly packed pad bag. Slinging it up over his shoulder, the man said,

"My lord, my lady, the doctor tells me the temperature has dropped another three degrees in just the last fifteen minutes. I fear I have to tell you that he says we must be leaving soon, or it is possible we will not be leaving at all."

"Tell the doctor he is as wise as always," said the woman. Then, turning to the man with the binoculars, she gazed at him with her private thoughts wishing sadly for one last time as she said,

"Shall we be going?"

"Yes," agreed the man, knowing no matter how long he

stared at the blasted, shattered corpse in the distance, that it would never move again. "Yes."

Gathering up the sniper rifle leaning against the frozen tree stump to his right, the man gave a hand signal to the others in the party that they should begin the trek down the trail back to their base camp. He paused for just a second so he might enjoy his achievement—trying to make the moment last as long as possible. Finally, though, the time had come to go on with life, to remember mundane things like the cold and the future.

Falling in behind the woman, the last on the trail before him, he looked off into the distance once more, oblivious to the light flakes beginning to fall. Ahead of the man, listening to the packed snow crunch beneath his boots, she turned her head and smiled, saying,

"It *was* glorious . . . wasn't it?"

"Yes," he admitted, knowing exactly what she meant. "Yes, it was."

And then they walked on in silence, following the doctor and the rest of their party down the mountain path to the relative warmth and safety of their tents. But after only a few more steps, the man caught the woman's shoulder with his hand. Stopping her quietly, he looked into her eyes with the desire she had come to recognize. She smiled again, as did he.

Then, holding her arms behind her, he lunged forward with his head and drove his teeth into her neck, ripping her throat out with one coldly efficient motion. She fell backward, stunned, mute, her life's blood pumping out across the snow. Her eyes glazing over, she stared up at the man whose love she thought she had—the man who had just murdered her.

And as she did, she felt her sustaining energies, what some would call the soul, slipping away—felt them flying into the cold-eyed figure standing over her.

"Glorious," he said, his tongue licking his lips. And then, when there was no life left within the dried husk at his feet, the man continued to make his way down the mountainside, toward the unsuspecting world below.

• • •

On the far mountain, the man in the white parka moved toward the figure in the tree. Looking up at the broken body, he felt a small sadness as he thought about what the violent death meant to him. He had not known the man hanging in the ice-covered branches, had never heard the name of the Confessor until the second the man in the dark cloak had pulled the trigger and slammed the holy man's lungs out through the back of his body.

"Tough gig," said the man in the white coat. Then he reached up to the Confessor's right hand and removed the ring from its index finger. After slipping it onto his own, he sighed at the weight of the responsibilities he had just assumed.

Yeah, he thought, the memories of fifty thousand years of human history flooding through him . . . real tough gig.

Slowly he turned and walked back the way he had come, wondering what was going to happen next.

1

"So who wants to go first?"

From his position behind his desk, the detective stared out through the ranks of the men and women that made up the management level of the Theodore London Agency—his agency. His job supervisors were gathered in the office on Friday afternoon to get the weekly reports out of the way. It was a boring, usual bit of routine, each supervisor taking his turn, reporting to either London or one of his partners on where all of their current investigations were at the moment.

"I'll take a shot at first place," volunteered Farley, a large transplanted Texan.

"Aw, stuff it, Farr," said Dommik, the ex–military man. "You pull this every week. Grab the first slot, float your tales, and then out the door."

"Hey, you snooze, you lose."

"Lose the cliché, you doughnut. I take first run today. Unlike you and your flimsy excuses, I've got a legitimate appointment tonight. For once the door's going to see my backside first. You read me?"

The detective sat back in his chair, pushing himself against the buttons holding in its punched leather. Normally by now he would have interceded, putting a choke on the boyish bicker starting up on the other side of his desk. He let the two go for once, though, suddenly filled with amusement at the pair. As he watched the two friends rib each other, he felt an ache of memory for the days when he had felt the same way, for when his life could still be lived on so simple a level.

His mind stretched back over his life, key moments exploding through his memory summed up for him in split-second pictures. He had been just like Farley and Dommik, young and waiting for his big moment in life.

He had seen service to his country and his city, and he had turned away from both to be by himself.

Something had pushed him to an instance of time into which only he could fit. The point had come when the world had filled with monsters to the degree where someone had to stop them. Fate chose Theodore London to be that person.

"Read this, amigo," growled Farley. "My honey lamb is expecting me and nobody thwarts the wants and wishes and desires of she who must be obeyed."

"Well," said London, ready to get things moving, "there's a first time for everything. Mr. Dommik . . . you had a report you wanted to make?"

"Yes, sir. I've already turned in my people's time sheets to Mrs. London and briefed Mr. Morcey on those three skip traces we inherited from the people down at Morrison, which just leave the . . ."

While Dommik talked and Farley fumed and the others in the room smiled good-naturedly at the big man's consternation, London listened to the ex–military man's report with one part of his brain, while he ruminated over the past with another. It had been a long time since he had thought about his contacts with the supernatural. When Lisa Hutchinson had first come to him she had pulled him and a number of others into a confrontation with a force from another dimension that shattered all of the survivors' worldviews. They were left with the knowledge that ghosts and vampires and demons were real things. Not just stories or hallucinations or myths, but real—as real as the floor beneath his feet or the window behind his head.

Dommik finished and Farley offered to fight anyone else in the room who wanted the second spot. Two of the agency's female supervisors set to teasing him, telling him they both wanted their shot at him. Farley implored London to save him from such an ungentlemanly fate, and the detective accommodated him. He never minded letting the big man twist in the wind once in a while. As even the Texan's best friend, McClullen, was wont to admit, Farley just had a style that begged to be stomped on from time to time. But fun was fun, and after the pair had had theirs London chastised them gently, then got everyone back to work.

Even as London listened to their reports, to the submission of their facts, as well as the question/speculation period where they all commented on each other's different problems, he still did it with just half his brain. The other half was dwelling back on the whirlwind period a few years earlier, when it seemed every other week brought a new menace to his doorstep. As the three of them closed out their end-of-the-week business together in his office, it was still the same.

Paul Morcey, a balding one time maintenance man who sported a nearly foot-long ponytail, loosened his tie. Glad the end-of-week reports were gathered he did not seem to notice his partner's distraction. In truth, he had noticed it, but he had also thought nothing of it. London was a man who followed the external world easily even when deep in thought. His wife had noticed his lack of attention, but had also paid it no mind, basically for the same reasons as Morcey. Work proceeded apace, the balding man and the young woman feeding the detective information, he accepting it in an almost, but not quite, absent fashion.

Finally, when they had finished everything except for the most minor of details, London suddenly interrupted their normal routine by pointing out the window. As he drew his two partners' attention to the view, he said,

"Maybe I'm just tired of working but tell me . . . when's the last time you saw a New York sky that blue? That perfect? Well?"

As both his wife and his best friend looked out over the city, the detective let his gaze fall down into the bit of green he could see, the few trees within his view that the dull ache of daily life in Manhattan had not yet killed. He stared at them for a long time, ignoring the people passing beneath their full summer branches. None of them seemed as interesting as the trees, not the woman with the feathered hat, the pair of bottled water delivery men, the dog walker struggling to hold her eight leashes, or the suit-and-tie types with their briefcases and hurried walks or even the large man in white with the long slick hair. London ignored them all, every second cranking his view closer until finally he was looking into the leaves, inspecting the veins running through them.

Shifting his interest, he inspected the set of trees for a long moment, looking for what life they might be hosting. He easily spotted two birds' nests and traces of city squirrels. Squinting, he took his examination closer, finding spiderwebs and a score of different insects. Then suddenly, he found himself identifying the various bruises and molds and fungi working their way into the bark.

Carrying this a little far, aren't we?

Startled by the sound of the voice within his head, London broke away from the window, turning abruptly back to his desk. Before he could explain his actions, his eyes suddenly bubbled over. Tears slid down both his cheeks while a dozen other voices in his mind—voices he had not heard in over four years—came awake with questions.

What? What are you crying about? asked one voice within his head.

Trees? We're losing it over trees now?

Maybe we've just been working too hard.

Yeah. Sure. And maybe you're just falling apart. First you're letting those two nitwits turn this place into a kindergarten with their bicker fest, and now this? What? Are you just getting goofy?

"Teddy?" came Lisa's voice, softly at his side. "Are you crying?"

"Jeez-it," said Morcey, moving forward out of his seat. "What's da matter, boss?"

"Nothing," answered London, feeling silly. "I guess I'm just getting old." Lisa and Morcey stayed silent. The woman pushed her chestnut curls back behind her ears and narrowed her eyes. Morcey pulled his mouth to one side, pursing his lips at the same time. Seeing the doubt in their faces, the detective told them,

"It's nothing. Really." The pair continued to stare uneasily, prompting the detective to admit,

"Well, all right. And . . . I know this will sound a little crazy, perhaps, but it's just that we push and push and push and when do we take a break? When do we stop and say enough is enough? I mean, we *are* rich. Are we doing it just for the money? For the fame and glory—of which I remind you there is none of in this business?"

"Teddy," asked Lisa, concerned about the change in her husband's manner, "what's going on? If this is just some male 'I'm over forty' thing, then okay. I can deal with it." Her voice grew light as she said, "That's my job." Then, however, the lightness retreated as she added,

"But, I would really appreciate being told if it's creepy-crawler time again."

The detective looked at his wife, genuinely surprised. Realizing his mouth was hanging open, he licked his lips to give himself a second's pause, then said,

"Sweetheart, I'm, I don't know . . . maybe I'm just tired of the routine. We used to be world savers, remember? We saved the entire world. Heck, why stop there? We saved the entire universe. More than once. This . . . this all"—he waved his arms around, trying to express dissatisfaction, but only looking like a man confused—"doesn't it seem, well . . . dull, once in a while? I listen to Farley and Dommik argue like a pair of overgrown kids and, I don't know . . . suddenly I just feel like I'm getting old and that there's never going to be anything exciting in my life again."

London focused his attention on his wife, only to be surprised at her reaction. Her blue eyes were open wide and unblinking. Her face was tense, the skin tight and rapidly draining of color. As he looked closer, he could see that her mouth was open slightly, small bubbles of foam moving back and forth on her lower lip were the only clue he had that she was still alive. The effect only lasted a moment, but it wasn't long enough to startle the detective, making him ask,

"What is it, honey?" As Lisa groped for an answer, their partner, ex–maintenance man Paul Morcey volunteered,

"What is it? I can field that one, boss. What it is, is that neither one of us can believe what we're hearin'. I mean, you kiddin' someone or somethin'? Yer talkin' about perfect blue skies one second, then yer starin' off inta space for ten minutes, and when you stop that, you start cryin' on us. Then, to crown that, you start goin' on about life being borin' because all the things from Hell we've pounded inta paste have stopped tryin' to put the nab on us." London squirmed in his chair uncomfortably as the balding man added,

"Since when are you upset about that part of our work bein' behind us? I thought worryin' about that kinda stuff stopped for you about the time little Kevin and Kate showed up."

London's eyes flashed across the right side of his desk to the picture he kept there. It was a photograph of himself and Lisa with their small son and daughter, taken only a month before on an excursion to Sesame Place. The four of them were in their bathing suits, all wet and laughing. The detective focused on the images of his wife and himself, forced to admit that neither of them looked much like people who missed fighting the forces of darkness.

Searching inside his mind, London asked all of the voices within his head what they thought was going on. The detective had long before developed the ability to consciously listen to the various facets of his own personality. He could argue with his own mind—as well as with the hundreds of ancestor memories he had tapped into.

What? asked one side of his brain. We can't shed a few tears without putting everyone in a panic?

Tears are shed for a reason. Have we got one?

Living in New York City is enough to make anyone cry. Not us.

Then what is it? What's going on?

Maybe Lisa is right. Maybe it *is* creepy-crawler time again.

Proof? he asked. Evidence? Feelings? Anything?

"Teddy?"

"Yes, sweetheart?"

"It's coming again . . . isn't it? This 'missing the action' stuff—something's coming, and the back of your mind is getting ready for it." She paused, then asked again,

"Isn't it?"

The detective felt his fingers stiffening. Their tips hard against the top of his desk, he felt them pressing down into the wood, felt the tension coming back at him as he did so, pulling its way up his arm. He winced as he felt his lower teeth grinding sideways against his uppers, his tongue pressed tight against the roof of his mouth.

Straining his senses to the utmost, he searched everything around him, reviewed all that had happened to him that day—the day before—everything that he had done, had heard, seen . . . thought.

Nothing, he told himself. No visions, no premonitions, no symbols, no signs—nothing at all. Nothing that has just fallen into place, no vague instincts, no worrisome nagging gut feelings . . . nothing to point to some winged nightmare disturbance coming toward us.

London went over all the information available to him in a moment, assembling an answer. He simply had no proof, no matter how substantial, that anything supernatural was heading toward them. Just the fact that he had looked out the window and seen a beautiful day, and for some reason started to cry. Looking out the same window again, he stared at the same trees. Whatever had set him off was there, hidden in the thickly leaved branches. The detective played back everything he had seen there in his mind, watching the trees move in the light breeze, watching the people move beneath them . . .

"What?" asked Lisa.

She had seen the spark in her husband's eyes—just the tiniest hint of a glimmer, but she had seen it. She had seen the look in his eyes before and she knew he had remembered something.

"What?" she repeated. "What was it?"

Not the trees, he thought, the people moving beneath them.

London closed his eyes for a second, sending his memory back to the people he had ignored earlier. Skipping over all but one, he focused on the man in white.

Large, he remembered. Long, slick hair. Tall, sure of himself, moving fast.

Headed this way.

The detective opened his eyes, startled. The voice he had just heard had not spoken to him in a long time. Blocking out everything in his memory except the man in white, London zeroed in on the man's face, and then remembered where and when he had seen him before. In a playful moment years earlier, he had named his revolver Betty and the knife he always carried with him Veronica. With nothing playful in his voice, he suddenly said,

"Come here, girls."

And then, as he reached down into the drawer where he kept his .38 and his blade, he let his hands find the weapons as he turned to Lisa and said,

"You were right. It is happening again."

And then, before anyone could respond, they heard the sound of the elevator stopping on their floor.

2

All three of them heard the slowing hum of an elevator car stopping at their floor. Their heads turned as one, all wasting a split second of time staring through the walls, seeing the elevator in their minds, waiting for the doors to open. At the clicking sound of the doors beginning to open, both Morcey and Lisa jumped up and started for the door.

"Sweet bride of the night," said the balding man, practically knocking his chair over. "I just knew the party wasn't over for good."

"Don't sound so anxious," added Lisa.

"Yeah, right," added London, his own hand dropping two empty half-moon clips into his drawer. "Try to show some restraint, would you? We don't really know what's coming."

Neither answered, hurrying to their offices to secure their own weapons. Despite his cautionary words, the detective had already hot-loaded Betty before they had cleared their chairs. As he slid the .38 into a partially open drawer his partners reached their own offices and their own weapons. By that time they could hear the elevator's metal doors sliding completely back into their walls, accompanied by the carpet-muffled approach of footsteps toward the door. Each of the agency members began counting off the steps in their heads. All of them knew when their time would be up.

"Thirteen," whispered London under his breath. As he did, the footsteps stopped just outside the agency's main door. The sound of the knob just beginning to turn seemed to echo throughout the offices as Morcey slid his always loaded Auto-Mag into the back of his trousers. He pulled his jacket over the large handgun and ran back into the waiting room, throwing himself onto a couch. As he grabbed a magazine, Lisa flew out of her office and slid into place behind the secretary's desk in the waiting room.

Get a grip, thought the detective, half to himself, half to his partners. Remember, we don't know what's going on here—who this guy is, why he's here, what he wants.

London did not stop to wonder if Lisa or Paul could hear him. He had realized years earlier that people in close proximity to one another—people open and trusting of those in contact with them—could always hear each other's thoughts on a subconscious level. He was as sure that they were receiving him on some level as he was that he had met the man coming through his door, indeed as sure as he was that the man coming through his door was the man he had seen heading for his building.

London also knew he would be able to hear the thoughts in both their heads—see what they saw—if he emptied his own mind and concentrated. Closing his eyes, he sat back in his chair, forced himself to take a deep breath ... to relax ... and then, he simply listened.

"Hello," came a male voice, working his way around the slowly opening door. "Is anybody home?"

"Come in, please," said Lisa, playing secretary, putting herself in the target seat to see what kind of attention the action would draw, consciously ready to send her husband what information she could. "Can we help you?"

"I guess," answered the man in white coming through the door. "That's what I'm here to find out."

As the door opened wider, Lisa saw a tall man, one quite overweight, but with the strength to carry it. He had long, dark hair that hung below his shoulders. As she took in his face, she noted that he was unshaven.

Two, three days' growth, she thought. Complexion looks good, though, so he's not living on the street. Just doesn't like to shave. Brown eyes—soft, easygoing, compassionate. Intelligent, though, humorous even.

Big, thought Morcey. Awkward, moves with that round man's bounce. Never quite smooth enough. Thick shoulders, wide, powerful—this boy could take some punish-

ment. Some things in his pockets, but nothin' suspicious.
What I can see of them. No bags, either. *Looks* clean anyway.

"What seems to be your problem?" asked Lisa, keeping
her attention focused on the man in white, her eyes going
deep into his, his into hers.

Her eyes passed over his hands, sending London more
information. The detective could see what she saw. He
noted their size—large, mittlike. His fingers were hairy—
far more wiry than the hair on his head. Several of his
knuckles seemed as if they had been broken over the
years. No jewelry on his neck, wrists, or hands, except for
a single gold ring on his left hand. Simple carvings covered the visible portion of the band, looking like a foreign
language—one that even London's ancestor voices could
not recognize.

"People," he answered, a thin self-amused smile stretching his lips. Morcey stirred on the couch, focusing on the
man's face. He looked at the smile, curious at its interpretation.

What's so funny? wondered Morcey. What Lisa said, or
what he said? What's the big joke, pal? And what's it
gonna cost us to find out?

"Any people in particular, sir?" asked Lisa, willing to
play whatever game the big man had in mind.

"Yes," he said. "Those would be the people that are trying to kill me again."

Then, without thinking of how unnatural his question
might sound, Morcey purposely drew the attention of the
man in white, asking, "Would those be people who, like,
tried to kill you and failed, or people who did kill you and
now want to do it again?"

"Very good question," answered the big man. "This
isn't going to be as hard as I thought."

"Not a good answer, though," came London's voice. As
everyone turned toward the back of the room, the detective
walked out of his office, hand extended, saying,

"My name is Theodore London. I'd like you to meet my

partners Lisa London and Paul Morcey." Coming up close to the man in white, the detective said, "That's a pretty serious problem you have, either way. Why don't we talk about it? Mister . . . ?"

"People call me the Confessor."

3

London raised one eyebrow.

Oh yeah, he thought, things are sure starting up again, all right.

"The Confessor, eh? And who exactly would it be that calls you this?"

"Everyone who knows me, or knows about me."

"And you say people are trying to kill you ... again. Well, as my partner asked, is that ..."

The Confessor raised his hand, begging the detective for a pause. When London granted it, the man in white said,

"Thank you. To answer your question ... I was recently murdered in a fairly brutal manner and I would like you to find out who did it. And yes, I do know exactly how that sounds. I'm not quite used to thinking of it in those terms myself. But since the story that explains it all takes a while, perhaps we could retire to your office?"

"Sure," answered London, caution intruding on his tone. He extended his hand, pointing toward his office, saying, "Please, go in ... have a seat." Then the detective turned toward his partners, asking them,

"Well, want to sit in?"

"Oh, yeah," answered Morcey in his best Curly Joe Howard imitation. "Coit'nly."

Lisa furrowed her brow, giving London a "what do you think" look, and followed the balding man into the detective's office. Taking a deep breath and then sighing silently, wondering what he was getting into, London returned to his desk, slipping himself into his chair as he asked,

"So, is it *Mister*, or ..."

"Just Confessor."

"Well then, Confessor, is that what I should have called you the last time we met?"

"You do remember," answered the man in white, his open face instantly revealing both his surprise and his pleasure. "Thank you. That's quite a compliment."

"Oh no," said the detective, "credit where credit is due. Our little talk did me a lot of good." Turning to Lisa and Morcey, London explained,

"The Confessor and I met briefly a number of years ago, in the gardens at Columbia University. It was right after Maxim Warhelski came to us with his . . . problem."

"The werewolf," said the man in white. London turned back toward him, staring, his eyes narrowed. The detective had thought no one outside his tight circle of friends knew about the agency's supernatural dealings. He was especially sensitive about the time half a decade earlier when he had been stalked by a massive werebeast from the beginning of time. Many of his friends had died at the thing's hands—too many.

London had followed the monster around the world until he found it in the mountains of China. After their confrontation, it had taken the detective the better part of a year to find his way back home. His homecoming had been stalled by a world-stunning calamity—the near destruction of the Earth by a runaway meteor. The two events and his wanderings had been tied together, and the year-long battle had been the last thing from beyond to happen to London. Since then, he had married, begun a family, and simply tried to make his way in the world like any other man.

"I'll bite," said London. Although he did not bother to deny the existence of the werewolf, he nonetheless forced his tone to stay even, working at not giving away the level of his concern. "How did you know about Warhelski's werewolf?"

"I came across an FBI man about two years ago. His name was Roth." The man in the white suit stared straight into London's eyes, saying,

"He had a great deal to talk about."

He knows everything. The thought flashed through the detective's mind. Looking back into the big man's eyes,

London could see that there was something serious going on in the man's head. Figuring that he had no choice other than to learn what it was, the detective said,

"I think we'd better start at the beginning. Why don't you tell us why you're called the Confessor. What that means, how it got started—you know, everything." The large man considered London's request. It seemed obvious to the detective that he had had something else in mind, but he acquiesced, saying,

"Sure, why not?" Then the man in the white suit clacked his teeth together sharply, his face going darkly serious. As Morcey and Lisa sat forward, the large man in the client chair focused his deep brown eyes on London, telling them all,

"I've been around for a long time. Or at least, the Confessor has. Let me explain. You see, the first time I—God, what would you call it?—manifested, perhaps? Whatever. The first man to think of himself as the Confessor lived before recorded time. I can't tell you where he was because the world has changed so much since then. Geographically, I mean."

The man in white could feel the emotions of those around him. There was confusion in the air. Resentment and traces of doubt hung over those he had come to for aid. Knowing that he had little choice other than to win them over, though, he closed his eyes for a second, marshaling his thoughts. Then, forcing a separation between the nearly overwhelming spirit known as the Confessor and his own self for the moment, he said,

"The Confessor is an identity that has existed for as long as there have been people. How it works I don't know. All I can tell you is that when one Confessor dies someone else takes over. It—the spirit of the Confessor—just reaches out and finds the next body in line."

The large man went silent for a moment, his eyes still and far away. Finally, without looking at anyone in the room, he said quietly,

"It was a few months ago when I got the call. The funny thing is, the last Confessor wasn't even dead yet.

They hardly ever are. Somehow, though, fate, destiny, whatever ... something reached out and made me— compelled me—to go halfway around the world. I found myself in the mountains in Switzerland, waiting for people to kill the old Confessor so I could take over his position. I don't know how I knew what to do, but I watched the whole thing take place ... through binoculars ... saw this party of about twenty track this old man through the mountains. I watched them blow him away with rifles from what looked like miles off. Then, when they couldn't see me, I moved in and took his ring."

The new Confessor held up his hand, displaying the symbol of his identity for all to see. With his hand still raised, he continued, saying,

"That's when everything changed. That's when I stopped being me and started being the Confessor. Suddenly all the old guy's memories were in my head—and the guy's before him, and the guy's before him, and ... you get the idea. What I'm saying is that instantly I could remember the Vikings sailing off to raid England, the Holy Roman Empire, villages in Africa—everything. I saw two of the Crusades, I saw the building of the Great Wall, Babylon, the Alexandrian Library. Everything—I've seen it. Everywhere—I've been there. Places I'd never even heard of before, let alone visited, were suddenly crystal clear in my mind. All of history was clear in my mind."

Morcey stared as if at the movies. Lisa sat back in her chair, her fingers threaded in her lap, thumbs tapping each other silently as she listened. London wore his professional face, the one that neither believed nor disbelieved, the one that merely waited and listened without passing judgment. Far beyond worrying about the judgment of others, the large man continued to talk.

"And then," he told them, "the urges began again. The same force that had dragged me around the world, making me find the body of the last Confessor—take his ring and his memories—now urged me to roam across the face of the planet ... made me look for my own sinners to listen to."

The man in white rose up out of his chair, not moving away from the space in front of London's desk, just needing to stand. Turning from side to side, facing each of the three with him in their turn, he said,

"Just like all the other men before me who've been moved to find the ring and put it on, I started searching out the scum of the Earth . . . or they me—I'm still actually not sure how it works. And what does it matter?" Moved by a sense of sudden urgency, one the detective could see in the changes in the large man's face—in the very air around him—London listened as the man in white said,

"Each of them would latch onto me as if I were their salvation. Each of them pouring out their horrors, telling me all the details of their particular crimes." Waving his hands, the large man spat,

"We live in a sick world, one filled with monsters. I've got all its rot in my head now. All its filth and corruption and sorrow. They come to me and they pour it out like gravy over Christmas potatoes." And then, finally having reached the point he wanted to make, the man in white said,

"And that . . . that's the problem. Several of the ones I've talked to recently—what they've told me—there're horrible things coming, Mr. London. War. Vast amounts of it. War and death and nations red with blood such as no one has ever seen. Not even me."

"Are you talkin' nukes?" asked Morcey.

"Worse. A thousand times worse." The man in white focused his eyes on London's, drilling the pain within him deep into the detective. His voice cracking, he said,

"I've talked to Hitler. I've listened to the sins of, and given absolution to, a man who oversaw the murder of millions of people. *Millions.* It took him years to do it, and before the end . . . in the end even his soul couldn't bear what he had done. And now, there's a force on the wind that doesn't even consider Hitler's work a start. Billions are going to die this time. I mean it. Billions."

But then, the man in white paused again, his left hand

curling into a fist. The air rushed out of him in a violent wheeze, one so stunning he fell back into his seat, grabbing blindly for its arms with his free hand. His eyes squeezed tight; his face that of a man trying to hold in a scream after a wave of pain—he talked through tightly clenched teeth, telling those assembled,

"It's funny. When we met, Mr. London, I was just Vincent . . . Vinn, Vinn . . ."

And then, slowly, his fist uncurled, his fingers straightening as he laughed. At first he tried to keep his amusement to himself. But then the noise of it grew louder as he stopped trying to disguise the sounds. Lifting his head, he stared forward at London through wet blinking eyes as he said,

"I can't remember."

"What can't you remember," asked the detective, knowing the answer.

"I've been able to hold it back so far," said the man in white, wiping at his eyes with both hands. "But each time I try to, to . . . to just be me again . . . it's always shorter and shorter. Now"—the man in white's voice broke into a series of bitter laughs.

"Now," he said, no longer bothering to fight back the tears, "I don't even remember my name."

And then, before any of the members of the London Agency could comment, the large man suddenly sat straight up in his chair. When he did so, London could see his face clearly. Gone was the wild desperation in his eyes, the hard lines creasing his round face with anxiety. Gone was the aura of confusion that had seemed to engulf him. Looking forward, and then to both sides, the man in white held out his hands, palms up, opening himself to those around him as he said in a voice deeper, calmer than any he had used so far,

"We're sorry. We did not mean to bother you."

And suddenly, London knew that the happy-go-lucky student he had met years earlier was gone, absorbed by a consciousness that had chosen the young man as its vehicle. Testing his theory, the detective asked,

"Do you remember your name now?"

"Of course," replied the man in white. "I am called the Confessor."

"Yeah," replied London, sadly, knowing his troubles were just beginning, "that's what I was afraid of."

4

"Whoa, Confessor," said London as the man in white headed for the door, "you've got some explaining to do."

"We are sorry," said the large man apologetically. "We have upset you." Looking around the room, taking in Lisa's and Morcey's faces as well as the detective's, he added, "All of you. It is best if we leave now."

"Oh it is, huh?" growled London, pushing himself and his chair back from his desk. "Just like that."

"We understand your problem," answered the Confessor. "You are feeling responsible for the pleas of the one who came to you. He begged your help and you feel honor bound to give it. Please, let this nobility pass. The one you wish to help is here. In the . . . how can I phrase it . . . *democracy* which is"—the man in white paused for a second, then continued, saying, ". . . us, his attempt to change future history has been voted down. We have nothing further to say."

"Nothing further to say?" repeated London. "You talk about billions dying, and then you tell us you don't want to say any more? What the hell kind of game is this?" Wheeling about in his chair, the detective ordered,

"Paul, get on the horn, pronto—see if you can find Father Bain." While the ex-maintenance man hurried out of the room, London stood, saying,

"Now you listen to me, I haven't had any trouble out of the goddamned Twilight Zone for years now. I was getting nice and comfortable just doing my job and going home at night to my wife and kids."

"Then, please," answered the Confessor in a haughty, almost snide tone, "go back to your schedule. Your place in what is coming has been foretold. You are not needed."

"The *man* you were before you became a committee

thought differently. He obviously thought your little group was making some kind of mistake—"

"He simply did not wish to surrender his individual opinion to that of the greater good. There is no further need for discussion."

London got up out of his chair, anger knotting the muscles in his shoulders, narrowing his eyes. He felt heat rising in his face—forehead, ears, cheeks—cold lacing his spine. His voice dropping down into a fierce range, he practically growled as he came around his desk.

"Now maybe you don't understand some of what I was telling you. I've seen this kind of shit before, and the double talk you're peddling now isn't putting me off. You might have noticed I said I haven't had any trouble with the supernatural for a while. Well, it has been a while." Stepping closer to the Confessor, the anger so visible in his face it made the man in white step back, London continued, saying,

"A long enough while for me to make a life for myself. A long enough while to get married . . . to have a couple of kids. Tell me, Confessor, in that long, altruistic history you mentioned earlier, have you ever been a father?"

"No, of course not," answered the Confessor sharply, his voice firm and clear. "Before the call—yes, many times . . . but afterwards—never. Ties to the outside world are not compatible with our duties."

"Surprise, surprise," responded London. "I would have never guessed. Well, let me tell you something about those of us who do have ties to the outside world. They make life real to us. They give us something to live for—and something to worry about. For instance, when someone tells you that billions of people are going to die, one of the first things that pops into your mind is . . . hey, are my kids going to be part of those billions? And even if they aren't, what kind of world is going to be left after a few billion people are killed? Is that the kind of world I want to leave for my kids?"

"Mr. London," said the Confessor, turning on his heel, "we are making our exit now."

"The hell you are."

The detective grabbed the man in white's shoulder, spinning him back around. He was surprised, however, when the Confessor leaned into the turn, bringing his left hand up to slap away London's right. He pressed his attack, bringing his right hand forward instantly, aiming it for the detective's throat. Any other man would most likely have fallen for the sudden, savage attack, but Theodore London was not any man that had opposed the Confessor in all his thousands of years.

The detective felt the second blow coming without even seeing it. Without hesitation, he stepped back far enough to catch the Confessor's wrist rather than take the blow. Stepping sideways, London jerked down the captured arm and then twisted it up, moving behind the man in white at the same moment. Then, shoving him forward, he slammed the Confessor's face into the wall, breaking the plaster beneath with the force of the blow.

"Lisa, make sure the outer door is locked, would you?" Without questioning her husband's actions, knowing what he was doing and why, the young woman moved off without hesitation, throwing both the door's locks and then going so far as to switch on their security system. While she did, London told the man in white,

"Nice moves, pops, but not good enough. Try and get something straight here, I'm one guy who doesn't care how many tough sons of bitches you're carrying around in your noggin. I'm the Destroyer, remember? I mush up guys like you for breakfast. Now, you want to start talking to me or you want to keep talking to the wall?" The Confessor strained against London's hold, but quickly found he could not move the detective. The side of his cheek pushed deep into the cracked plaster, the smell of paint and dust in his nose, the man in white said,

"You do not understand. We cannot break the vow."

"What vow?" asked London. Letting up on the pressure he was using to hold the Confessor in place, he asked,

"What are you talking about?"

"We cannot reveal what others have told us. We cannot.

That is why people trust the name of the Confessor in the first place." The man in white wheezed, sucking down a large gulp of air as best he could with half his mouth and one of his nostrils pressed closed against the wall. Calming himself, the Confessor steadied his nerves, relaxing all of his muscles. Feeling what was happening throughout the large man's body, London cautioned his prisoner, saying,

"Don't try it. If you think I'm going to fall for you going limp, you're not as smart as you think you are. I'm not as concerned for your comfort as you might hope I am."

"And what will you do?" demanded the Confessor, sudden rage turning his arms and legs to iron. "Will you hold me here against this wall forever?"

"No," answered the detective. "I'll just put a bullet in your head and wait for the next Confessor to show up for your ring. Or maybe I'll just put it on myself and see what I can get out of it."

"You wouldn't dare," snarled the man in white.

"Billions are going to die," said London, his voice cold and thin. "And I can tell from your little coy act that my family is supposed to be a part of the dead. You don't know me too well. I dare plenty." And then, without knowing why, a voice within the detective's brain told him,

Send Lisa to her office.

Without questioning the rightness to the feel of the command, London said,

"Lisa, would you go to your office?"

The woman started moving instantly, too used to the detective always having a good reason for anything he said or did to question him. She stopped in the doorway, however, thinking that she might not understand exactly what he was asking.

"Teddy," she asked, suddenly realizing that she did not know what he wanted her to do. "What is it you want me to do?"

"I want you to go to your office."

"I understand," she told him as a suspicion that something was wrong began to dig its way through her. "But *why* do you want me to go to my office?" Struggling to hold on to the Confessor, the detective told her,

"Because I . . . I . . ." And then London suddenly realized that he did not know. Searching through his mind for the voice that had given the command, he found it buried deep within him. It was the voice he heard only once in a great while . . . not one of his ancestors, all of whom he had learned to talk to, but some other, primal part of him. It was a distant voice, one that only spoke at the most crucial of times—the one other people called intuition. Taking hold of his, he asked it,

What was that all about? Why did you think Lisa should be in her office?

Protection, came its answer.

London stood away from the Confessor, slightly dazed, wondering what his mind could be talking about. What had it realized, he asked himself. What had it come across that he had not seen, had not noticed? Then, as the split-second of self-questioning ended, the detective pointed out the doorway, shouting,

"Go! Now!" As Lisa ran for her office, London yelled,

"Paul! Get ready—something's coming!"

The ex–maintenance man came running from his office, pulling his Auto-Mag free.

"What's doin', boss?"

"I don't know, but I can feel it." Turning toward the Confessor, London asked,

"Any ideas, smart guy?"

But then, before the man in white could answer, a sense of something moving toward them made the detective yell, *"Down!!"*

London and Morcey hurled themselves to the floor instantly, just as a score of bullets smashed through the windows behind them.

5

Glass exploded throughout the room. Broken bits of wood and brick ricocheted off every surface, slivers of glass and steel embedding themselves in the ceiling, walls, and floor. Incendiary bullets followed the lead ones, splattering the walls with popping bursts of chemical fire. As more bullets followed the first wave, the straight lines of patterned fire began to eat their way into the wall as Morcey shouted,

"Somebody don't play too nice, do dey, boss?"

"Hey," answered the detective, "that's all right. Neither do we."

London inched his way across the floor rapidly, slicing himself open in a score of spots on the scattered glass as he made his way to the windows. The ceiling sprinklers came on, raining down on London and Morcey, adding to the confusion. The chemical-based flames paid scant attention to the water, however, merely causing the fires to smolder, multiplying the insanity in the office. Ignoring all distractions, though, the detective pulled Betty from her spot in the drawer as he went past, thinking rapidly as he crawled along,

We're on the thirteenth floor. That spray came in on a downward slant. I didn't hear a helicopter ... so what the hell could they have used to do that? For that matter, who the hell *is* our mysterious little 'they'? Are they after the Confessor or us—or both? Who cares right now? Most important, where did they shoot from? ...

Suddenly the waves of gunfire coming from outside abruptly ceased. Just reaching the blasted windows, London's mind flashed,

And why did they stop?

And then, realizing there was only one reason his at-

tackers would have stopped saturating the office with gunfire, the detective yelled,

"Lisa! The hall door's next."

"Already on it, sweetheart." The woman had shoved a
large, two-drawer hanging file cabinet across the front of
the door to her office. Now she crouched behind it, waiting, one gun in her right hand, another on top of the cabinet in front of her. Seven clips were laid out in a row next
to the second H&K P-7 at her elbow.

While she had been positioning herself and London had
been making for the windows, Morcey had flung the back
table and one of the heavy client chairs into the doorway
leading from the detective's office to their reception area.
Steady behind it with his Auto-Mag, all three of them had
just reached their positions when the wave they had been
expecting hit. Whoever had attacked the agency had blown
the outside windows as a distraction. The real threat hit
their front door the moment their outside forces stopped
laying down cover.

Although Lisa had locked the door minutes earlier, the
approaching forces were not slowed down. Plastic explosives took out the entire doorway, jamb and all, sending it
hurling into the room in a cloud of smoke. As it bounced
off the opposite wall, a pair of figures came through the
opening created by the explosion, moving fast, guns
spreading fire throughout the reception area. Lisa felt the
impact as several slugs plowed into the file cabinet in front
of her. Returning fire, she sent two 9mm slugs through the
head of the first of the invaders.

Then the young woman ducked down as the second in
line returned fire in her direction, setting himself up for
Morcey. The ex–maintenance man fired next, the thunder-
ously powerful Auto-Mag round passing completely
through the body of the second man in the doorway and
into a third. Instantly, though, another pair—one man, one
woman—came in low, up and over the backs of the dead,
leaning into their attack.

Both sprayed the room with bullets as they entered, filling the air with the smell of burning powder. Lisa was

forced to throw herself back into her office as slugs blasted into the file cabinet, so many hitting that the heavy drawers were actually knocked backward. Covering her, however, Morcey was able to get off two careful shots. One hit the first attacker in the shoulder, spinning him around violently, his arm torn away from his torso by the devastating shell. The second round slammed into the woman's breastbone, blowing her chest open, her back erupting as the bullet passed through, spraying the wall behind with blood and shattered vertebrae.

No sooner had the second assault team been stopped when a new shower of slugs was fired from out in the hall, explosive rounds so powerful they blasted away parts of the wall. Listening to the chaos behind him, London wondered,

What the hell could they be using out there?

Ignoring the commotion, however, the detective left their outer defense to his partners as he risked taking a look out through the shattered remains of the window. Doing so, he saw no trace of who or what had fired on them from the outside. He had been correct—there were no helicopters in sight, no auto-gyros, gliders, or any other type of flying machine. The detective threw the full range of his senses outside; he detected no smell of engine fuel or jet-pack chemicals, no sight of recent heat trails. There were no metallic echoes falling away from the building. No trace elements in the air of anything except the recent hail of bullets.

Ummmmmmmmmmmmmmm, the single note trailed through London's head. No sign of anything. Well, as Doc Goward used to say, when you can't find the obvious, look for the things that are not there.

Narrowing his eyes down to the thinnest of slits, the detective shifted his vision through the spectrum of known light, suddenly stopping in the infrared. What he saw puzzled him at first. He had discovered a heat trail, thin and clean, one that had passed their window twice, apparently in a kind of corkscrewing figure-eight pattern.

"Good Jesus Christ," London muttered aloud, his eyes

going wide as he realized what he was actually seeing. "Now I *have* seen everything."

Narrowing his eyes again, he followed the pattern, tracing it in the air until he found what was causing it. Keeping the object at the end of the trail pinned with unblinking eyes, he slowly stood up and slid Betty into his belt, flexing the muscles in his shoulders unconsciously. Staring forward, he ignored the water beating down on him from the ceiling, ordering his body to filter out the smoke all around him.

Like Lisa and Morcey, his ears had already gone into shock from the deafening thunder created by the vast number of reverberating gunshots that had been fired in the office. Ignoring the loss of that one sense, he let his subconscious track what was happening behind him through the vibrations echoing through the floor. Consciously, however, the detective had only one purpose, to not lose sight of the pinpoint circling in the air some thirty blocks from the building.

"Come on, you bastard—come on back."

And then, suddenly, those attempting to force their way into the agency halted their attack. London blinked involuntarily, missing a beat as the fusillade of destruction blasting behind him suddenly ceased. Sharpening his gaze, the detective was not surprised to see the pinpoint he had been watching streaking toward his building once more. Flexing his fingers, he pulled Betty from his belt, holding the .38 lightly as the distant figure drew closer.

"All right, kids," whispered the detective, talking to all the voices within his head. "It's showtime."

All of London's ancestors who had ever held a gun, who had ever fired an arrow at a bird in flight, all the minds in his racial memory that understood anything about the physics of intersecting angles melded themselves together, opening their storehouse of experience to the detective.

As the approaching spot in the sky hit the twenty-block mark, London raised his .38 to eye level. By the time he circled his shooting hand's wrist with his other hand, the pinpoint was only ten blocks away, gaining in speed and growing in size. In the split second it took to cock Betty, the racing thing was only five blocks away, moving at at least seventy miles per hour. As London's finger slid inside the trigger guard, the form had cut that distance in half and had begun to raise its own weapons. Not needing to cut things any closer, the detective's body tightened, feet rooting to the floor, spine bracing for impact, arms steeling against recoil.

The detective fired once, twice, three, four times. All four bullets found their target. The first entered the head, the second and third the torso, the fourth the neck. The figure crumpled against the smashing impacts, its maniacal speed cut in half as each slug cut into it while London fired again and then again, finally stopping its forward motion completely.

As the detective stared, the figure hung in midair for a moment, blood pumping wildly. Then it crumpled in on itself and finally surrendered to gravity. When it began to fall a long moment later, London moved forward, actually leaning out of his window to watch it plummet downward. Somehow in the back of his mind aware that the figure's accomplices had retreated, he took the time to study the pattern of the thing's descent. After all, he had once seen winged, humanlike things that could fly, but he had never actually seen a man who could. Especially a man who had no mechanical devices except guns. And especially a man who was supposed to be dead.

6

"Boss!" shouted Morcey, screaming even though he was only inches from London's ear. Pointing behind the detective, he shouted again, "Look!"

London understood. Despite his extraordinary abilities, the detective had been left as deafened by the explosive force of the attack as his partners. His eyes following the length of the ex–maintenance man's hand, London saw what it was that had caught his partner's attention. Crumpled in a heap at the far end of London's office, in an ever-increasing pool of scarlet, was the body of the Confessor, his white suit soaked through with blood. In spite of the still-pouring sprinklers, the two men crossed the room, heading for the still form in the corner. Neither of them held out the slightest hope, however, that the large man might still be alive.

"What'll we do, boss?"

London stared at the bullet-riddled corpse for a long moment. Then, knowing that whatever he was going to do he had to do fast, the detective bent down and pulled the golden ring from the Confessor's right hand. Wiping away the worst of the blood, he held it under the shower coming from the ceiling, letting the sprinkler finish cleaning it for him. As the last of the blood drained away in thin pinkish ribbons, London turned to Morcey and said,

"Lock this in the strongbox, will you, Paul?" The balding man stared at his partner for a moment, then understanding suddenly flashed through his eyes.

"Oh, I getcha," he shouted. "I remember. This guy said that he took the ring from the last Confessor. So, you're figurin' that whoever the new Confessor's gonna be, he's gonna hafta show up here to get the ring."

"Right," answered London, going through the dead man's pockets to see if they yielded anything else perti-

nent. The sprinklers finally stopped pouring. Not seeming
to notice, the detective kept searching, telling his partner,
"It's not going to do us any good if the thing's just locked
up in some precinct house property room. Besides, I'm
awful curious to see who shows up to claim it next."

"And whether or not they can tell us anything about the
end of the world," added Morcey. "*This* particular end of
the world, anyway."

"Don't get too droll," cautioned London. Pulling a thin
billfold from a hidden pocket inside the Confessor's vest,
the detective pored over its contents, looking for any kind
of a lead. As he thumbed through its meager contents, he
continued shouting back to his partner, saying,

"Yeah, sure, we've saved the world. More than once.
Yeah, we're real James Bonds. But before we get too
smug, let's try to remember how many millions have died
while we were saving everyone else."

"Ah, yeah, I know," answered the ex–maintenance man,
moving off to lock away the Confessor's ring. "But if I
hafta stand here with a dead body in the room creepin' me
out and all, and try to psych myself up for takin' on God
only knows what this time around . . . hell, the least I
oughta be able to do is remind myself that when it comes
to kickin' monster ass, that at least we *are* the best in the
business."

Not responding to his partner, London stood up as Lisa
came into his office. His eyes met hers, the look in his letting his wife know that he wanted her to talk first. Without
hesitation, she reported,

"Everyone that's still out there is dead. Anyone else that
was around is gone. We put down our small-scale invasion
a little too permanently. No one out there is going to be
answering any questions."

"No time to worry about it," answered the detective.
"Lisa, get out of here now. Go home, tell Lai Wan what
happened, and the two of you secure the brownstone. I'll
have my beeper if you need me."

Knowing that he had said all he was going to, Lisa
turned and headed for her office. She knew better than to

waste any time with pointless questions—knew that not only would London have told her anything else he wanted her to know, that she might need to know, but also that the police would be there soon, and that after they arrived no one would be going anywhere.

As she grabbed her coat and shoulder bag and headed for the elevator, Morcey returned to London's office. As he did, the detective held up a small rectangle made out of thin, stiff cardboard with a series of holes punched in one end. Showing it to his partner, he asked,

"Paul, you know what one of these is?"

"Yeah. It's one of them new program keys they're usin' in all the hotels nowadays." Taking it from the detective, he looked it over, saying,

"Looks like the kind they punch a new code for every time." Understanding what London was going for, the ex–maintenance man jumped ahead of his partner, saying, "I doubt Lai could get a fix on this."

Morcey's reference was to Lai Wan, a top psychometrist the agency had used many times in the past. She could read the past of any object she held, but as the balding man had said, she did have her limitations. Defining his thoughts on the subject, he told London,

"There wouldn't be enough history in it. People holdin' it wouldn't leave an impression strong enough for her to grab onto." Holding it up to the light, the ex–maintenance man mused, "Obviously this must be the key to the Confessor's room—right?"

"That would be our best guess," answered London. "Of course, there's probably at least two hundred hotels in Manhattan using these by now."

"All the more reason," said Morcey, "for me to get my ass out of here."

"That and the approaching gendarmes."

"Oh, *oui, oui*," answered the ex–maintenance man with a laugh, pocketing the key while heading for the front door. "Now there's a big consideration." Stopping in the doorway, he turned long enough to ask,

"Listen, how long you think they'll keep you tied up?"

"No idea. Check in at home. No matter what, I'll keep Lisa posted on whatever's going on."

"Solid, boss," answered Morcey, disappearing out into the hall. Through the floor, London could feel the heavy hall door opening and closing, letting him know that the balding man had not been foolish enough to wait for the elevators. Indeed, it was only a few seconds later when he could sense two of the elevators opening. Heavily armed police officers swarmed out of both cars and into London's office.

They burst into the reception area, leaping over the bodies, several branching off for both of the side offices while the main body of them went straight forward. Throwing themselves into London's office, they found the detective sitting behind his desk, calmly cleaning Betty. As they all went rigid, aiming their assault weapons at him, he said,

"Too late, boys. Party's over. I think there's still some cole slaw in the fridge, though. Help yourselves."

Before any of the rank and file could answer, a commanding voice from just behind them said,

"Oh, well listen to that. We've got a comedian among us." As the officers parted enough to allow the speaker to make his way through, London looked up, as interested in whoever was approaching as they were in him. A tall, slender man with thinning hair and a black-and-gray mustache came through the crowd. Giving his men the signal to stand down, he walked up to the detective's desk, his hand out in front of him.

"The murder weapon . . . if you please?"

"Murder weapon?" asked London, looking up into the officer's face. "There's only one murder victim here, and he's lying in the corner. I'm not sure which weapon killed him, but this one in my hand is the only one that didn't."

"Oh, and I'm to take your word on that, am I?"

"Yes," answered London, smiling. Looking up into the officer's face, he stared unblinking into the man's eyes, telling him at the same time,

"My name is Theodore London. I will now tell you exactly what happened. The man in the corner came into my office roughly a half an hour ago. He said his name was the Confessor. He claimed the world was in danger and that billions of people were going to die."

The officer with the thinning hair blinked, unable to meet London's perpetual gaze. The detective pretended not to notice, continuing with his story uninterrupted.

"Then, before he could tell me anything more, the crew you see all around you attacked. I did the best I could to hold them off but, as you can see, I was not entirely successful. As for the murder weapon, my guess is that it's down in the street somewhere. The windows were shot out by a man who attacked from the outside. My assumption is he fired the killing shots."

London broke contact with the officer's eyes, releasing the tall man from the grip of his voice. The policeman stepped back with a jerking motion, seemingly as if having broken free from a set of chains. As he did, a trio of firemen arrived. The officer, grateful for the distraction, began to snap orders to both the firemen and his own people. Then, after they were set to work, checking for the cause of the fires, collecting evidence, cordoning off the offices, and all the other duties involved with investigating a crime scene, the head man turned his attention back to London. Moving toward the detective's desk almost with apprehension, he said,

"You're not going to make this easy on us, are you?"

"Officer . . . ?"

"Lieutenant . . . Lieutenant Swartz."

"Lieutenant, I will make this as easy as possible. Unfortunately, the circumstances you've just put yourself into will not make this easy."

Swartz stared at London, keeping a few extra feet of distance between himself and the detective. He regretted not demanding London's weapon when he had first been put off, but the force of the detective's will had held him back. In the first few seconds of their confrontation, London had shown him who was in charge, not through any show of force, but simply by laying himself open to the lieutenant, letting him see what he was up against.

Despite his years of experience, the lawman did not know what to do. At any other crime scene, he would not have allowed an obvious suspect to control things as he was allowing London to do. But, he told himself, he seemed to have no other choice. There was simply something about the detective that all his instincts told him he had to believe. He did not like the fact that his men had seen him back down from London, but then, he did not like anything he had seen or heard or done since he had arrived.

Looking across the detective's desk, he stared at London, wondering how the man could be so calm. He could see the evidence of an attack all around him. It certainly appeared to Swartz that the detective's offices could have been attacked from the outside. He had counted up the number of bodies on the way in. The bullet holes everywhere, the scorching on the walls, the holes blown in them from explosive rounds—he had seen it all, counting and cataloging everything on a subconscious level. Decades on the job had given Swartz an ability to assess any crime scene almost instantly. He was one of the best in the business, a man whose instincts could always tell him in a matter of seconds what was going on, and what he had to do to make sure what went on was what he wanted going on.

Now his instincts were telling him that the only chance he had was to listen to the man sitting on the other side of the bullet-riddled desk. Pursing his lips, he made a small, unconscious noise, then said,

"So you think circumstance has made a mess of things, do you?"

"Yes, Lieutenant, I do," answered London. Slipping Betty back into her drawer, the detective looked up, saying, "I hate to drag people into these things. I'm going to be perfectly honest with you. I have no idea whatsoever what is going on here. I don't know what the big threat is that the man calling himself the Confessor was worried about. But obviously," said London, motioning with his hands to indicate the ruin all around the two of them, "there was something to his fears."

"Yes," agreed Swartz in a sarcastic tone. "Obviously."

"I know you can't turn your back on something like this. I understand your duties. You seem like a man who takes his job seriously." London tilted his head, feeding back to the lieutenant the personal facts he had learned from the man just by being in his presence.

"You don't take graft, turn a blind eye, or like being pushed around. You're tough on your men and tough on yourself. You've already thought about how much face you lost when I backed you up a minute ago, and you've already put it aside in consideration of the fact that you can't let your pride stand in the way of something where billions of people might die. You've decided that I'm not a nut case, but you can't figure out what to do about me."

Swartz smiled, beginning to warm to London. Knowing that the detective was right, he wrinkled his lips for a second, then passed his tongue over his teeth and said,

"You know, for a man in a soaking-wet suit who could get himself slapped into a jail cell for any of . . . oh, what? Say, eighteen different reasons . . . you certainly manage to carry yourself well."

"It's a talent," answered London.

"Yeah," answered the lieutenant, admitting that he needed London more than the detective needed him. "Well, we're going to need some talent if we're going to get this thing solved."

"Yes," agreed London, knowing exactly what he was saying. "We certainly are."

7

Morcey walked down the hotel hallway, headed for his twenty-seventh room 1514 of the afternoon. The short strawberry blonde walking behind him remained silent, concentrating more on watching their backs and the doors around them than anything the ex–maintenance man was doing. When Morcey had left London earlier, he had taken the key to the woman, an electronics expert named Cat who had worked with the agency numerous times in the past.

Using the tools of her trade, it had taken her no more than a few seconds to crack the card's bite pattern. The printout she got from it told her that it had been programmed to open a room somewhere listed as 1514. Its program specs also told her the manufacturer of the key system equipment. A quick call to an old friend gave her another printout, one with all the hotels in New York City that used that particular system.

"So," she had asked Morcey, "that give you everything you need to know?"

"Not quite everything, of course," answered the balding man, taking a deep breath in response to the size of the list. "But it's a great start. Thanks, Cat."

Morcey did not look at the woman as he spoke to her. He was too absorbed in the length of the printout in his hands. Studying his expression, the electronics expert asked,

"Something's up, isn't it?"

"Sure," answered Morcey absently, planning out his next move. "Why else would I be here?"

"No," insisted Cat, the hair on the back of her neck beginning to tingle. "I mean ... something *special*. Something spooky. It's Frankenstein time, isn't it?"

Morcey looked up from the hundreds of names on his list. As Cat caught the set of his eyes, she exclaimed.

"It is! Something's going on again."

"Yeah, well, it looks that way," he admitted. "Maybe."

"Maybe?" responded Cat. As the woman closed down her operations desk, she asked, "What do you mean?"

"We've had some weird talk, yeah . . . but the creatures of the night haven't bothered to show themselves yet. So far it's just been guys and gals with guns."

"Monsters with guns?" quizzed Cat.

"No, no pistol-packin' mummies or nuthin'. Just a simple, old-fashioned armed invasion." Years earlier, Cat had faced down both a horde of vampires and an unstoppable werewolf with London and his team. She had loved the excitement of the challenges, the thrill of the fear levels such mind-exploding dangers had pumped through her—the vindicating satisfaction of having lived through both encounters. Because of her insider status, Morcey did not hesitate to tell her the Confessor's story, and what had happened afterward. Grabbing for her all-purpose carry bag, she said,

"Sounds good. What'll we do first?"

Morcey considered arguing, not wanting to drag someone too far into the dangerous situation he and his partners had suddenly found themselves in—but before he could say anything, Cat changed tactics on him, asking,

"And tell me, how's Lai Wan? You two still getting along?"

"Yeah," the balding man had answered, "sure. Everythin's peachy. How about you and Margorie?"

The look on Cat's face told him everything she had hoped it would, sparing her from having to say it, from having to ask to be included. One glance told him that the electronics expert and her lover were no longer together. Suddenly he understood why putting herself on the line would be desirable. Without more than a moment's hesitation, he put aside the notion of keeping Cat out. After all, he told himself, it seemed fairly obvious that they were going to need help of some kind along the line. At least the short computer whiz did not need to be briefed on what it was the agency did.

Cat had seen at least half of the horrors that he had at London's side, had swallowed her fear and dug in and fought alongside the rest of them. If she wanted in, he figured she was in. That decided, the pair had taken a look at the list of hotels and formulated a plan. First they decided to ignore the outer boroughs, hoping that the Confessor had been staying in Manhattan. After that, they had called all the hotels on the list, eliminating all those less than fifteen stories high. Then, armed with a list of only sixty-three possibilities, they had begun to move around town in Cat's Honda, going from hotel to hotel, looking for the room 1514 that their key would open.

"Okay," said Morcey in a whisper, holding the key above the magnetic lock, "and now, for my next trick . . ." The ex–maintenance man slipped the plastic rectangle into the lock slot, saying, "Presto." And then, after twenty-six tries, he was rewarded with a green light instead of a red one, and the sound of the lock's internal magnetic seal separating.

"Will wonders never cease?" he muttered, shoving the door open. "We're finally in."

The pair shoved the door open the rest of the way, entered, and locked it behind them. Quickly they moved into the main chamber, looking about them for any signs of trouble, recent entry, or just anything that might seem out of the ordinary. Once they were satisfied that everything was normal, Morcey ordered,

"You take the bathroom, closets, and all the drawers. I'll crash his luggage."

"We looking for anything in particular?" asked the strawberry blonde, checking to see if anything might have been stashed in the bathtub, or hidden beneath the vinyl toilet seat cover.

"Won't know it 'til I see it," answered Morcey honestly as he dug through the first of the two large leather overstrapped bags sitting in the corner. "You know the story, you've got just as good a guess as I do. So, let's just look and hope the Bible was on the money."

"The Bible ... ?"

"Yeah, you know ... 'Seek and ye shall find.' "

The two searched on in silence after that, tearing through the hotel room with practiced efficiency. The bathroom proved to be hiding nothing much, as did the dressers, the bed, and the luggage. Morcey had found only one thing of interest, a knife in the second bag, its blade tangled with thread. It was not a particularly lethal blade, nor did it show any signs of having been used for anything sinister. The ponytailed man left it with the Confessor's extra shirts and pants, moving on to the rest of the room. He checked the rug next, but could find no spot along the molding where the wall-to-wall carpeting had been pried up.

The pair continued on, however, looking everywhere. They checked under every piece of furniture, pulled out each drawer to search underneath for anything that might have been taped to their bottoms. Cat checked the inside of the toilet-paper roll and lifted the lid of the toilet tank, running her hand under the water to see if anything had been stashed in it. She even checked the bathroom pipes and the shower head to see if they might have been removed recently.

While she did, Morcey went over the mattress and the box spring to see if anything had been slipped between them or if they had been opened so that something might be inserted in one of them. He looked inside the light fixtures, behind the pictures hanging on the walls, in the folds of the drapes, and inside the air conditioner. Sadly, however, none of their searching turned up anything of consequence.

Standing in the center of the room, the ex–maintenance man stood still for a long moment with his eyes closed, thinking to himself, running through a mental tally sheet. One by one, he checked each thing they had done off the list, trying to see if there was anything they might have forgotten. And then, suddenly, it hit him.

You dope.

Without a second's hesitation, Morcey crossed the room to the corner where he had left the Confessor's luggage. Tearing open the second bag, he pulled out the knife he had found earlier. The balding man pulled loose some of the bits of fiber stuck to the blade and then held them up to the light, trying to determine their color. Unable to do so from such a small sample, he held the bits of thread between his thumb and forefinger, moving them back and forth as he tried to determine the feel of the material. Then he knelt down, getting the nape of the carpet between the thumb and forefinger of his other hand, moving it back and forth in the same manner. As he did, he shouted with excitement,

"Cat! C'mere."

When the computer whiz entered the main room, she found Morcey on his hands and knees, running his hands over the carpeting. Before she could ask, he said,

"I shoulda thought of this earlier. Jeez ma knees, I laid enough industrial carpeting in my time to know what a plug of it looks like stuck in between the hilt and blade of a knife. Come on, give me a hand."

"Give you a hand with what?"

"I think the Confessor slit the rug so he could shove somethin' underneath."

"Wouldn't we see the hole?" asked Cat.

"Not if he double-sided some heavy-duty tape and then pounded it down. It's how we use'ta fix splits all the time back when I . . ." And then, the ex–maintenance man's fingers found what he was looking for.

"Got it!"

While Cat watched, Morcey dug his fingers down into the carpeting and pulled back. The rug lifted with the sound of peeling tape. And then, reaching underneath, the ponytailed man pulled forth a double-letter-sized manilla envelope. Pulling open the top, Morcey looked inside, finding a few miscellaneous papers and a set of computer disks. Not wanting to waste any time, he stuffed the envelope into his inner jacket pocket, made sure there was nothing else under the rug, and then said,

"Okay, let's split." As the two moved out into the hall he told Cat, "Gotta thank you for everything. Bill the agency for your time at your regular rates. We may not have a client, but I'm sure we're still doin' good enough to be able to cover ya."

"Hey," asked the electronics expert, suddenly angry, "you trying to stiff me out?"

"No," answered Morcey as he pressed for the elevator. "It's just that I've done everything the boss wanted me to do. Now I gotta find out what's next." Swallowing hard, Cat said in a whisper,

"This isn't a client/payment/ho-hum kind of case. Come on, this is the good stuff. This is . . . is the real meat."

"Real bloody meat," said the balding man, referring back to the carnage in the agency offices he had told the woman of earlier. Ignoring his reference, she told him,

"I know. But I'm a big girl—all grown up and everything. If I get in over my head, I can swim back to shallow water all on my own. I can take care of myself." And then, as the elevator arrived on their floor, she looked up into Morcey's eyes, searching for a trace of sympathy she could appeal to. As the doors before them began to slip open, she said,

"It's not a school day tomorrow, and . . . well, it's not like there's anyone waiting for me at home. Anymore. I can stay out and play as long as I want."

Stepping inside the elevator, Morcey punched the lobby button, then made a sweeping motion with his hand, saying,

"Hey—room for one more, I suppose."

Smiling, Cat stepped into the elevator, asking,

"One more 'what'?"

"Jerk, I guess," answered Morcey.

And then the doors slid shut, and the car began its crawl back to the lobby.

8

London walked up the front stairs of his building, a sedate three-story brownstone on one of the last tree-lined streets left in lower Manhattan. Lieutenant Swartz moved in step next to him, observing everything he could. As the detective opened his front door, the policeman noted that the building had no buzzers for its various apartments. Looking at London, he asked,

"You own this building?"

"Good guess, Lieutenant."

"How the hell does a private ticket punch up this kind of credit?" asked the officer skeptically. "From the looks of things, you've got yourself a pretty good setup with your agency, but this is real money."

"I came into some real money a few years back," answered London as he pushed the front door open for Swartz. "A guy paid me ten million dollars to go to Hell and get his soul back from the devil for him."

Swartz stared, wondering if he was supposed to regard what the detective had just said as a joke. London had already given the officer some details of what they might be up against—hinted to him of some of the things he and his friends had faced over the years. Throughout their talk so far, however, the detective had not made light of any of the things he had told the policeman. Something deep inside Swartz pushed his panic button, warning him that London had not suddenly started kidding him then, either. Stepping into the building's foyer, the lieutenant took in the well-worn marble of the floor, the high gloss of the sharply polished wainscoting, the clean cuts in the glass of both the windows and the doors.

The building bespoke money to Swartz's trained eye. Maybe London had not been paid ten million dollars to go to Hell, thought the lieutenant, but he had certainly been paid something close to that amount somewhere along the line. As the officer continued to study his surroundings, he followed the detective, until London shouted out,

"Oh, honey, I'm home."

Lisa stepped out of a doorway on the second floor and looked over the railing down at her husband. Before she could say anything, however, the thundering sound of little feet slapped against the hardwood floors above the detective, almost drowning out the shouts of their owners.

"Daddy!" cried out both of London's children, bursting out from the same room from which Lisa had emerged. The pair raced past their mother, running for the banister along the building's main stairway.

"Catch me, Daddy," shouted London's son.

"No, me, Daddy," cried his daughter. "Catch me."

The detective positioned himself at the bottom of the stairs, arriving just seconds before his son. London caught the boy under his left arm, his daughter under his right. While Swartz watched, the detective pretended to be staggered by the act, spinning around and around in the foyer, twirling himself and the children wildly about until he finally gave in and tumbled to the floor.

Lisa came down the stairs, her scowl the solid, unblinking frown of a mother trying to decide whether it was her children or her husband who needed to grow up more. Before she could say anything, however, a cold voice came from behind them all, catching everyone's attention, almost shocking Swartz.

"Children. Time for lessons."

"Yes'm, Auntie Lai."

"Coming, Ye-Ye."

The officer wheeled around, finding himself staring at a tall, slender Chinese woman dressed in black. As the girl and her younger brother scrambled across the room to both sides of the woman, Lisa came forward, introducing herself and everyone else present to the officer.

"I assume you are Lieutenant Swartz. Teddy phoned to tell me that you would both be coming here. I'm Lisa London. These are our children, Kevin and Kate. And this is our friend and the children's guardian, Lai Wan."

Neither of the children spoke to Swartz. Instead, they both looked him over with curious eyes in a manner the hardened policeman found unexpectedly unnerving. Gently pushing the pair of children back toward the door through which she had silently entered—moving them seemingly with her presence alone—the Chinese woman drew her large black shawl closer around her shoulders, saying,

"Lisa has told me everything I did not already know." Then, taking a breath as if what she wanted to ask took some preparation, she steeled herself, then gave voice to the troubling question to which she already knew the answer.

"Lisa was correct, was she not, when she said that it has begun again?"

"Oh, yes," admitted London. "It's begun again, all right."

"Then we will be occupied as long as you need us to be occupied, Theodore."

"Thanks, Lai," answered the detective, dusting himself off. "I'll let you know whenever we get finished."

The woman nodded and then turned to go back the way she had come. The children, their smiles and giggles gone without a trace, followed her to the door, moving as silently as she did. Lai Wan and Kevin disappeared through the shadow-masked door in the front of the foyer, but Kate stopped at its threshold, turning to look at Swartz once more.

She stared at him for a long time, watching him as he absently brushed at his moustache. He looked back at her, not knowing what else to do. Then, suddenly, she broke eye contact with the policeman and followed her brother and teacher, disappearing as they had. The lieutenant stared at the empty doorway for a moment, then turned and said,

"Spooky nanny there, Mr. London, Ms. Hutchinson."

"Lai Wan is more a friend of the family," said Lisa,

heading back up the stairs. As her husband and the officer followed her, the policeman asked,

"Is there some reason her name seems familiar to me?"

"Possibly," answered London. "She's one of the top psychometrists in the business."

"Of course," said Swartz, snapping his fingers. "The Felson case . . . the Anderson disappearance and, and, the Smefling jewel robbery . . ."

"She's been able to provide some small services to the police in the past," said London as they neared the second-floor landing.

"Not bad for a 'spooky nanny.' Eh, Lieutenant?"

"No offense intended, Ms. London."

"There hardly ever is, is there?" answered the young woman. "But it always shows up, nonetheless." As the trio reached the landing, Swartz told Lisa,

"Ma'am, you want to blame me for whatever is going on, go ahead. I'm used to it. But as a partner in a private investigations firm . . . one whose offices are at present a multiple crime scene . . . you might want to think of me as more a teammate than the enemy."

Lisa knew the lieutenant was only trying to feel his way through the strangeness of the case they all had before them. She could remember when she had first discovered the world beyond what most people regarded as reality—remembered the trauma she had felt while being hunted by winged monsters. Now, she thought, things are flying again. But she was unable to hold herself in check, snapping at Swartz instead, telling him,

"Think of you as a teammate and not the enemy? I'll tell you what I think of you as—trouble. You think we're some kind of joke—that after you spend a little time with us, that after you find out what our *real* story is, you'll be able to figure it out and then slot us off with all the other nut jobs you've dealt with in your time." Reaching the door to the Londons' main living area, Lisa turned back to Swartz, snapping,

"Well, let me tell you, Lieutenant, night is falling, and you've still got your sunglasses on. How about a few questions? Tell me, *teammate*—is a crucifix any good against vampires? Do werewolves go down when you shoot silver bullets into them? Is the devil real, Lieutenant? You know the name? The devil—Satan, Lucifer, Beelzebub—that guy? Does he really walk the Earth, looking for souls to tempt? Think fast, Lieutenant. Your life could depend on you having the right response. Your life . . . and the lives of your *teammates.*"

After that, the woman merely glared at Swartz, her stare daring him to comment. Breaking the uncomfortable silence, London said,

"I'd make some kind of nervous comment to defuse the tension here, but unfortunately, Lieutenant, she's absolutely right. Sure you don't want to just throw me in the clink for murder? Your sanity might have a better time of it."

"Now, look here," answered the officer, tired of being pushed away from his usual position as the center of authority. "I've been on the the police force in this city for twenty-one years. I've seen bodies pulled out of sewers, the trunks of cars, and shallow graves from here to the Sunrise Highway. I've locked up men who thought kids younger than yours were the perfect place to shove their private parts, people who sold rat poison in school yards as cocaine, and guys who beat grandmothers to death for spare change. Maybe Universal Pictures didn't make movies about any of them, but that doesn't keep them from being monsters." Blood filled Swartz's face as his anger rose. In a cold, crisp tone, he told Lisa,

"Now, I've been awfully patient here. I've listened to your husband's theories on things, and against what some might think should have been my better judgment, so far he isn't locked up waiting for the boys from Bellevue to peek in through his ear. So, if we're really going to have dinner here, cut me off a big piece of slack and serve it up, okay? Because, honestly, I'm getting awfully hungry for some."

Pushing against the door to their quarters, Lisa held it

open as she turned to London, talking to him as if the lieutenant had suddenly disappeared.

"Well, he's got the bluster. Now I guess we'll just have to wait until things start going bump in the night to see if he's got the hardware to back it up." Then she pushed the door the rest of the way open and disappeared inside the apartment beyond, letting the door close on the two men behind her. London, trying his best to hide his smile, leaned on the door and opened it for Swartz, saying,

"Welcome to my home, Lieutenant."

The policeman followed without further comment. As they entered the living room, London led the officer to his study. The offer of a drink brought a request for rum. The detective told Swartz to make himself comfortable, promising to return in a minute. Left to his own devices, the lieutenant wandered about the room, letting his job instinct guide him. It was not too long before he was standing in front of the large, hanging mirror that was the obvious focal point of the room.

Swartz studied the mirror, wondering what its significance was. Framed in an ornately carved rectangle, the policeman could not help but notice that streaks had been burnt into both the glass and wood at some point in the past, as if a laser beam or lightning had glanced along the length of it. Two objects were mounted above the mirror in crossed fashion. One was a remarkably heavy-looking sword, the other was a single antler. As noteworthy as the brutal weapon was, it was the antler that captured the officer's attention. It was a large, twisted thing, covered with a thin layer of dried, bristling, deep scarlet fur—all of it oddly cold to the touch.

The lieutenant wondered about the unusual trophy, then noticed the table under the mirror. The thick, leafy fern in its center nearly obscured the things on it. Swartz picked up one piece, a round ornately carved ivory box, its surface covered with a parade of elephants following each other trunk to tail. From the deep yellow of the ivory, the policeman wondered just how old it might be.

"Couple thousand years, I believe."

Swartz turned to stare at London. Realizing what he had done, the detective apologized, saying,

"Sorry. I try to wall off people's surface thoughts when I'm outside. I'm afraid once I get in my own home I tend to get a little too comfortable. I'll try to be more careful."

"You read my mind," said Swartz, more uncomfortable at that moment than he had been all day. Turning away from London, he looked back at the wall, his eyes zeroing in on a series of eleven framed photos hanging in a straight line. They were all dark, the ones toward the end somewhat out of focus and erratic. The lieutenant looked them over, making out a humanoid form that appeared to be running down a forest trail toward the camera. The figure grew larger in each frame, although not necessarily clearer, until the final shot showing mostly a scarred chest and canine snout.

Swartz stared. His mind became transfixed by the single detail. A snout? he thought. Like a dog? Like a wolf?

Wheeling around, a sudden rush of nerves chilling him, the officer asked,

"What is this? Some kind of bad spook-house exhibit?"

"I told you what you were getting into here, Lieutenant," answered London. "Did you think I was kidding? Did you think that telling you we believed in werewolves was some kind of setup for an insanity plea bargain?"

"I didn't, I mean . . ."

Swartz turned back toward the photos, his eyes locking on the last picture again. He looked over his shoulder at the detective, then back to the photos, then back again toward London. Turning back around to face the detective head-on, he asked,

"Tell me you accepted all of this without browning out. Tell me someone started chattering in your ear about monsters and things from Hell and you didn't bat an eye. You just swabbed out the barrel of your revolver and said 'let me at 'em.' Right? The wolfman, the mummy, Dracula—no problem for you. Being a superior mortal and all."

"No, Lieutenant," admitted London. "When Lisa first came to me I had my doubts. Luckily one of those 'things from Hell' you mentioned followed her to my office. If it hadn't been for a little timely intervention by my partner, I'd have been dog meat and, well, actually, the world would have ended and we wouldn't have had to have this conversation."

Swartz looked at London, knowing from his years of experience—having listened to every type of liar there is—that the detective was telling the truth. Perhaps only, thought the policeman, what he believes to be the truth. But if he's kidding himself, his wife and the nanny sure seem to be falling for the same line of hooey.

Before he could comment on what London had said, however, the telephone rang. Swartz almost jumped out of his skin when the bell sounded, cursing his nerves for failing him in such an obvious manner. But even as the lieutenant tried to compose himself, London answered the phone, finding Morcey on the other end of the line.

"Find something?" he asked his partner.

"Oh, yeah," answered the ex–maintenance man. "We turned up the good stuff this time."

"We?" asked London.

"Cat and me. I signed her on to help me crack the key thing. Now I can't get rid of her." The detective smiled as he heard the sound of a small fist connecting with what he assumed was Morcey's back. Ignoring it, he asked,

"So, what have you got?"

"Something that should be seen—not talked about on the phone."

"That juicy?"

"Ahhhhh, let's just say better safe than sorry."

"Why, Mr. Morcey," said London dryly, "you're getting cautious in your old age."

"Maybe so, boss," answered the balding man. "Maybe so. We'll see how you feel when you get here."

"Where's here?"

"Pash' . . . ah, I mean . . . Lacey's."

"We'll be there as fast as we can."

"We?" asked Morcey.

"I believe Lieutenant Swartz will be joining us."

"You're bringin' in the cops this time?" said the ex—maintenance man. "And you got the nerve to call me cautious?"

9

"What brings you here?"

"What brings me where, Grandmother?"

London stood inside the door of the battered old shell of a building, staring down at a thin stick of an elderly black woman. He had been forced to enact a certain number of rituals just to get the door of the building opened for him. Now, the real testing began. Filled with a dark fire that put the lie to her true age, the old woman answered him,

"To dis place."

"What place be that?"

"You choke to name dis place?" asked the woman, her voice the sound of dry reeds cracking underfoot. "You run from de thought to name dis place?"

"This place has no name, Grandmother. One cannot name what is not there."

"Den enter what is not . . . ," said the woman, waiting for London's response.

"And be where there is nothing," he replied.

"You no visit me for a long time, London boy."

"You mean," asked the detective with trepidation in his voice, "ever since I got your son killed?"

"You no take Pa'sha's hand, lead him to the other side. Dat boy beggin' for the black robes to swim down for him for too many year before he met you." The old woman stepped back from the door, her customary way of allowing people to enter her fortress home. Her son had left it to her when he had been torn to pieces by the werewolf in the photos on London's wall. He had been a weapons maker and dealer, and a warrior of no mean skill. He and London had helped each other many times over the years . . . had been blood brothers. The detective had always been amused by the massive weaponeer's cautious traits.

The two had believed London would be the first to die. It was not the only thing they had been wrong about.

"But why for you come to me now? You make nice words to me after Pa'sha get hisself killed, but you no speak again after. You sent the death day flowers, but you no come see your brother get lowered into the ground. Why you come now?"

"Mama Joan, when you were burying Pa'sha I was on the other side of the world, looking for the beast that killed him. It took me months to find it, and a year to get back, but I finished the thing off. After that, I . . . I just didn't think you'd want to see me. So I stayed on my side of the line and I left you alone. Now, however, things have changed. There's some bad demons a-flying. I need my brother's help, even from the beyond. I believe Paul is here . . . he should have told you some of this by now. Right?"

"Yes, London boy. That one be here with the Cat girl, down in the underground with Lacey. You go get your friend in the car and come back. I wait the door for you."

The detective smiled, not bothering to ask Mama Joan how she knew Swartz was waiting in the car around the corner. The old woman smiled back, knowing the reason for his. Then, just before he left to fetch the lieutenant, she said,

"You know, dis place, it miss your smile."

"Well, truth be known, I've missed the smile this place brought me."

And then, wordlessly, Mama Joan reached out toward London. Without hesitation, the detective reached toward her, accepting her embrace, enfolding her within his own. As they hugged, it crossed both their minds that neither of them had ever even made to touch the other before, not in all the long years they had known each other. Understanding what they were doing, though, they broke their hold on each other, wiped their faces clean of any trace of emotion, and then backed away from each other as the old woman said again,

"Go get the policeman. I wait the door." But as London started to leave, Mama Joan caught his arm, telling him,

"I like this sweater."

Before leaving his home, the detective had changed out of his wet clothes and into something more practical for keeping out the damp chill. Smiling again, London told the old woman,

"Lisa made it for me."

"I thought so," answered Mama Joan, moving the material of the sleeve back and forth between her fingers. "It's got the feel of a woman's love in it." Holding the sleeve a moment longer, she said,

"She feels ... satisfied. You finally marry dat sweet thing?" The detective began to answer, but before he could actually say anything the old woman looked deep into his eyes, and then smiled as she said,

"Married—yes. And even children. Maybe you learn something from come dis place so many times, after all." Then the smile vanished as she said, "Go on, get him. Sudden I think maybe you got no more time to waste."

London went to the corner, waved Swartz on, and then waited for him. When the lieutenant arrived, the detective started them both walking back toward the door, keeping their pace exceptionally slow so he could prepare the policeman for where he was about to go and what might happen there.

"Now remember, for your sake more than mine, this place doesn't usually make a habit of opening its doors for policemen. You *will* conveniently forget everything you see and hear—right?"

"I understand how a deal is made, London," snapped Swartz, tiring somewhat of the detective's unorthodox procedures. "I think I can behave myself."

"Try real hard, Lieutenant," said London as they neared the front door. "This place might look like just one more rat's-assed dump, but it's a bunker you and your men couldn't breech without cannons. Don't talk to the old lady at the door. Trust me, she doesn't want to have anything to do with you or any small talk you might want to

make. Break any of her rules and all you do is open yourself up to the Murder Dogs that could be behind any or all
of the doors in the place."

"Murder Dogs?"

"A colorful name, granted, but an accurate one. They're
a tough bunch, but all they want from you is to be left
alone. Just try and remember one thing," added London as
they came up on the door, "whatever you might think of
what these people do, they did help save the world . . .
more than once. Those of them that are still alive, anyway."

As they approached the door it swung open from the inside, Mama Joan allowing them both to pass. The pair
cleared the doorway, but as they moved forward, Mama
Joan suddenly stepped into Swartz's path. Before he could
do anything, she drew her fingers across his face, leaving
four thick scarlet lines from the right side of his forehead
to the left side of his neck. As he began to protest, she set
down the bowl of blood she had dabbed her hand in and
said,

"You quiet. Dis the mark you wear while you in dis
place. If I call for kill, my pups, they know who to kill.
And, please, do not seek to be that white-man kind of
clever. You try wipe away, the pups they kill, I say or not."

"Do you have any idea who you're talking to?" growled
Swartz, both angry and embarrassed.

"Yes. I be talkin' to one little man, locked in dis
place—surrounded by guns and hate and only kept alive
by the thinnest of lines. Do not break dat line, Lieutenant
Swartz, and you will live to clean your face and regain
your fragile dignity when you be gone dis place."

The officer turned to look at London. He gave the detective a harsh stare, which London returned. Not knowing
what else to do, Swartz turned back to where Mama Joan
had been, only to discover that she was no longer there.
He had heard none of the doors in the hall either open or
close. He had heard no noise at all. And yet the old
woman was gone. The policeman turned to stare at London again, but the detective only shrugged and said,

"What do you want from me? Come on, we've got more important things to do than fight with each other."

"So you keep telling me," answered Swartz.

"Well, that's because it's the truth," replied London, walking down the hall. "But it's good of you to be keeping track."

The pair started down a circular staircase at the end of the hall, one marked with signs declaring it unsafe. Swartz worried about them at first, but as they descended, he could tell the warnings were just a ruse. Once in the basement, they followed a twisted path until they finally came to the building's main workroom. Swartz's trained eye could not help roving, trying to spot clues as to what kind of operation the place's inhabitants were running. Everything in the room had been draped with large sheets, however—some cloth, some canvas—to foil such an attempt.

In the background, Morcey and Cat waited, seated at a large workbench covered with computer monitors and littered with electronic gear of all types. Next to them was a thin black man of medium height. He stood and crossed the room as soon as London and Swartz entered. The lieutenant noted that he was forty-five to fifty-five years old . . . also that he had extremely dark skin, several visibly bad teeth, close-cropped hair, a pair of eyes that did not match each other exactly, and a scar roughly three inches long on his left cheek. London only saw an old friend, and greeted him as such.

"Lacey—long time, no see."

"Dat's right. And whose fault is dat?"

"Ah, check, please," said London, smiling. The thin man's scarred face broke into a smile, his broken teeth a beacon in his obsidian black face. Grabbing the detective's hand, Lacey pumped it vigorously. As the two clasped each other's shoulders with their free hands, the thin man said,

"Dat's right, you got dat right. Better be leavin' a jumpin' big tip, too. Oh, bright rain on the cane, you been

gone too long. The daddy-man's spirit ... it been askin'
about you. We knew you'd be comin' soon."

"What's this, London," asked Swartz abruptly, "travel
bulletins from the other side?" The detective wheeled
around abruptly, pointing his finger like a steel rod at the
lieutenant as he snapped,

"This is my brother's home—you got that? You're here
on sufferance, *Officer*. Just keep your yap shut and try to
learn something." Then London invaded Swartz's head,
sounding a message directly inside his mind.

*I told you to be quiet in here. If you think I won't let
Mama Joan and her boys do what they want with you, you
are sadly mistaken. I'm no get-out-of-jail-free card. This is
their island in your city, and you're on your own. If they
think you're trouble, you'll never live to see the
outside—so do yourself a favor and shut up.*

Swartz shuddered, not so much from the threat of violence or death implied by London's warning, but from the
warning itself. The detective's voice, sounding in his head,
had been horribly unnerving. The lieutenant had been staring directly at London's face. The detective's lips had not
moved. He had seen the faces of the others in the room as
well. None of them had heard London's admonishment.
Only Swartz. And in that moment, the policeman finally believed not just on a few surface levels, but on all levels of
his brain, that something beyond his ken was happening.

Only a split second had passed since the detective had
spoken aloud. The lieutenant fumbled for the right words
to say, then for any words at all, but he was not able to
make a sound. Suddenly he found himself without focus,
cut adrift, without a place in the chain of command. Used
to being the top dog, he was more than uncomfortable
finding himself in a room of people who were investigating a crime, a room where everyone else was more in the
know, and more in authority than he was. As he tried to
say something, London put a finger to his own lips, saying,

"Not now. You're just learning. Listen." Then, the detective turned back to Lacey and said,

"All right, we're here. We're ready. So tell me, what are we here and ready for?"

"Dis be some bad juju, as dey used to say in the old movies. Me, now, I just be an old boom-boom man. Sell a little boom, buy a little boom—I'm no player for dis new world. Runs too fast for me, it do. But, Cat here. She still playin'. She the bright light. Even when the daddy-man go on, she stay here, work her day from the same table as always. All the Murder Dogs, we stay here, but we got our eyes turned back at dat old world. Cat, she got her eyes lookin' forward, toward dat world dat's comin'. She's got the goods. You take a look. You tell me if'n you sees anything you likes."

All attention in the room shifted to Cat. The small electronics expert shrunk in on herself, the weight of Swartz's impatience and London's ability to pass judgment crushing her for a moment, forcing the breath out of her. The moment passed unnoticed, however. Taking a deep breath, she said,

'Ted, you been feeling like there's something missing from your life? Not enough zip? Not enough zing? Not enough excitement?"

"Oh, possibly," answered London.

"That's good, that's good," answered the strawberry blonde as she reached for a stack of papers on the table next to her. With a biting edge growing in her voice, one that implied anger as well as fear, she continued, "That's real good. Because have we got a vacation package for you."

"Cat," asked the detective with concern, "you sound a little bothered."

"Oh, I just might be," she admitted. Then, looking London straight in the eye, she told him,

"The last time I saw you, we were trying to take out a thing that couldn't be stopped by guns or bombs or fire or anything. I not only helped you with that mess, I got your ass out of the worst of it. You took off without so much as a thank-you, and I didn't see you again for years. Doesn't do a woman's ego good to be treated that way.

But . . ." Cat's voice froze for a moment into a desperate pause that let everyone listening know that despite her cool exterior, she was indeed more than a little frightened. Thawing her voice, she finished by saying,

"Let me put it this way, you get the world out of this mess . . . and I'll forgive you."

10

"Well," answered London, wondering what could have shaken the normally tightly wound Cat so profoundly. "I guess I better try to do my best. Just what the hell did you two find anyway?"

Morcey held up the original computer disks and the papers he had found under the rug. Passing them over to the detective, he said,

"As you can see, the Confessor's room surrendered its secrets."

"Withholding evidence, Mr. London?" asked Swartz in a whisper.

"Letting your ego interfere with our investigation again, Lieutenant?" answered the detective just as quietly without bothering to turn toward the policeman. Accepting the small handful from his partner, he listened as Cat said,

"The papers are pretty meaningless . . . just number patterns, miscellaneous words interspersed. Obviously a code, but for what, we didn't know. We headed back here to see if we could access the disks, but we couldn't beat the code."

"Why not?" asked Swartz.

"Six-hundred-character security label."

"What?"

"That's right, Your Honor," answered Cat, sarcastically. "The gherkins who rammed this stuff onto the disk came up with a securing label that takes over five minutes of straight keyboarding just to reach access. And of course, that's if you know the code. If you don't, you guess forever. We're talking a completely unlimited number of possibilities."

"But that's uncrackable," said Swartz.

"That's right," answered the electronics expert with a wide grin.

"But you called London saying you had news for us."

"Right again, chief."

"Then that means you cracked it—and in only a few hours."

"Isn't he just the smartest thing," said Cat to the rest of the room, affecting a deep southern drawl. Switching back to her regular voice, she said, "Relax, Kojak, before the rest of your hair falls out. It wasn't all that hard." The short woman leaned back in her chair, clearly enjoying the moment she had carved out for herself. After a few seconds of gloating, however, she leaned forward again, saying,

"We busted our heads for a long time, I'll agree. Hell, it took the first two hours of me turning this stuff inside out just to find out what we were up against. Then we got smart. And, as much as I'd like to take credit for everything, it was Paul that came through."

"Lai Wan, really," added Morcey as all turned to look in his direction. Without waiting for anyone to ask for an explanation, he said,

"We just called home. I guess it was before you guys got there. Anyway, we told Lai what the problem was, and then read her what we had. She concentrated on it for a while, then suddenly, which I guess is no big mystery for you now, she cued in on the answer. It only took us about fifteen minutes before she was able to dictate the password code, which left us with enough information to crack the nut. Of course, as soon as she knew we had everything we needed, she told us the kids had to finish their lessons and she went back to helping them."

"Quite the nanny," said Swartz in a voice that suggested he did not believe what Morcey had told them. "A psychic that can divine passwords over the telephone? No laying on of hands? You're spreading it thin, London."

"Lai Wan's my wife, Kojak," answered Morcey, annoyed at the lieutenant's tone and what it implied. "We've got what they call a good rapport. She couldn't do it with anyone else like that, 'cept maybe the boss."

"Oh, so you've got a good rapport with your partner's wife, do you, Mr. London?" The detective held up his hand to Morcey, whom he could sense was already coming off his stool to confront Swartz. Not bothering to turn to face the policeman, London answered,

"I've got a good rapport with everybody, Lieutenant, even holier-than-thou badgeketeers. Now, if we can stop getting bogged down in how we found out what was on the disks, let's get down to discussing what it is that's on them."

"You got it," answered Cat. Punching in a series of commands on the keyboard closest to her, she ran through a series of screens until she finally reached the point in the material that she wanted to show the others.

"Now," she said, keeping her eye on the scrolling text in front of her, "I don't think these files were made by your friend the Confessor. I think he, shall we say . . . appropriated them somewhere along the way."

"Any ideas where?" asked London.

"No. No, not really. But on the face of things, it doesn't seem all that important, either." And then the woman leaned out of the way of the monitor in front of her so the others could see its screen. Clearing the way for them, she said, "Here, take a look."

The two newcomers stepped in closer, ready to learn what everyone else in the room already knew. London allowed Swartz to step in first. He knew the policeman had been pushed aside too often and that he needed something to hold on to. The detective, on the other hand, was more interested in reading the emotional level of the others. As he and the lieutenant stepped up to the screen, he felt strong emotions bubbling to the surface in all the others. The three of them had looked over the material earlier, had had the time to get used to it.

Now, however, as he and Swartz moved forward, Morcey, Cat, and Lacey began to review what they had seen in their heads, each of them wondering what the detective and the policeman would have to say, each of them reevaluating their own feelings against what they projected London's feelings would be. As they did so, the detective could feel more than a rise in tension from them. He felt a growing terror, a horror so cold and all-pervasive that suddenly he was quite curious as to what could be causing it. In some ways, reading the people around him took him somewhat aback.

Morcey had been with him since the first. The pair had faced all manner of nightmares together. For the balding man, the news of each new beast and menace had always been like a tonic. Once he had left his life as a janitor and stepped into the role of monster hunter, he had begun to live for each new confrontation. But now, his fear was as thick as that of the others, a dread that London could tell dated back to Morcey's childhood.

It's like the bogeyman, or something, thought London. All of them—it's something that all three of them have feared since they were old enough to fear anything at all.

But, asked another part of his brain, what could that be? What is it that three people that different, from such different walks of life—all of them different ages, no less—could have feared—*so completely*—since practically the day they were born?

And then, the detective stepped forward toward the monitor. As he stared down at the words on the glowing orange screen, Cat said,

"So, what do you think? Is this a case for the London Agency, or not?"

The detective stared over Swartz's shoulder, taking in the contents of the computer's screen. Scanning all of the data before him, it did not take him long to see what it was that had the others so worried. His mind rolled it all over. A man who claimed to belong to a lineage dating back to the beginning of time tells them someone has confessed a monstrous evil to him. He is killed by a legion of warriors, one of whom cannot only fly but perhaps even cheat death itself.

And why is he killed, whispered a voice in the back of

London's mind. Why, so the secret of two hundred missing nuclear warheads could be protected. That's why.

With a voice almost cracking from sudden dryness, the detective answered,

"Yes, Cat, I see your point."

11

"I'm telling you, *Mister* Morcey," said Swartz, slamming down the receiver in his hand, "I told my people to check everything. Not only the streets, but the walls and rooftops of all nearby buildings. They did a ten-block sweep. That's a lot of man-hours for this city to pay for. They didn't find any trace of a body anywhere near your offices. If there was a flying man outside your window, he didn't fall anywhere where the city of New York could find him."

The balding man started to answer the lieutenant, when London's voice came from behind them,

"Then that clinches it, all right. They're back."

"Who's back?"

"A man I killed a few years ago," answered the detective, a regretting, somewhat disbelieving tone in his voice. He paused for a long moment, as if he were thinking about some initial memory. Then suddenly, he made a small rueful sound, finally adding, "And ... I would suppose ... a few of his friends, as well."

The lieutenant sputtered, still having trouble keeping his balance when the detective said such things. Having no choice other than to raise officially objective questions, once he caught hold of himself, Swartz said,

"Oh, that's it, eh? First off, you couldn't have missed with any of your shots—awww, no. A man is flying— *flying, mind you*—at your window, and you pop him with six shots, one right after another. Bam, bam, bam—bam, bam, bam. You ... why, you couldn't possibly miss. Not the great Theodore London. And then, when his body isn't found after the biggest square-inch search the city's seen in the last twenty years, it's not because you missed, or, or even because he just floated away—oh, no. Either of those would be too easy. No, it's because he's some guy who rises from the dead."

"Hey," shouted Morcey, sliding off his chair. He held himself straight with defiance as he said, "I got two words for you, pal. One's a verb, the other's a pronoun. Why don't you just stuff it for a while?"

"And why don't you give me something solid to work with?"

"The hell with you, Kojak. We gived you solid."

"Right—flying men."

"Goddamned right, flying men," shouted the ex–maintenance man, his jaw hardening. "You've had your people check it out. Were there any helicopters over the city at that time, in that area? Did anyone find a report of a plane, a balloon, even some loopy parachutist? No. But your people also reported to you that our windows were definitely shot in, not out—didn't they? You know that someone was outside our windows and I'll bet your people have also done the ballistics to tell you that they weren't shot out at close range, or from a trajectory matching any of the surrounding rooftops. So why don't you just get with the program and stop dry-heaving all over us?"

Morcey and Swartz stared at each other, fingers just beginning to curl into fists, blood starting to flush their faces. Tension had gotten the better of both men—tension born of waiting without having anything constructive to do. Tired of listening to the pair bicker, Lacey looked up from the chamber mechanism he was cleaning and said,

"You two make a lot of air, you know that? Why no you can't sing the same song—just for a little while, heh? Nobody asking you to marry each other, but you could fall in love . . . just a little, for sweet ol' Lacey, maybe?"

Morcey glanced at his watch. It had been four hours since Cat and London had first bent down over the printouts and papers which were their only leads. So far, all the group knew was that someone, somewhere, had managed to pull together a private arsenal of 223 nuclear bombs. Some were atomic, some were hydrogen, and a few were neutron. Most of them were suspected of being unstable— just as likely to blow up whoever set them off as those they were set against.

But that was all they had: a list of the bombs, the countries they had come from, and in what condition they were suspected to be. The rest of the codes and lines of facts they had had added up to nothing more in all their hours of study. Lai Wan had come to Mama Joan's to, as Swartz had put it, lay hands on the papers to see what she might have been able to discern. Sadly, she had not been able to find anything. The disks had been duped by the Confessor, and the papers he had hidden were not originals. He had made copies of the originals on a copying machine. And, as the psychometrist told them,

"I am sorry, but I cannot tell you what any of this means beyond the surface material we can all read. I could tell you the password only because the Confessor had known it. It is unfortunate but true that he did not know what these papers meant, or what further there is to tell from this rest. If he did, I would be able to tell you. But I cannot. Gentlemen, Cat, you must forgive me, but I cannot tell you any more."

And then she had taken her leave, returning home to help Lisa wait with the children as the others wrestled with the problem at hand. Lacey had pleaded ignorant from the beginning, ignoring the challenge of trying to decipher the puzzles. Morcey had joined him quickly, doing no more than glance at the pages and various computer screens before admitting defeat. The lieutenant—never much for mind puzzles—had given in quickly as well, leaving the game of rearranging the pieces of their enigma to the detective and Cat.

That, however, had left the three men with nothing to do except get on each other's nerves. Swartz's talk with his own captain, gathering in what little the police had learned, had done little for his temper. London swept it aside, however, saying,

"Gentlemen, we've got no time to waste. Something beyond the scope of what any of us has had to deal with for a long time—some of us forever—is back and they've gotten hold of a lot of very bad toys."

"What's the story, boss?" asked Morcey.

"Remember a guy by the name of Martin Tabor?"

"Tabor, Tabor . . . ," said the ponytailed man with a thoughtful drone. He rubbed his knuckles into his cheek for a moment, then suddenly remembered, "Oh yeah, the C.P.A. of the damned."

"That's the guy."

"What about him?"

"That's the guy I think I shot flying at our windows."

"Tabor?" said Morcey with a wondering tone. "Tabor can fly now? Tabor's shooting off guns?"

"And apparently leading non-vampires in attacks against us," added London, not happy at all with what he was saying. Swartz came forward, his mustache twitching as he moved his upper lip back and forth. In a voice more interested than belligerent, he asked,

"Who's the suspect?"

"Martin Tabor is a vampire we killed a few years back."

"Vampire, huh?"

"Yes," answered London. The detective reined in his sarcasm, giving the lieutenant the benefit of the doubt.

You must have let him in on this for a reason, a voice reminded him, as London said,

"Vampires. They don't suck blood from anyone's necks and they don't sleep in dirt or coffins . . . at least, it's not necessary. They don't command legions of rats or wolves, and they don't turn into bats. . . ."

"But they do fly?"

"Yes, Lieutenant, they do—as of today—seem to fly. They are real, Swartz." London looked into the policeman's eyes, and then told him,

"They've been alive for thousands of years. Not all of them, but some. We killed their king a while back, a man who had been a sorcerer before Solomon. We killed Hercules, too. We thought we killed Tabor."

"Look, dead wizards and Greek gods I don't know from. But, trying to take this all serious for a moment, let me ask you . . . ," Swartz paused, part of him wondering where he was going, part of him willing to wing it. Having finally found something in the case he could latch on to, he threw away his reservations for once and asked, "Are you sure it was him? Are you swearing positive identification?"

"It looked like him, yeah—what I didn't shoot up—but it was more. It had the . . . I hate to put it to you this way . . . but, it had the *feel* of him."

"That little fuck is back," said Morcey in a somewhat distant voice. Hearing the edge to it, Swartz turned to him and said,

"You're the one who got this Tabor, aren't you?"

"Yeah," admitted Morcey, openly. Wondering if he was about to be charged with something, he compounded his admission, making it purposely clear by adding, "That was my distinction."

The lieutenant paused for a long moment. Then something changed in the room. A voice from the back of his mind, one that he always trusted, suddenly asked him if he was going to believe what he knew—*knew*—deep down was true or not. It laughed at him when he tried to take a tough line with it, asking him who he thought he was fooling. Finally, knowing when he had made up his mind, he simply added quietly,

"Guess you didn't do a very good job."

"No," agreed Morcey, his eyes narrowing, his lips thinning out into a long, humorless grin. "I guess not."

"Hummmm," said Swartz, reflecting the balding man's thin smirk. "Guess we'll have to think about fixing that."

"Yeah, maybe we will." The ex–maintenance man took a step closer to the policeman, and then said,

"And maybe I should be tryin' to take a few things inta consideration here. You ain't never been involved with nuthin' like this before. Yeah, sure, I know you think you've seen a lotta shit, but this is different. I've seen a bunch of people in your same position—thrown inta the middle of one of these things—no idea what to do. No idea about what's real and what ain't. It's hard, 'cause you wanta just, like deny it all, make excuses, wish it away. It's just natural."

"So you trying to make nice to me all of a sudden?"

asked the lieutenant in his I'll-call-a-truce-if-you-will voice.

"Yeah," answered Morcey, "I suppose so. But only 'cause if I do and you keep actin' like a creep, then it'll give me an edge of moral superiority."

Swartz stared at the balding man for a moment, and then as the phrase, "In for a penny . . ." flashed through his head, he started to laugh. It was definitely a giving-in kind of sound, a chuckle of defeat that signified he could not find any reason to continue fighting. Turning back to the detective at that point, he said,

"You didn't come out here to referee. What'd you find out?"

"We've managed to crack a few lines here and there—we think. Putting together what we have, there are two hundred twenty-three nukes out there. If we're correct, there are fifteen major divisions. You know, ten here, fifteen there, three here, what have you. We don't know where anything is . . . yet, but we do have a lead."

"Spill," said Swartz, warming to the trail.

"We found an access point; it looks as if a number of freighters of Panamanian registry will be trying to move quite a few of these warheads into the country on the West Coast."

"All the bombs are coming into America?" asked the lieutenant with a shocked voice.

"No," answered London. As Cat walked through the door with a new printout filled with information, the detective said, "they're apparently being spread throughout the world. But we traced a number of these vessels to their next port of call, and they're due in San Francisco next week."

"That doesn't give us much time," said Swartz, wondering just what he should do. His brain offered a dozen different suggestions. tell his superiors, alert Interpol, call the FBI, the State Department . . .

Get a leave of absence.

The lieutenant heard the voice in his head, taking a second to realize that it was not one of his own. Looking at the detective, he bunched his brow down over his eyes, staring with a questioning look. London smiled, and then said,

"You heard me."

"Are you saying we do this ourselves?"

"No, I'm saying . . ." But just before the detective could finish his answer, the phone rang, echoing shrilly in the metal-filled basement. Lacey answered it, finding it to be the outside line he had given Swartz to use to stay in touch with his department. The lieutenant took the receiver, talked to his people for a moment, then asked them to hold on while he said,

"We left people at your office, you may remember."

"Yes," answered London, flatly, leaching any kind of commitment from his voice. He could feel the anger coming off Swartz, the anger whipping back and forth within his thin, middle-aged body. Knowing the officer was under tremendous pressure, able to tell what had happened from the sorrow in the man's eyes, the anger in his blood-reddening neck, he gave him the moment he needed to talk without erupting.

"There were two dozen of them there—a few more, actually," he said after a moment. "More than half of them were armed. At least eight of them heavily."

Swartz shut his eyes then, the pain of what he had been told too much for him to bear all at once. Those on the other end of the line waited patiently for him to come back. They saw no need to rush him, either.

"Are they all dead?" asked London softly.

"Not yet," answered the lieutenant numbly. "They're getting statements from the three that are still alive."

"Maybe we should go up and take a look," suggested London.

"Maybe we should go with our eyes open," added Morcey, patting the bulge under his arm.

"Oh yeah," agreed Swartz. Pulling out his own sidearm, he dropped the clip out of it and then held it up to eye level. Looking at each cartridge, he snapped the clip back up inside, then chambered a round, saying,

"And our fucking glasses on."

Lacey ran his upper teeth over his lower lip, then pulled an ammunition belt from a drawer next to him. Strapping it around his waist, he said,

"My, my, it's always so much fun to play with da white boys. Dey come up with such interesting games."

12

Man, thought Morcey, I thought there was a lot of blood after they killed the Confessor.

Everywhere the ex–maintenance man looked, the scene was one of scarlet horror. Bodies had been torn apart, arms pulled free from torsos, with long strings of ribboned meat hanging from them, trailing across the floor. Who or whatever it was that had come in on the officers and civilians investigating the crime scene in London's office had been quick and thorough. Men and women had been slaughtered equally, their bodies violated with a ruthless sense of completeness.

Officers of all ranks were scattered throughout the agency's suite. Most were barely able to function, hampered by either numbness or rage. Many were red-eyed from the sight of friends and co-workers treated so horrifically. Several had been forced to leave the scene, filled with shame but unable to stop themselves from crying. Those that were able to stay forgave them, however. Those who were not crying surely wanted to.

Never before in the city's centuries-old history had the police suffered such a devastating loss. The dead had not just been killed—they had been *used*. Some had been battered through the wall, heads and arms in one room, legs in the next. One had been impaled on a large shard of glass still standing upright in one of the shattered window frames, his eyes deliberately pierced with long, daggerlike slivers. Another had been twisted into a monstrous tangle—arms and legs intertwined, his head removed and placed in a line of heads on the top shelf of Morcey's closet.

The gruesome row was the most disturbing sight in the office. Each of the heads had been carved to appear as if it were wearing some sort of grotesque clown face—

oversized lips, starburst eyes, et cetera—each one was a unique horror, distinct from all its mates. The heads had been surrounded by some sort of thick, dark gray dust, its design reminiscent of the fake snow used in department store Christmas windows. A number of the dead's badges had been propped up in the heavy, charcoal-colored particles as grotesque decorations. Then, after setting the scene, the mutilators had torn the closet's sliding doors down to fully display their handiwork. So far, the sight had forced everyone back out of the room only a few seconds after they entered.

"Sweet bride of the night," muttered Morcey softly to himself as he left his office, as happy to leave as any of the city investigators. "I bet Lacey and Cat'll both be glad they had to stay with the car when they hear about this. Ohhhhhhh, man—oh, God."

"Not pretty," agreed London.

"Pretty? No, I guess not, boss. Not when you gotta step over the pools of blood 'cause they're stretched out like rainwater in the street."

The dead were not the only thing that was different, however. Although it was not noticeable at first, more had been done than just the killing of the policemen and woman. The detective's office had been wrecked. Whatever damage the first crew had done had been practically negligible in comparison to those who had come after. Besides the heavy toll in human life, every bit of furniture had been smashed. London's desk had been splintered, torn apart down to the nuts and bolts that had held it together. The leather of his chair had been shredded as if by claws. Holes had been torn in the walls—even the floor and ceiling.

As the detective and his partner moved into the main office, they found Swartz standing there, pulling down a lungful of smoke from his third cigarette since they had arrived. Not normally much of a smoker, he had lit one up in the elevator on the way up to the agency's floor, as if possessed by some knowledge that he would need the thick, nicotine comfort within it. After the door had opened and he had witnessed the carnage that began in the hall, he had had no problem chain-smoking his way through that one and the next . . . and the next. . . .

Lighting a fourth from the burning filter of the third, the lieutenant fought back a hacking fit prompted by the smoldering plastic fibers. After that, he ground the filter out on his sleeve and stowed it in his pocket to keep it from getting mixed in with whatever evidence the new forensic team might be able to gather. After a particularly forceful exhale, he turned to London and said,

"So, what's your guess? Were whoever hit this place out to do just what we can see they did, or was this a regrouping move? In other words, did they come again wanting the same thing they wanted the first time?"

"Meaning, are we dealing with cop killers or detective killers?" When Swartz nodded his head a millimeter, London went on. "I wonder. Actually, I've begun to wonder if both attacks were made by the same group. I've been thinking."

"About?"

"About, Lieutenant, just what *this*"—spreading his hands, London indicated the bodies and destruction all around them—"this was all about." Then, looking around at the dozens of officers and lab men and detectives moving about his office, the detective asked,

"Do you think we could get off somewhere a little more private? So we could . . . talk?"

It took Swartz a moment to realize that the detective wanted to ask or tell him something the policeman might not want his colleagues to hear—not because it was anything he might want to hide, but because it was most likely something the lieutenant himself would have trouble accepting, let alone his fellow officers. Giving London another nod, Swartz took a deep drag on his cigarette and then walked them out of the crowded main office, back out into the reception area. After a second's consideration, the lieutenant chose Morcey's office for the simple reason that no one else wanted to go into it. Then, after the three had gotten themselves inside, Swartz asked,

"So, what's up? You divine something out of the ether of the spirit world?"

"No. Just a little old-fashioned deductive reasoning. Of course," said London, not unkindly, "I've got a few facts to go on that you don't."

Swartz stared at the row of heads in the closet. He heard the detective's words, but they could not tear his eyes from the horrifying sight. London and Morcey gave the lieutenant a moment of silence, waiting for him to come around. As they stood, watching him from behind, he said,

"So, I guess us big dumb cops are pretty fortunate, then, eh?" The pair said nothing, simply standing quietly while they watched the tension growing in the policeman. The detective could actually see sizzling waves of heat sluicing away from the officer's upper body. And then, as Swartz's head began to vibrate, his shoulders shaking with anger, he continued speaking, his voice filling with rage.

"I mean, just thank fucking God we've got the divine resources of Theodore Fucking London and his facts from nowhere to fix everything up for us. Just what would we poor idiot slobs do without you?"

And then, as he stood transfixed in front of the closet, a single drop of blood fell from the shelf. It broke away as if on cue with Swartz's last word, falling with a spinning motion until it hit the carpet below, splatting quietly into more of the dust that had been used to decorate the heads. At that moment, the lieutenant's last shred of sanity fell away.

Leaping forward toward the closet, he slammed into the shelf, screaming and thrashing, kicking the dust on the floor and flinging the heads this way and that. Other officers burst into the room instantly, recoiling from the sight of Swartz throwing heads about the room. London and Morcey moved forward as quickly as they could, each of them grabbing one of the lieutenant's arms. They made to restrain him, but he threw them off with an incredible surge of strength. The detective recovered his balance quickly, however, and was then able to reverse his direction, catching hold of Swartz again before he could return to his attack on the obscene shrine the killers had left behind.

Holding up his hand to the policemen crowding into the room, London said,

"Stay back—it's okay. The lieutenant only saw a rat headed for the . . . remains."

"A rat?" questioned one of the police detectives, instantly rebuked by London, who shouted,

"Yes. A rat. A rat in the closet. The lieutenant doesn't need anyone pampering him or worrying about him. He's just fine. Aren't you?" asked the detective, calming Swartz with his touch, repeating the question to give the policeman something to zero in on.

"Aren't you?"

"Ah, yeah, yeah," Swartz answered weakly, still somewhat dazed by the rapid adrenaline rush his body had hit him with and then the counteracting orders London had sent his brain. As the policeman reeled to get himself back under control, Morcey turned to the officers crowding into his office, telling them,

"He's goin' ta be okay. Why don't you guys take a breather? We'll fix 'im up."

Mostly glad for an excuse to leave the room of horrors, the others filed out, leaving the wild-eyed Swartz to London and his partner. As the last of them left, London asked the lieutenant in a whisper,

"Are you all right?"

"Yeah. Yeah, yeah. Sure. I'm fucking peachy."

"Well, then, let me say what I wanted to before." As Swartz turned toward the detective, London stared into his eyes, searching for whatever strength the man had left. He had been subjected to the sight of dead friends torn apart and used as playthings by monsters. On top of that, he had been presented with proof that there were flying people, immortals, vampires, and werewolves in the world all on the same day that he discovered that more than two hundred nuclear warheads were in the hands of a dangerous group of lunatics. The detective knew that he would only be able to handle any new information if he were walked through it in a familiar manner. Keeping his eyes locked on the policeman's, London told him,

"I've begun to wonder if we were actually attacked by vampires before or not."

"What do you mean? I thought you made a positive ID on this Tabor character?"

"I did. And like I told you, it took six slugs hitting him dead on to slow his approach and knock him out of the sky. But the others attacking at the same time, they went down a lot easier, right, Paul?"

"Yeah. You know, I didn't think about it before, but they went down pretty much like regular folks. Whaddaya think it means, boss?"

"I don't think we're facing a cover. I think someone out there is marshalling troops—attacking us on different fronts, like any good general." Swartz stared back at London, returning the detective's dark gaze watt for watt. Then, feeling his strength returning to him, he said,

"You've got something more to say—I can see it in your eyes. Spill."

"Glad to. The dust in this room, I've seen it before." Looking down at the scattered heaps of gray all around them, London said, "This is what happens to a living thing when a vampire drains it of its life force. When they totally empty something of its sustaining energies—no matter what it is, grass, people, apples, dogs, whatever—this is what's left."

As Swartz and Morcey stared at the dust all about them, the detective confirmed what both men's minds were already suggesting to them.

"I'd say it's a safe bet to conclude that this is what's left of your missing officers."

And then the lieutenant gave in. His body sagging, he stumbled across the room to the still-intact chair behind the remains of Morcey's ruined desk, falling half into it, half across the desk. Hiding his face in his hands, he lay across the top of the desk, weeping. Tears burst from his face, drenching his sleeve and the wood below. Neither London nor Morcey said anything. Both knew what acceptance of the world beyond did to most people. In truth, the detective was not worried about Swartz. He could see that the rage in the lieutenant had subsided, that he was pulling himself together.

After a few minutes, unashamed of his outburst, the officer sat up. Sitting back, wiping at his face with his sleeve, he said,

"You said earlier that the Confessor's ring is what gave him the secrets he came to tell you. I saw the Confessor's body out there in the other room. It doesn't have any rings on it."

"No," answered London. "We took it."

"Then why doesn't one of us slip it on so we can unravel all the secrets he did and get to the bottom of this?"

"I appreciate the fact that when you decide to believe in something you go all the way, Lieutenant," said the detective, "but it's not quite that simple. Remember, you may learn all the secrets, but then you won't want to tell them."

"I'm willing to take that chance," answered Swartz, his mustache bristling, "hand it over and I'll show you."

"Not that easy," interrupted Morcey, drawing all the attention in the room. "I locked it in my office safe," he continued, pointing out a section of the wall that had been torn out violently. "Considering the evidence, I'd say there's not much point ta debatin' the pros and cons of putting on the Confessor's ring. Basically 'cause we ain't got it no more."

Swartz pulled at his thin face, smoothing his mustache back into place as he said,

"That's just swell. Now, on top of all our other problems, all we have to find out is who, out of all the different freaks that stormed in and out of this place today, took the ring."

And at that moment, a new voice came from the doorway,

"That, gentlemen, would be me."

"And," asked Swartz in a voice that was almost a scream, "who the hell are you?"

The man in the doorway was old, but not feeble. His hair was mostly white, his body straight and thin. Regarding the lieutenant casually, he answered,

"My name is Bain. What's yours?"

Before the policeman could respond, Morcey cut in with introductions, saying,

"Father Bain, meet Lieutenant Swartz. The lieutenant is rapidly on his way to becomin' a believer. Lieutenant, you may remember the father from a few years back. He's the one the papers were all callin' 'the miracle priest.' "

"At your service," said the old man, making a surprisingly agile bow in the policeman's direction as he added, "delivering souls to our Almighty Father is a specialty. Might I interest you in our two-for-one special?"

Ignoring Bain, Swartz turned to London, demanding,

"Is this guy a real priest or just another one of your little hobgoblins?"

"Father Bain was, at one time, the Right Cardinal Bain, spiritual head of the diocese of New York. You may remember him as one of the hundreds of thousands who disappeared during the Conflagration. His reemergence into society as a miracle worker shouldn't have disturbed his credentials any. You are still ordained, aren't you, Father?"

"Oh, yes, my son," answered the priest seriously. "To the best of my knowledge they haven't tried to take that away from me . . . yet. I suppose it helps that officially they don't think of me as a living person anymore."

"All we can hope for in this world," said Morcey, extending his hand to the priest. "Right, Father?"

"Indeed, my son, indeed," answered Bain. "As Jesus said—in this world, not of it."

Taking the ex–maintenance man's hand, he shook it earnestly, saying, "Good to see you again. Are you still living in sin or have you made an honest woman of that beautiful girl, yet?"

"Yeah, yeah," answered Morcey with a chuckle. As the two broke off their handshake, he continued, "Somehow, believe it or not, we found a little time in between rounds of savin' the world to get married. We even tried ta find ya ta do the service, even with me bein' Jewish and her a Buddhist and all, just to keep it in the family, so to speak. But . . . as you might realize, you ain't been that easy to find lately."

"True, enough. Although, as you can see, I got your message today."

"And wasn't that convenient?" broke in Swartz's voice. "No one can find you . . . how long? Years, was it? And yet you're Johnny-on-the-spot when the time comes to interfere in an important case."

"Lieutenant," said London with a quiet voice, "try to remember that the father *is* one of the good guys. Besides, if he did manage to get in here and get the Confessor's ring in between the attacks, I'd say we owe him." Turning back to the older man, London said,

"Why don't you tell us what happened, Father?"

"Not much to tell. I got the message that Paul had called this morning down at the Callahan Mission. Funny thing, though, when you think about it, I guess it isn't . . . not to us anymore, I would suppose." Noting from Swartz's look, Father Bain knew that he had lost the policeman. He explained further, adding, "Apparently, I checked in there to see if I had any messages only a few minutes after the message was left. First time I had checked in weeks. Just got an urge—don't you know?"

The father smiled widely at the lieutenant, who merely scowled, crossing his arms over his chest. Ignoring the policeman, Bain added,

"I did call, but there was no answer."

"You had me lookin' for the father just about the time we got hit by the first attack," said Morcey. "I only had time to leave the one message before Tabor and company started shootin' the place up. When the father called we was probably gettin' too shot up to hear the phone.'

"Makes sense," agreed London. "Go on, Father. You were saying?"

"Yes. Anyway, the fact that there was no answer started to nag at me." Directing his next sentences to Swartz, the elderly priest said, "We're not much for calling each other lightly. Not that we're not friends, but we really don't gather unless something important is going on. Too much to do in this world," he sighed sadly, saying, "I suppose. Anyway, I decided to make my way up here. I hadn't spread the gospel in this part of town for a while, so I thought, 'why not?' "

An officer stuck his head in the door at that moment, calling for the lieutenant's attention. While Swartz apologized for the interruption and went over to confer with the policeman, Bain lifted his hand, showing London that he was wearing the Confessor's ring. He made a motion with his head and his eyes, moving them in the direction of the lieutenant. Knowing what he meant, the detective gave his head a slight nod, pursing his lips into a "he's okay" formation. Then, once the interrupting officer was gone and Swartz was back, the father said,

"So I came up and found quite a few policemen buzzing about the place. At first, they were set upon denying me access. But, well, you know how persuasive I can be, eh, Theodore?" When London nodded, letting the lieutenant know that the priest could indeed talk his way into just about anywhere, Bain moved his head to indicate that he was flattered, then said,

"Anyway, it was readily obvious to me that none of you were here. Part of me—that little voice that always knows when something is just not right, you know—was quite insistent that I should leave at once. But another part of me—that rare whisper that can come in and countermand any thought, no matter how grounded it might be in common sense, insisted I stay. When I asked it what I would want to stay for, all it could say was that 'I knew.' Finding that most peculiar, I simply stood still for a moment, closing my eyes, searching my mind for what it was that I thought I knew. Before I could help myself, I had come into Mr. Morcey's office and opened his safe."

"How did you do that?" asked Swartz.

"Do what, Officer?"

"Open his safe? Did you have the combination?"

"Not consciously. But I guess I had it within me to figure it out. I did not question the forces moving me. They seemed . . . right somehow, and so I allowed them to continue to move me. In seconds, they had opened the safe, pulled out the Confessor's ring, and then they deserted me. Suddenly, I was alone again, holding the ring, with only one thought in my head, to run as fast as I could. Not being one to question the directives of Providence, I took flight. I would suppose only just avoiding"—he waved his hands gently around himself, indicating the devastating carnage to all sides—"all of this."

"If you've got the Confessor's ring," said Swartz, wagging his finger at Bain as if just putting something together in his head, "then what's the answer . . . for all of this? What was it done for? What the hell's going on?"

The elder priest stared at the officer for a short moment. His eyes narrowed, he tried to decipher what the lieutenant meant, but he could not. Finally, London said,

"Before he kicked on us, the Confessor said that putting on the ring had been the catalyst for him . . . that after he did it he could hear the voices of all the previous Confessors in his head." The detective recapped the story of the man in white for Bain, trying to bring him quickly up to speed. Gauging the reaction the father was having from the expression on his face, London finally asked,

"Nothing like that for you, though?"

"Sorry, my son. If this really is some sort of unbroken kind of thing, then I would imagine that means I'm not the one fate has picked to be the next Confessor."

"Now wait a minute," snarled Swartz. "You say you're led here by a mysterious compulsion, that you open a safe without the combination because of an urge, and then after you get the ring another whim hustles you out of here just before all the carnage. But, with all of that, you're not the one who's supposed to put on the goddamned ring?!"

"Now you listen to me," answered Bain in a low, growling voice crisp with hinted thunder. "There's an old saying that wise men pay heed to. 'The Lord works in mysterious ways.' Ever hear it? Ever give any thought to what it means? Don't strain your secular little brain, I'll explain it for you. It means that once you open yourself up to God and his plan, you no longer have to worry about anything. That there is no more strangeness, no more purposelessness—that right and wrong suddenly have very definable borders and that where you are supposed to be at any time and what you are supposed to be doing are things that are suddenly clear. Clear like the sky after the cleansing rain." Moving forward, his voice growing a notch, the father closed the space between himself and Swartz, saying,

"My life is clear to me, Lieutenant. I know who I am and what I'm supposed to be doing. Whatever my God tells me to do, I do it. Without question. When you walk the brimstone lane, watching for devils, it pays to memorize the rule book and do whatever the coach tells you . . . no matter how much your own opinion might differ." Then, folding back the drooping sleeve of his cloak, Bain pulled off the Confessor's ring and handed it to Swartz, saying,

"Here—you think this is a trinket out of some Spielberg movie. You try it. You find an off/on switch—you tell me all about it."

The policeman accepted the heavy piece of jewelry. Holding it up for inspection for a moment, he hesitated only slightly, then jammed it on his finger. Morcey, Bain, and London all stood silently, waiting for the officer's reaction. Finally, the elder priest asked,

"Any revelations, Lieutenant?"

Swartz curled his lips for a moment, ready to throw words back at Bain simply to make himself heard. But then he checked himself, a part of his brain reminding him that finding out what was going on was more important than any amount of ego-soothing schoolyard banter. Looking at the thick band of gold on his finger, he admitted,

"Nothing I recognize as very legitimate."

"Then," said Morcey, tired of getting nowhere, "what do we do next?"

"Next," answered London, moving toward the door, "we go see someone who *can* tell us something."

It only took the others a few seconds to follow him out into the hall.

14

"Still working this late?" asked London. "No rest for the weary, eh?"

The woman behind the desk was of mixed blood, in her late twenties—tired from too much work and edgy from too much coffee. She sat surrounded by books and files on all sides, her desk covered with papers as well as unopened letters and packages. She looked up sharply upon hearing the detective's voice, an equal mix of surprise and fear playing across her face. After her initial moment of shock finally passed, she leaned back in her chair as far as it would go and then spoke.

"Oh my, my," she said, her voice sharpened to a sarcastic edge, "now I must admit I never really did expect to see any of you again."

"What's the matter, Joylyn?" asked Morcey. "You not up for surprises anymore?"

"In this world," answered the woman behind the large oak desk, "there are surprises and there are surprises, and then there are surprises. Your little band has been known to deal in all kinds—all of them being the kind most people don't like." Turning to London, the woman asked.

"How about it, Theodore? What kind of surprises are you dealing in these days?"

"Now, now," answered the detective, turning aside her sarcasm. "If I were to tell, then it wouldn't be a surprise anymore, now would it?"

"I'll take my chances."

"Well, now, that's good to hear," said London with a thin, sarcastic drawl. Pointing into the woman's office, the detective urged the others to enter, saying, "As long as you're still willing to take a few chances, we'll take that as an invitation to come on in. I believe you know everyone here except for Lieutenant Swartz."

The woman's name was Joylyn Featherstone. She had been a graduate student working for one of London's colleagues the last time the detective had seen her. That had been years ago. During the time her beauty had not faded. If anything, her high cheekbones, a gift from her American Indian great-grandmother, had become even more accentuated. Her enthusiasm for investigating the supernatural—at least on the level the London Agency tackled its investigations, however—apparently had not.

The colleague of London's she had been employed with had been killed by the werewolf. Joylyn, only a few credits shy of having her teaching credentials at that time, had completed her studies without her mentor, doing her dissertation on his works. It had gotten her a doctorate and her late boss's office and most of his classes. Professor Zachary Goward had been Columbia University's unchallenged authority on religions, superstitions, and the supernatural. His philosophy and theology classes had been highly praised. Joylyn had not yet come close to equaling his ability to mesmerize an auditorium full of students. But she had found her own approach to the same material as well as managing to get it across without boring any of her listeners.

"I assume there is no stopping you?"

"No," answered London. "Not really. Not unless you want the death of billions on your conscience."

Joylyn's eyes narrowed down into thin slits, her nostrils expanding as she exhaled harshly. The woman crossed her arms tightly across her abdomen, cutting herself off from the others in the room, unconsciously increasing her defensive pose by allowing her fingers to curl into fists. She made to throw London's words back at him—had her words picked out—but before she could Father Bain put up his hand, cutting her off with the gentle motion as he said,

"It has been a long time, Ms. Featherstone. Everyone here, with the exception of Lieutenant Swartz, of course, knew how close you were to the late professor. We are not cruel men. We know you cannot see us without seeing him. But we are facing a terrible foe now, one whose face and powers we do not know—one who has all the advantages at this point, except for two." Stepping back from the woman's desk, Bain spread his arms, pushing himself down into a pleading pose as he said,

"We are in desperate need of your help to understand one of these. If you could trust for the moment that the fate of the world really might be in the hands of your courage, it would be most appreciated."

The woman waited for a long moment, then finally allowed her features to soften. None present would have gone so far to call her expression an actual smile, but at least her frown had disappeared, which to those who knew her was a good enough starting point. The relaxing of her face released the tension in her body. As her face lightened, the mood in the room lifted instantly. All of the men relaxed as she did, glad to see that their impasse had been conquered. Sitting back in her chair, uncrossing her arms from her chest, she gave all the credit of her mood shift to the elder priest, saying,

"Guess it wouldn't do to cross Father Be-Blessed, now would it?"

"There are those who would agree with you," answered Bain in a light tone. "Of course, there are also those who wouldn't." Growing serious, Bain added,

"Whichever view proves to be true in the long run, please . . . allow me to thank you. We really do require your assistance. If even half of what we suspect is actual, then the world is in monstrous danger."

"Don't say it," said Joylyn, half-serious, half-joking. "It's the end of the world, right?" When none of the men said anything, she stopped moving, her mouth half-open. Summoning up what strength she could, she said,

"Oh, no, not again."

"Well," responded London, encouragement in his voice, "Maybe not. Not if we get moving anyway. And, with that thought in mind, I'll get us right to the point. Tell us, do you recognize this ring?"

Father Bain, wearing the heavy gold band he had taken

back from Swartz, raised his hand and removed the ring, passing it over to the young woman. Joylyn took it from him with the ends of her nails, instinctively keeping the oils in her skin away from its intricately carved surface. Holding the ancient piece up to the light, then moving it closer to her eye, Joylyn mused for a moment. Something about the ring did indeed seem familiar to her. Then, suddenly, her eyes widened almost to the point of exaggeration, pushing her dark skin back until her shock was readily evident. Placing the ring on the desk in front of her, she continued to stare at it, completely absorbed by her study of it as she asked in a faraway voice,

"Where did you get this?"

"Off the hand of its dead owner," answered Morcey.

Joylyn looked up suspiciously. Leaving her seat, she pulled down a lime green three-ring binder from a set of eighteen such volumes on the uppermost shelf directly behind her. The set was one Goward had put together over the years, one she had not yet been able to add to. It contained all of the material he had cataloged but for which he could not acquire original copies. Copies he had transcribed by hand of Tibetan scrolls, photocopies of pages from priceless books from various corners of the world, photographs—anything of which the professor did not have an original ended up in the oversized lime green binders. Finding the page she wanted, the current head of Columbia's Phenomenological Research Department laid the book open on the desk next to the ring, and then said,

"You're not supposed to be able to do that, Mr. Morcey."

'What's that, ma'am?"

"You're not supposed to be able to take this ring off its owner's dead hand. Mainly, because he's not supposed to die." Picking up the ring, Joylyn held it to the light again, looking over the carvings once more, this time comparing them to the sketches in her binder as she said,

"I mean, I assume you're telling me that this is the ring of the Confessor. Right?"

"Yes," answered London, softly. "That's what we were

told. Now we're looking to you for confirmation. Granted, this whole mess is only a few hours old, but it's already almost out of control. You may have heard about some troubles in Midtown earlier today."

"That was you?" she asked, quickly correcting herself by adding, "Sure, of course. Blood spilled by the gallon, firefights in Midtown Manhattan, heads lined up like toys, I should have known . . . right?"

"People know about the heads already?" said Swartz with a growl. "That information was supposed to be kept out of general circulation." Directing his question to Joylyn, he asked,

"When did you find out about that? And where? What station? Or what paper?"

"Nothing like that, Lieutenant. News of that type travels fast in the paranormal underground. Someone decapitates that many people and then uses the heads for a display, certain people can't help but hear about it. I got a message over the fax about an hour ago." Looking up into Swartz's face, seeing what the leak meant to him, she added,

"Sorry, Officer. I didn't create your leak. I just got splashed by it. Besides, just looking at you I can see you're new to this. In fact"—the woman leaned forward a bit, studying the policeman's face, looking into his eyes—"I'd say you were *real* new to this. How long—just today?"

"What difference does it make?" snapped Swartz.

"Oh, oh," said Joylyn. "On the edge. You guys better take it a little easier on this boy. I'm not the expert, but I think he's seen all he can take for the moment."

"Takin' it easy on people ain't what this kinda work is all about," said Morcey. "Remember?"

"Yes," answered the young professor coldly, "I remember all too well. I remember helping to bury Pa'sha Lowe one day, and then Dr. Goward the next. I know just what this 'kinda' work is all about." Turning to Swartz, she said,

"I sure hope you do, too, skinny. You'd better know just what working with this crew is all about. Don't think that

badge is going to protect you from what you're going to
see here ... if you live long enough to actually see the
things that start crawling out of the woodwork when these
guys show up."

"Isn't she sweet, boss?" said Morcey. Before anyone
could reply, the ex–maintenance man told Swartz, "Do try
to keep in mind that we don't actually show up until the
things have already started crawling out of the woodwork."

"Enough," barked the lieutenant in a demanding voice,
one well used to giving orders. "I'll take care of my own
mental health, thank you very much. And if I might sum
things up here, no one wants to pull you out of your little
room full of books, so you can stop worrying. All we want
to know is ... in your expert opinion, is this the Confessor's ring or not? And if it is, what else can you tell us
about him?"

"In my opinion ...," she said the words almost as a
question, but then summoned up her conviction and
stepped fully into the case, answering, "yes. From what information I have, and just from the simple fact that the
London Agency is involved, yes—if there is really a Confessor, then this is probably his ring."

"If there really is a Confessor ...?" asked Swartz.

"Yes, *if* there really is a Confessor. Did you ever hear of
him before today? Do you even believe in him yet? In a
man who's walked the planet since the beginning of time,
forgiving the sins of all he meets, no matter what they've
done? Do you?" When the lieutenant just stared, the
woman told him,

"I know what you want, but I can't help you. I don't
have any information on where the Confessor came from,
or where one can find him, or anything like that. All the
facts I have on the name are on the page you're looking
at, and most of them are about the ring. Outside of that,
until today, the notion's just been another legend to me.
But then, like I said, until I met your friends here, Lieutenant, werewolves were just another legend to me. Okay?"

"Yeah," answered the policeman. "Sure."

"All right, then," said London. "You got everything you need now, Lieutenant?"

"Sure. We came to see if there was anything to this story about the Confessor. Fine—I suppose we really do have his ring, so now I guess I can safely believe in at least that much of the story and figure that we probably aren't on a wild goose chase. So now we go off to see what else we can find out before the whole world ends. Yeah, sure, I've got everything I fucking need except for someone to make some sense."

London stared at the officer, hoping that he would be able to help the policeman stay close enough to sanity to keep him from impeding the detective's investigation. Swartz was not open to the beyond, not one given to leaps of faith. His was a world of facts and logic and things proved beyond shadows of doubt. He was used to being in charge, to solving crimes with clues and informants, directing his small uniformed army throughout the city to do his bidding. Taking a backseat on a ride into the unknown was more than unsettling for the policeman. It was harrowing, an action designed to push him to his limits. Knowing that everyone present in the room was concerned about his ability to work with them, he said,

"Look, you can stop making the worried faces, okay? Yeah, sure, I'm not happy to have to admit that just the way you people take all this shit so seriously, vampires and rings that tell people what to do and, and werewolves and . . . and everything else . . . has pushed me as far as I'm willing to go. Normally I'd be working on locking you all up—fuck, fuck! Normally? Normally you'd already be locked up—you and you," he said, pointing from London to Morcey. Pointing then to Bain, he continued, saying,

"And you, too, for that matter. Theft is still a crime in New York, no matter what half the citizens seem to think. But too many people I knew got murdered today and—despite how much I think you and yours are full of shit, London . . . ," his voice dropped to a much softer level as he finished, saying, "I have to admit that my gut thinks you know what you're doing."

"Take it from me, Lieutenant," added Joylyn unexpectedly, "it doesn't get any easier. I've seen people killed around our Mr. London as well as you. But I don't think any of it could have been avoided. As much as I hate to admit it, for whatever the word of an overeducated black college professor is worth to you, he really does seem to know what he's doing. As much as anyone else in this business."

And then a finality settled over Joylyn's offices, one that told everyone the meeting was over. The detective made his good-bye, thanking the professor for her help, and for her if not kind, at least honest words. Morcey and Bain said their good-byes as well, while Swartz gave the woman his customary curt nod, as much of a farewell as he ever gave anyone. Then the four men pulled themselves together and headed for the door. As they did, however, the young woman stood up from behind her massive desk and called out,

"Father Bain . . . ?"

"Yes, my child . . . ?"

"You said that your enemies had all the advantages except two. My guess from context is that the Confessor's ring was one advantage. If I can ask . . . what's the other one?"

"Why," answered the priest, almost startled, "the one all of the righteous have . . . prayer."

Joylyn watched the four men leave, watched their backs disappear down the hall, disappearing around the corner. And then, as she heard the old building's ancient elevator begin to move toward her floor, she went back to her desk. Sitting down behind it, she closed her eyes and pressed her palms together, and for the first time in years, tried to help the four men in their work by turning to the universal advantage Father Bain had mentioned.

"You've done a lot with this place since the last time I was here, my son."

It took the four quite some time before they made their way back to London's building. The time had grown late. The children had been put to bed several hours earlier. Both Lisa and Lai Wan had waited up for London and Morcey's return, assuming that at least Swartz would be with them. Cat and Lacey had gone from Mama Joan's to London's after the detective and the others had left to help watch over his family until he could return.

"Thank you, Father. Wish it was still early enough for you to see the kids."

"Next time."

"If there *is* a next time," said Cat. She stood in the foyer of the building, stepping back as the men entered, the pump-action shotgun in her hands not unnoticed by any of them. Pulling a small, palm-fitted communicator from her belt, she thumbed the open channel switch, then said,

"Lacey, you still alive?"

"Funny lady," came the thin man's voice. "You sure make a guy feel his confidence, you know that?"

"What I know is that Dick Tracy is back from running all over the city and leaving the protection of his family up to us. You want to come down for the fill-in?"

"Sure. Pour out some stiff black for me, will you? It's cold on this roof. You know?"

The electronics expert smiled at the communicator as she said, "Yeah, I know. C'mon down. I'll save the biggest mug they've got for you."

"Thank you, sweet girl. I be there as fast as I can."

For any normal person in such a position, removing the roof guard would have been a bad idea. Not for London, however. Neither he nor Cat, nor any of the others present who knew him for that matter, were very worried about the possibility of the detective's home being successfully invaded as long as the detective himself was there. They had seen him *feel* the approach of too many things to lose faith in his abilities.

Also, they knew no place else any safer. Years earlier, London had cut all leads to himself. His mail was delivered to his office. All his credit cards, bills, and the like, were routed through the agency, or through second, third, and sometimes even fourth masking levels.

There was no paper trail to lead anyone to his home or to his family. Nor was there a psychic one. Both London and Lai Wan had done their best to cut off their home from the outside world, to remove all traces of their families. As far as anyone knew, theirs was an apartment building occupied by two families, the Munsens and the Bennetts.

As the troupe filed in, with the doors locked behind them, Lisa came out of one of the upstairs doors, stopping on the second-floor landing for only a moment before starting down the stairs. As soon as she had her husband's eye, she asked,

"So, what did you find out?"

"Lai's still awake—right?" When his wife nodded, the detective answered, "Let's get everyone upstairs in one place, then we can go over everything. I'll tell you all the long and short of it, which is, sadly, not much."

"Imagine," she told him, "one of these things not being easy from the word go. There's a surprise, eh, lover?"

"Yeah, right," answered the detective sourly. "Save the comedy, Mommy, will you? And let's just try and get through this one as best we can."

Lisa agreed with a nod and then turned and headed back upstairs, knowing all too well what her husband meant. They had been married too long for her not to be able to interpret what he needed at any given moment from the tone in his voice, just as he could do the same with her. At that moment, she could tell that London needed a quiet homemaker. He needed her to get drinks ready, hot and cold, and whatever she could dig out to go with them. He also needed her to serve and clear without saying much except for the occasional required social amenity, and to ask people what else they might need.

The main reason he needed all of that, of course, besides the obvious, was to enable her to blend into the background. With everyone focusing on him, they would pay her no attention, which would allow her to observe everything that happened from a vantage point no one was guarding against. Even if Swartz or Bain, or anyone for that matter, were trying to hide anything from London, they would not have much of a chance of keeping it hidden from both of them.

When she reached the top stair, the tired young woman gathered up her remaining strength, mentally wrote herself an IOU for a year's sleep, and then pushed off for the kitchen. The detective led the others up the stairs after her. Just as he reached the second-floor landing, however, he suddenly felt something moving off to one side in the shadows. With one arm held up behind him to warn the others to caution, he felt the air ahead of him with practiced ease. But after only a split second, he put his hand down as he called to a sleepy-eyed Kevin to come out into the open. Trying to stifle a yawn, the boy remained seated, calling to his father in a blurred voice. London went over to his son, asking,

"What are you still doing up? And sitting out in the hall in the dark, for that matter?"

"I was waiting for you. I had to tell you something." The others moved around with the good-natured patience of adults taking pity on a parent. Ignoring them, the detective told his son,

"Well, I hope this is important. Spill it, what's up?"

"Daddy, Kate and I played with the Ouija board after you went out." While some of the others smiled, London kept his expression even, waiting for his son to finish.

"We asked it what was happening, and what was going to happen, and all that kind of stuff."

"And what did it tell you?" When Kevin beat around

the bush for a moment, the detective reminded his son sternly that not only was it past his bedtime, but that he himself had a lot more to do that night and could not afford to waste time. Kevin told his father that he was sorry, then said,

"We couldn't get much . . . just that there was a lot of bad stuff going on, and that a lot of people were going to be killed and all, and that you were going to go to King Kong."

"King Kong?" asked London.

"Oh, goof," said Kevin, suddenly embarrassed. "I mean Hong Kong, the board said Hong Kong."

"Was that it?" asked London. The detective's head instantly filled with a chorus of voices, all of them giving their opinion on the boy's message. Worried more about his son than what he had said, London shoved his ancestors aside, ignoring all of their comments. When his son said that he had given him the entire message, the detective told him,

"Then it's time for bed. Thank you for being so concerned. Now scoot."

Kevin gave his father a hug and a kiss, then waddled off down the hall to his bedroom. After his door closed, Lai Wan came drifting out of the shadows from a point farther down the hall. When London asked why she had allowed Kevin to sit out in the darkness, she told him,

"He had something very important to tell you. He went to great lengths to trick me into leaving him in the hall unobserved so he could wait up for you." A warm smile crossing the woman's face, she said quietly,

"It would not have been very sporting of me to have kept him from doing so."

London frowned, tilting his head to one side. Knowing that the psychometrist was not one to overindulge either of the children, he started on after all of the others, saying over his shoulder,

"You could have taken a message."

"Yes," she said, catching hold of his arm, keeping him back for a moment, "I could have. But I must ask you now: What went through your mind, through your senses, when Kevin told you about Hong Kong?"

The detective stopped for a second, considering what the woman had asked him. Swimming back in his mind, he listened to the voices flooding his head once more. As he did, they started chattering at him again, all throwing in their opinions. London was surprised to see how many of them put stock in what the boy had to say. Turning to Lai Wan, he told her,

"To be honest, I seem to think there's some merit in what he said."

"I wondered myself," she answered in a quiet voice. "So, after I told them to put away the board and to stop being so foolish, I sent them to brush their teeth and then went to consult the globe in your den. I entered the room without turning on the lights. Goin to the globe, I spun it and then lay my hands on it." Releasing her grip on London's arm, the psychometrist indicated with a wave of her hand that the two of them should start moving again so as not to fall too far behind the others. As they walked, she kept their pace deliberately slow as she continued to whisper.

"Keeping my thoughts only on what has happened today, I concentrated on all that you had told us . . . pushing all else from my mind. As I moved my hands about, I felt a tug guiding them across its surface. Whatever the force was, it took my hand straight to where it wanted to, urging me to stand my finger to a definite point."

As the pair reached the door to the second-floor apartment London and Lisa used as their main living quarters, the detective asked,

"So . . . do I have to ask?"

"Yes, you do."

Frowning again, not at all sure what kind of game Lai Wan was playing with him, he asked the psychometrist in a tired, frustrated voice,

"Did your finger stop on Hong Kong?"

"I do not know."

Staring unblinking into the woman's dark eyes, he

searched for some clue as to what kind of game she might be playing with him. Then, finally, he asked,

"All right—I'll bite. Why don't you know?"

"Because the spot my finger had stopped on was blistered and cracked. The paint had been burned away . . . the metal beneath was still warm." As the detective stared, not knowing what to say, the psychometrist told him,

"But yes, I will admit . . . it was the spot where Hong Kong should have been."

The assembly had gotten smaller. Throughout the night, they had gone over every fact they had, backward and forward. They had examined the globe from London's study, they had examined the Confessor's ring. Swartz had had copies of all his people's reports sent to the detective's home. He also had photographs of all the evidence that had been collected and cataloged . . . from both in the street as well as from London's office—in short everything connected with the case thus far—sent along with the reports. Officers had continued to arrive for over an hour, some bringing handfuls of envelopes, some bringing boxes. Not many of them had cared to stay.

Don't blame them, thought the lieutenant. If I could turn back the clock and forget everything I've seen today, I wouldn't stay here, either.

Swartz fought the internal battle of fear as well as any who had joined forces with the London Agency over the years—better than some. He kept telling himself he had seen a lot in his time . . . that whatever was going on this time, he would find a logical explanation for it. But still, the little things continued to prey on him: the casual acceptance by everyone around him of the most bizarre interpretations to events, the constant references to werewolves and vampires . . . talk of traveling to Hell itself, and monsters from other dimensions.

Or, he thought, that damn creepy Chinese babe and her laying on of hands. No matter what she says, they all take it as gospel. She says Martin Tabor is back, they all nod their heads. I want to know who Martin Tabor is, they tell me he's a vampire they killed a few years ago. Oh, says I, but if you killed him, how's it he's running around again? No problem, says the ghostbusters. Vampires have a way of bringing their own dead back to life, they just have to round up a couple dozen people and sacrifice them. That's all.

"That's all," the policeman had muttered to himself. "Yeah. Sure. But of course. *That's* all."

No one noticed, however, for there was nothing unique about what Swartz was doing. After the amount of time they had put in on their problem, the lieutenant was not the only one in the Londons' large dining room muttering to himself. The group had stayed up through most of the night going over all of the material the police had brought to them. They had discussed everything they knew as fact and then moved on to their speculations. After that they had broken up into smaller groups, working on this or that problem, looking for new angles, and then throwing out their new angles to the rest, looking to see what the others may or may not have to add.

Finally, however, after a straight seven hours of mostly going around in circles, the sun was well on its way up into the morning sky and most of the assembly was asleep. London had sent Lisa to bed hours earlier. Like all parents, they knew the kids would be up far too early, and that one of them should be awake enough to deal with them. Morcey had turned in early as well, agreeing with his partners that if London were going to stay up all night then it would probably be best if he got some sleep so as to be fresh in the morning.

Cat had stayed up most of the night using her mobile computer system to track leads around the world. Working for hours at a stretch, the electronics whiz studied the materials the Confessor had brought to London's office, searching after the whereabouts of the warheads listed. The woman was looking to find some sort of pattern in the seemingly random movements of the weapons, hoping to be able to come up with their final destination. Before she could discover anything conclusive, however, she found herself wasting too much time correcting errors made only because of her inability to concentrate. Making Lacey pledge to wake her in half an hour, she had curled up on the larger of the two couches in the Londons' living room.

Lacey did not wake her. She did not think he would. Looking down at her, frowning even in her sleep, he had told the others,

"Crazy female—gotta be the big winner every time or she can't live with herself. When she wake up, tell her it's all my fault and let her kick me over it. That girl don't get some sleep, she's gonta start walkin' inta walls."

"And where will you be?" Swartz had asked. "Just so we can direct her to you."

"Iz'll be on da next couch over. Where'd you think, mister policeman?"

Lai Wan had smiled to herself, watching the lieutenant bristle at Lacey's little joke. Despite her amusement, however, she despaired for the officer, wondering if he would be able to adapt to their situation in time before something truly beyond his ability to comprehend came along. She could feel his confusion coming off him in waves, flowing over the walls he continued to build between himself and the others.

After Lacey had curled up on the other couch, she had gone over to the table where the officer had several dozen piles of evidence scattered before him. Sitting in the chair to his left, she had said,

"Finding anything, Lieutenant?"

"Actually . . . no."

"That is too bad. I have done what I can here, for now. I myself am going to turn in for a while. Before I do, though, I thought I might offer you a piece of advice."

"And what would that be?"

"As the Londons' daughter Kate once told me, 'you should loosen up a little.' I say this as kindly as I can . . . truthfully . . . meaning no disrespect to either you or your station. You could be a great asset to this investigation, but you must stop looking for the simple types of criminal motives you are used to dealing with." Motioning with her hand, she pointed toward the window as she said,

"Whatever is happening out there it is not going to be any kind of crime you are familiar with. If Mr. London is right—and for what my word is worth to you, I am certain he is—then an undying force is behind what is happening. Everything that has happened is the work of a cabal of vampires, undying fiends who live on the energies of others. Countless thousands have died at their hands—your fellow officers whose heads you found may not even be their most recent victims. I warn you, Lieutenant, for the sake of your sanity, not to mention that of the entire world, do not look for the same motivations you would normally seek out in this case." His face a defiant wall, the policeman answered,

"Sorry, lady. I've been at this game a little too long. Whatever it is that's going on out there, there's going to be a logical explanation for it."

"Of course there will be, Mr. Swartz. I never said vampires were illogical, sir. I merely attempted to point out that what may appear to be logical to a being who cannot be killed, who lives on the life force of 'mere cattle such as ourselves,' might not appear logical to you or me."

With that, the psychometrist excused herself from the table, said good night to London, and silently left the room. Swartz watched her leave, and then looked around to assess the situation. London was at the other end of the large dining room table, going over a printout of the disks the Confessor had brought. Everyone else was asleep except for Father Bain, but the Lieutenant did not see where he could bother the priest at that moment and simply turned back to the envelopes spread out in front of him.

The reason Swartz had not wanted to disturb Father Bain was that the priest had settled into his own corner of the room shortly after the group had gone over all the facts they had for the first time. Bain had known that he could not help them in analyzing facts and evidence. Getting down on his knees, his face to the corner, the elder priest had shut himself off from the others and begun a prayer vigil, beseeching his Lord for guidance on behalf of all those present.

None had disturbed the holy man. The priest had prayed throughout the night, taking no rest, nor food or drink. Indeed, when some of the others had done so, neither their chatter nor the smells coming from what they had made for themselves caught his notice. Until the sun came up he had stayed rigid in his devote pose, the mental connection between himself and his God unbroken.

Once the first rays of morning reached the old man, however, he finally gave in, admitting that the flesh had its limits. Apologizing to London, he called out, saying,

"I'm sorry to trouble you, my son, but I'm afraid I'm going to have to stop for now."

"That's fine, Father. Get some rest."

"No, you don't quite understand. My knees have . . . have become the knees of an old man, I guess. I can't stand."

Instantly the detective bounded up out of his chair and crossed the room, coming up alongside the elder cleric, helping him to his feet before Swartz could even stir. As the pair moved across the room slowly, London asked him,

"Tell me, Father, exactly how does confession work?"

"Well," answered the priest, counting off on his aching, nearly crippled fingers, "first, the penitents must be truly sorry for their sins. Second, the penitents must resolve to not sin again, to the best of their ability."

At that point, the pair reached the room's oversized ottoman. As Bain slid down into it gratefully, he continued, saying,

"Third, absolution is obtained from the confessor; penance is given and performed. And all of it leaves the confessor bound by his oath of silence, and nothing and no one can compel him to reveal what has been admitted under the seal of confession." Holding back a yawn, the elder cleric added,

"Of course, this all might not apply to your man in white the way it does to us."

London thought about what Bain had said for a moment. Thinking of another question, he looked down but did not ask it. The priest had fallen asleep before the detective could ask.

Postponing the question until later, London returned to the main table. Looking over at Swartz, he marveled at the

man's stamina. Despite the fact the officer had been awake
for at least a straight twenty-four hours, he still seemed remarkably in control of his faculties. Of course, the strain
was taking its toll. The lieutenant's eyes were heavily
bagged, his thinning hair matted against his light-bulb-
shaped skull. As the policeman stroked his mustache, the
detective sat back down at the table, asking,

"So, you see any reason to go over any of this stuff
again, or is it time for a nap?"

"I can keep at it just as long as you can, London."

"Well, I'm glad to hear it," offered the detective sarcastically. "But that doesn't actually answer my question.
What I wanted to know was whether or not you were tired
enough to want to stretch out and see if some sleep will
help settle your thoughts or not?"

Swartz bristled instantly, a reaction London had become
far too used to by that point to give any thought. What did
catch his attention, though, was how quickly the lieutenant
caught hold of himself and pushed his anger aside. As the
detective held his tongue, waiting to see what was going
on inside the policeman's head, Swartz sat back, pushing
his chair up on its hind legs. Rubbing at his eyes, he let go
a tremendous yawn, one so comically loud it forced London to hide an embarrassed smile. Then, wiping at the
sleepy feeling that had settled on the skin of his face, the
lieutenant asked,

"So tell me, London . . . you really believe the sh—ah,
everything you've been peddling to me for the last . . .
ummm, ah, however many hours it's been?"

"Yes—not just to give you a hard time, or anything—
but I'm afraid I have to stand by all of it."

"Including this stuff about vampires?"

When the detective merely nodded, using the same
wide-eyed, tight-lipped expression he usually reserved for
those times he was trying to convince his children of
something, Swartz took the look in, turned his head from
side to side, and then let his head hang for a moment. His
eyes closed, he drew in a long, deep breath, then let it
back out slowly. At the end, he stopped himself from

drawing another breath for just a moment, denying himself oxygen for as long as he could before his body overruled him and flooded his lungs once more. Bringing his head back up, the lieutenant said,

"Okay, so there are vampires in the world. If that's the case, then let me ask you something."

London concentrated on the new look in Swartz's eyes, wondering what it signified. Willing to play along with the policeman to find out, he said,

"Anything you want."

"You people said before that these aren't like . . . what? What do I mean? Umm, like movie vampires, or something. They don't grow fangs and suck blood and sleep in coffins and shit. You said they murder people and just suck up the energy from the dying bodies. It's not blood, but like, well . . . people's *souls* they're after. Right?"

"Yeah . . . ?" said London, suddenly growing interested, wondering where the officer was leading him.

"Then, okay. Let's suppose everything we have so far is correct. Suppose we do have a bunch of vampires who have a shitload of nuclear weapons at their disposal." Taking a deep breath, Swartz closed his eyes as tightly as he could, grinding the sleep out of them. Then, knowing he had to pose the question in his mind, he opened his eyes again and asked,

"A couple of hours back, your nanny said something to me. She said that I should try figuring out what is logical to a vampire. So I'll ask you . . . is it logical to think that these fucks might set off their bombs just to kill people so they could suck up a million souls at one time?"

London's first impulse was to tell the lieutenant that he was wrong. When the detective had first come up against an enclave of vampires, they had explained the way things worked to him. Anyone could become a vampire—all they had to do was kill someone. Come up behind them and beat their brains in. Murder was the conduit to another person's soul. The vampires had cautioned London, however, telling him that the effect did not work from a distance. Guns, burning people to death, gave no return. No, they had assured him, it had to be up close and personal.

But the detective had effectively put that myth to rest for them when he had accidentally proved that someone who could walk the dream plane, who could touch people's souls from a distance, could draw in any number of souls, no matter how their living bodies had been dispatched. Martin Tabor had been one of the vampires to whom London had clumsily revealed this information. If it had been Tabor that the detective had seen, perhaps Swartz's theory explained some things—like how the previously ineffective vampire had not only returned from the dead, but had learned to fly in the bargain.

Maybe it did explain why the nuclear bombs had been gathered, and what a coven of vampires would want with them. Maybe it also explained why they would have scattered them all across the globe in twos and threes. If there was no . . . enemy . . . to be challenged—if *everyone* was the enemy—if every soul on the planet had been targeted by Tabor and his followers . . .

"London? London!"

The detective looked up suddenly, shocked to find Swartz standing over him, shaking him. Seeing that London had snapped out of his reverie, the lieutenant let go of the detective's shoulders, saying,

"When I asked you about vampires using the nukes to suck up a lot of souls at one time you went blank, like you were in a trance or something. I didn't know what to make of it, but I didn't want to take any chances, so I thought maybe, I don't know, that I should snap you out of it or something." Moving back a few paces, the policeman added,

"Sorry."

"No," answered London, still not back on quite the same level of consciousness where Swartz was. "Don't apologize. That's all right—honest. And no, there was nothing wrong, nothing to worry about; I wasn't being possessed or anything."

"Then what . . . ?"

Heading across the room, London opened a cabinet behind his bar. Pulling out two glasses, he grabbed a bottle of Jack Daniel's and held it up, making a gesture with it that the lieutenant interpreted correctly.

"Sure," said the policeman. "Why not? But can I ask the occasion."

"Oh yeah," answered the detective. Holding both glasses with one hand, he poured four fingers of the smooth sour mash Tennessee whiskey into each. Then, as he passed one off to Swartz, he said,

"The occasion is the fact that, as much as I wish you weren't, you are absolutely right. Yes—a group of vampires with nuclear bombs *could* use them to suck down a million souls at a time. Yes—absolutely."

The two men stared at each other for a long moment. As they sat, unblinking, London added,

"They could set them off, one after another, and no one would know who was doing it, or why. Countries would blame terrorists, each other, but what would it matter? Every time another bomb went off, bang, millions would die, and the vampires would just keep channeling the lost lives into themselves and giving themselves new super powers."

Swartz stared at the detective intently. Rotating the tumbler in his hand, feeling the liquor whirling around the inside of it, he said,

"So, what next? We drink our drinks and then follow the kid's advice and go to Hong Kong?"

"You know . . . ," said London, absently, his eyes fixed on the caramel-colored liquid in his glass, "before all this started, I was never much of a drinker. A little wine once in a while, that was enough. Then I started having monsters coming through my windows, and before you know it, I develop a taste for the hard stuff."

"I can top you," answered Swartz. As the two men stood up simultaneously and walked toward the other, extending their glasses in each other's direction, the policeman said, "I don't drink."

"Well, trust me," said London, a smile spreading across his face, "we live through this . . . I'll bet you start."

The two men touched their glasses together and then lifted them and drank heavily. The lieutenant knocked back almost half his tumbler before the liquor hit his stomach and cut his breath off, choking him for a few seconds. Smiling back at London after his coughing fit had subsided, he said,

"Yeah, I'll bet I start, too."

And then, just as the two men lifted their glasses a second time, the detective's head twitched. Dropping his tumbler, London had just enough time to knock Swartz to the floor before the first of the grenades burst through the window.

"Lisa!!"

The detective's scream filled the house, sounding in every corner of the brownstone just a split second before the first of the explosions. As he and Swartz scrambled for cover, the lieutenant fumbled for his service revolver while London sent a mental blast to everyone within the building except his children, jolting them all awake instantly. Five rocking shocks went off before either man could do anything—one after another—filling the air with tearing shrapnel.

"Check Bain!" ordered London, sliding across the floor, leaving Swartz behind to do as he had been bidden without considering that the lieutenant might do otherwise. Going through the door, the detective hit the hallway quietly but at a skid, finding gunmen already flooding through his front door into the foyer. Instantly he calmed himself, sending his feeling throughout his home. Within half a second, he knew where all the people who were supposed to be inside were, as well as how many intruders there were to deal with. At the same time, however, three of the invaders took note of his presence on the upper landing as well.

"Up there!" shouted one of the two women in the group below.

"Target prime," announced the force's leader, pointing at the detective. "Do him—now!"

The order directed the attention of the entire invading force coming in his front door, just as London had intended by posing for them. Instantly their guns were raised as one, their focus intent on bringing down the detective, ignoring all the other doors around them for the moment. Having set himself up as a target simply to give everyone else in the building time to react, London stood his ground defiantly, while at the same time dividing his brain, setting aside a part of it to keep feeding him information on all of his attackers, leaving the rest to deal with his immediate enemies.

Suddenly, the detective's time sense divided down into microseconds. Below him, as hammers were being drawn back in what appeared to him as slow motion, his senses scouted out through the building and beyond it, keeping tabs on the rest of the attackers. As the same weapons' triggers were pulled, reports began to flood his brain, telling him where all the remaining gunmen were. And then, twenty score explosions filled the brownstone's spacious foyer as a storming hail of bullets tore upward toward London. Throwing himself not to one side or the other, but backward, he twisted his pose to allow the torrent of lead to pass by him, burying itself in the wall and ceiling behind him.

From below, it looked to the invaders that the detective could not possibly have escaped harm. London could feel a certain relaxation coming from them, their body language showing they were already hunting out other targets. Shaking his head, the detective summoned up all the spare energy he had. As he did, a voice within him slowed his hand, reminding him,

Don't expend everything you have on these ... There are more on the roof and in the street. Forgo hot anger—deal in cold retribution.

Thinking to himself, Well, when you're right, you're right ..., London calmed himself. In the real-time second that it took for him to do so, several of the invaders realized that he was still standing and readied themselves to fire again. Sneering, the detective thought,

Now.

Instantly, pellets of solid energy sprang from his head, traveling with the speed of light toward the men and women below. Incapable of missing their defenseless targets, the shining projectiles smashed through the helmets of the invaders and then imploded against the frontal plates of their skulls, exploding their heads open in a bloody display that splattered every wall and a great deal of the floor. One after another, the bodies crumpled and fell haphazardly, guns dropping, limbs twitching—every one of them suddenly nothing more than the empty husks of formerly living beings.

Before London could relax, however, machine-gun fire from a pair of weapons slashed through the doorway, coming at him faster than any movement he could make. Closing his eyes, reflexively the detective threw a wall of energy up in front of himself. The barrier was thin in spots—able to shield London from destruction but not from the force of the bullets. The wall of lead buckled the detective's barrier backward. It pushed him with an incredible ferocity, bouncing him off the back wall.

London's head was bashed violently into the plaster, his teeth slamming together, just missing his tongue. He staggered forward, badly bruised and disoriented but not crippled. Concentrating as best he could on the last two invaders below, he reached out for their minds, sending mental fingers into their subconscious levels. Then, even as he squeezed away the pain in his chest and legs, he gave them both the silent command to look at the other, affecting them so that they saw their teammate as himself. Instantly both men fired, splattering each other with deadly hails of close-range bullets.

"Better than you deserve," muttered London, spinning on his heel to head back into the dining room. "All of you."

Before he could reach the room, however, he met Swartz, who was coming out at a run, shouting,

"The priest's been hit."

As the lieutenant hit the landing, his eyes focused instantly on the carnage littering the landing below. As he continued to stare, the detective told him,

"So were they."

Then, before further comment could be made, London spun around, sensing movement behind him. As the door to the upstairs bedrooms cracked, he said,

"It's all right, sweetheart. I'm fine. Keep the kids with you and head into the kitchen."

"Are you sure?" asked Lisa, her head coming around the sheltering door.

"I know the bedroom's stronger, but we've got some more visitors on the roof."

Lisa London did not bother to question her husband further. If he told her there were more gunmen approaching from above, she knew he was right. Both Swartz and the detective stood guard for the few seconds it took her to hustle the children along the landing into the kitchen. Both of them wanted to stop with London, ask him if everything was going to be all right, ask him to come along with them and their mother. Both knew not to, though. The detective had entered both their minds, urging them to be brave and to stay with their mother.

As the trio passed, however, Lisa blurted,

"Need any help?"

London noted the pistol and box of shells in her hand. Trying to maintain his balance against the staggering pain in his chest, he waved her on, saying,

"You keep it. God knows I can't be everywhere. Lock yourselves in and kill anything that moves."

"My husband," she shouted to Swartz, waving her gun as she held the door open for Kevin and Kate. "He's so considerate."

"Yes, ma'am," answered the lieutenant, actually glad to have something he could sink his teeth into. "I'm sure he's a treasure."

As the two men heard the kitchen lock clicking into place, the detective told Swartz,

"I'm headed upstairs. There's more of them outside, but I get the feeling they're waiting for some signal from the ones already inside." Pointing at the remains of the helmets the invaders had been wearing, London said,

"Look at their headgear." Swartz studied the bits and pieces he could see, noting the resemblance between the paramilitary look of the bodies below and those from the day before. Wondering if the detective felt the same way, he asked,

"Think this is the same bunch as the other day?"

"Same style—hit out of nowhere, broad-daylight attack. They let us spend the night worrying about when they'd hit us, let the sun come up, let us feel a little relieved, then they hit. I have to admit to wounded pride, too—I really didn't think anyone could trace me here." Opening the door to the upstairs, London finished, saying,

"Score two for the other side. I'll give them credit—they're not stupid."

"I take it they're not vampires, either." When the detective stopped and stared, the lieutenant pointed below, saying,

"They all died after just one shot." London nodded, adding,

"Right. But there are vampires in the house. Two in the basement, five on the roof. The ones in the basement have human backup," added London, letting Swartz know what he expected of him. "You might want to pick up Paul on the way down."

Then, just as London was disappearing through the doorway, the policeman shouted,

"By the way, what the fuck did you hit those guys down there with?"

"I thought them to death," shouted back London as he started to make his way up the stairs.

" 'Thought them to death,' " Swartz repeated. "Good trick. I'll have to learn it."

Then, with his service revolver drawn—and great trepidation—the lieutenant began to make his way down the stairs.

18

Auto-Mag in hand, Morcey led the lieutenant into the sub-level of the brownstone. The pair had found each other in the stairway leading down into Morcey's apartment. The ex–maintenance man had gotten out of bed just seconds before the attack, which was why he had had time only to throw a suit coat over his pajamas and grab his revolver and the trouble bag he kept under his bed. After Swartz told him what London had said, Morcey nodded and, reversing his direction, he beckoned the policeman to follow him as he said,

"I know all about it. My wife told me what happened. I was just comin' to get you."

"How did she know ... ?" Swartz started to ask in a whisper, catching himself in time to say, "Oh, yeah—right. She can probably just, ah ... what? Feel them through the floor or something?"

"Something."

"So what did she ... feel?"

"Eight of them all together," answered Morcey. His revolver already cocked, he moved down the stairs carefully, telling the lieutenant,

"Two of them seemed to be sharin' in givin' the orders. I figure them for vampires, which makes the other six just cannon fodder. Look for them to be in front. Try and save your best stuff for the vamps. It takes an awful lot of lead to bring one of them down."

Swartz did not bother to answer, content to absorb the knowledge he needed to stay alive. Suddenly, he did not care any longer what he was up against, what name it went by. The day before, a number of people who carried the same badge he did had been treated like stockyard cattle. Now the killers were back and he was going to have his chance at them. They could all be dressed like Hammer

Film Christopher Lees and turn into bats before his eyes for all it mattered to him. All the lieutenant cared about at the moment was payback.

As they inched their way downstairs, Morcey continued to whisper to the policeman,

"Lai said they were movin' through the downstairs without any trouble. It's pitch black down there so my guess is they're hooked up with infrared. Probably miked into one another like they were yesterday." Switching to his imitation of Bugs Bunny, Morcey whispered,

"Which, as if I had to tell ya, means we're really gonna be up against it here, copper."

"We're the good guys," answered Swartz. "We're always up against it, cueball."

The two men looked at each other and grinned, both understanding the other's need for humor at that particular moment. Then, knowing that their time was running out all too quickly, the policeman asked quietly,

"Is your wife safe?"

"She knows where the enemy is five minutes before they get there. She'll make her way up to Lisa and the kids without any trouble. Believe me, they'll be as safe as they can be. Besides, she's got Selby with her."

"Selby?"

"The dog."

"I didn't know you had a dog," answered the lieutenant, a bit surprised.

"We don't," said Morcey with a twinkle in his eye. Then, before Swartz could ask, the balding man made a "stop" motion with his hand. Sensing that the intruders were close at hand, he reached into the bag hanging off his shoulder and pulled out an unlabeled gray canister and a small grenadelike device the policeman did not recognize. Then, putting his back against the wall, he took a deep breath, shut his eyes, and concentrated, listening for movement, listening for any repetition of the noise that had put him on his guard. It had been a tiny sound—cloth against wood, maybe—but it had been enough to let him know he had found the enemy.

Taking another deep breath, he tried to visualize the room beyond, worked at figuring out where he would position eight people if he were moving them forward through the same space. Picturing them in his head, he focused on the point man, gauging his probable position from the sound he had heard. Letting his breath out slowly, he took another, eyes still closed, waiting for his counterpart on the other side of the door to move again, waiting for the same sound he had heard before.

Suddenly, Morcey's eyes flashed open. He heard the same muffled sound again, a scraping of fabric along rough cement. Instantly he knew exactly where the forward member of the enemy was. Holding his hand up to Swartz again, Morcey pantomimed that the lieutenant should cover his eyes. Then, watching as the knob turned in the door in front of him, he thumbed free the release on the grenade, waited for the door to open, and tossed it into the next room.

Morcey turned his back immediately as the next room exploded in a fierce flash of white light. Not waiting a second, the balding man turned open the safety valve on the gray canister and tossed it in behind the flare bomb, then slammed the door shut. Screams erupted on the other side of the door, followed by gunfire which ricocheted off the walls and blasted through the doorway. As caramel-colored fumes began to leak through the new holes in the door, the ex–maintenance man followed up his opening attack by returning fire.

He fired indiscriminately, emptying his Auto-Mag. The small hand cannon's blasts echoed and reechoed throughout the basement, rendering both him and Swartz temporarily deaf. Then, even before reloading, Morcey forced the lieutenant back from the door, screaming into his ear,

"Don't breathe the fumes!" Swartz merely stared at him, his eyes demanding a reason, as the ex–maintenance man pulled a fresh clip from his bag. Letting his empty brass drop out onto the floor, he shouted,

"Poison gas!"

"Poison?"

"We're playin' for keeps here, Lieutenant. Remember?"

But before Swartz could reply, the door in front of the two men was struck from behind. The blow was massive, savage, a ringing smash that seemingly knocked it from its hinges. When a second blow followed, Morcey turned and fired through it again. The lieutenant joined him, firing alongside him into the unknown. Both men pumped round after round through the door, hoping to hit whatever lay behind it. Even as they did, however, the withering attack continued, blow following blow. Bits of wood flew in all directions, some pushed in by bullets, some pushed out by the tremendous power of the attacker on the other side.

Just as Morcey and Swartz stopped to reload, the severely weakened door finally gave way, crashing out and down, slamming against the floor. As wisps of gray fumes rolled in across the floor, the two men backed away toward the stairs. Both finished loading their weapons as two figures pulled themselves out of the sub-basement. One male, one female, they hobbled forward, each suffering from monstrous gunshot wounds. Blood spilled out of them, splattering the floor, trailing behind them as they moved forward.

"Two!" gasped the woman in surprise, her voice hacking as her lungs tried to repel the gray poison she had breathed in. "Only two."

"Makes you feel stupid, doesn't it?" answered the man, crimson leaking out over his lips.

But then, as Swartz stared in horror, the cascade of blood began to staunch. Both figures began to heal before his very eyes. One bullet—probably from the lieutenant's service revolver, judging from the small amount of damage—had caved in the side of the man's head, slicing away his ear and actually exposing his skull. As Swartz watched, he saw the chipped bone begin to knit, pulling itself together even as the vampire's skin began to boil around the wound, flowing to cover it, hair springing out again.

Morcey made ready to fire, but as he raised his arm, the policeman grabbed it, screaming,

"They're ... they're ... they're *healing*."

"Sweet bride of the night," shouted the ex–maintenance man, struggling with the lieutenant. "Let go of me, ya nut job! We gotta do 'em now before it's too late."

Trapped by his own terror, Swartz stumbled as Morcey knocked him aside. Then, free of the policeman's grasp, the balding man took a step forward, watching the spread of the gas, raising his Auto-Mag to fire as he said,

"You think *that* made you feel stupid ..."

And then he fired at point-blank range, sending his first three shells into the male's midsection, blowing the vampire's body into two sections. As the man's torso flipped backward, his head falling into the rolling fumes, his legs stood for a moment on their own, then teetered forward, collapsing into a heap a few feet from the rest of the vampire's body. Morcey had chosen the male as his first target because not only had he been closer but he was not as badly wounded as the woman. Turning his attention to her, he swiveled his aim before she could close on him. Her shaking hands inches from his body, he jammed his Auto-Mag against her face, once again breaking her re-forming nose open and immediately sent two rounds through her head. Then, not content to relax, he pulled the trigger again and again, sending shells into both bodies. Moving his hand cannon to a joint before he fired each time, he blew their arms from their sides, heads from their necks, legs from their bodies. Then he reloaded ... and did it again.

By the time he finished, his arm was aching from firing his massive weapon so many times. Stumbling to the stairs, he fell against them, panting from exhaustion. As he watched, however, he saw individual pieces of the vampires still flopping in the curling smoke rolling across the basement floor. He knew the poison had dissipated by that time. Michael Roth, the London Agency's contact in the FBI, had secretly passed a case of the bombs on to Morcey several years earlier, making sure he was carefully versed in its use. By then, it would have been safe for the ex–

maintenance man to walk through, and no more than an ir-
ritant to the vampires. Pulling himself upward, he said,

"Gotta take care of dem bastards." Before he could
move away from the railing, though, Swartz said,

"I've got it."

Moving forward, propelled by enough boiling hate and
rage and adrenaline to overcome the chilling fear that had
tried to cripple him, the officer pointed his gun at the female's twitching back, and with his arm rock steady, fired
directly into her spine twice, shouting,

"That was for Murray Sanderson."

Turning to the man, he shot his desperately flopping
torso again and again and again, screaming,

"And that's for Bill Peters, and Leslie Carragone, and
Jimmy—you fucks!"

Sending his last bullet into the male's head, he then
crossed the room to a barrel he spotted in the corner, one
filled with odd lengths of wood and pipe. Pulling out a
yard-long section of heavy steel, he crossed back to the
barely distinguishable heaps of flesh still quivering in their
piles. Raising the shaft above his head, he brought it down
on the man's head, splattering his skull, sending bits of the
vampire's brains splashing about the room, yelling,

"Take that, you bastard."

Moving around the cellar methodically, the lieutenant
beat every part of both bodies, raining blows one after another, screaming all the time. Tears ran down his face as
he raged, smacking at the throbbing legs and arms and torsos, calling out the names of his fallen comrades.

Finally, however, Morcey grabbed his arm, pulling at
him to stop. Swartz spun around, his eyes crazed, his lips
flecked with hanging strings of thick spittle. He almost attacked the balding man, but managed to catch himself just
before he could swing at him. Understanding, the balding
man said,

"It's okay. It's okay. They're dead. We got 'em. You
smeared 'em. They're finished."

"It's not 'okay,' " snarled the policeman, jerking away.

"They killed Murray. Murray and Andy and Leslie and Pete—fucking killed Fat Pete, and, and, and—"

"And now they're dead," said Morcey. "But there still might be some in the house."

Understanding instantly, Swartz leaned the steel rod against the wall and pulled out his revolver. Raining his empty brass across the floor, he pulled out two half-moons and slapped their contents into his .38, reloading it in seconds. Then, hefting his rod again, he turned his unblinking eyes toward Morcey and said,

"More in the house? Let's go find them."

19

London took the steps to the top floor silently, gliding from one to the next, making no sound whatsoever. Above him he could hear small bumps and scrapes, letting him know where his enemies were. As he continued upward, he sent his senses back down through every board and brick of the house. He kept the fingers of his being out constantly, monitoring his family and friends as well as searching for any signs of more attackers. He could feel Morcey and Swartz moving toward those in the basement. By dividing his attention into compartments of his mind, he could also clearly follow the movements of everyone else in the building: his wife and children as well as Lai Wan, Lacey, and Cat as they moved about the lower floors, looking for each other, caring for Father Bain, securing weapons, searching for places to hide.

"Keep your chins up, little darlings," he whispered, sending the message to his children. In the back of his mind he felt a warm touch, a blend of love and fear and trust that appeared for a soft moment, then disappeared. He knew it had come from Kevin and Kate, and their burst of faith made him smile as he continued to climb.

As he neared the third floor the detective slowed down, flexing his muscles as he moved, stretching out his arms and legs as he approached the floor where the invaders were moving around. London had sucked in the energies of those he had slain in the foyer, calling all of their souls to him, treating their life energies as just another breakfast.

Their souls were small, human things, warped from misuse, but he would use them nonetheless. The detective had never taken a human soul on purpose before, not only disdainful of the practice morally, but afraid of being seduced by the taste for easy power. As the voices of those he had sucked to him pleaded for release, he silenced them all with a thought, none of their pleas meaning anything to him.

You come into my home intent on murdering my children . . . and you're asking for mercy? Shut up. I'm going to enjoy sending you all to Hell.

From that moment on, their voices were silenced within his brain. Their power coursed through him, bursting within his muscles, but London knew it would not be enough to last him long if he got into a tight situation.

Have to conserve power, he thought. And if we do, I think we know the perfect way.

Stepping back against the wall near a small, curved display alcove, the detective picked up the thin, high table that always filled it and moved it down the hall. Then he returned and sat down in the alcove, crossing his legs as he worked at putting all thoughts of what was happening out of his mind. Forcing himself to forget the vampires, to forget the danger to himself, to his family, to his friends and the rest of the world, he pushed all of it aside. Cutting himself off from recent memory, even from his ancestral voices, he thought of the time he had spent years ago in China.

He visualized the mountains, remembering the cold, the lay of the snow and ice that filled the canyons he traveled through and past and over. He sent himself back in time in his mind, felt his hands inside his gloves, felt the ache creeping into his fingers from the biting cold. He brushed at the hair creeping out from under the hood of his parka, sneaking down over his forehead.

It felt stiff, both from the frost in the air and from weeks of going unwashed. And then, suddenly, London realized he was no longer in Manhattan, no longer in his home or in his hallway. For all intents and purposes, he was in China, sitting cross-legged in the snow, his back not against the wall of his alcove, but pressed into a massive crack in the rock face behind him. He could feel snow, blowing through the air, coming to rest on his face, melting on contact with his cheeks, only to refreeze on the stubble of his beard.

Listening, the detective could hear the wind that was moving the snow. He could hear patterns opening within it, sliding different bodies of air past him at different angles, different speeds. Finally letting his eyes open, he took in the dazzling panorama of peaks before him, his breath breaking free from his body as he gasped in astonishment. He had been so preoccupied the last time he had been on the same trail, he had not seen the purple streaks that ran through the peaks in the distance, had not noticed the way many of the mountaintops ranged to one side or the other, not rising up like the postcard mountaintops most Americans were used to.

Then, as he shielded his eyes from the reflecting sunlight bouncing upward from below, London heard someone moving on the trail above and to the left of him. Watching the silver of his breath swirl away before his eyes, he listened intently, trying to determine all he could from whoever was approaching.

More than one, he thought. As he listened, his racial memory sprang forward; ancestors who knew mountains, who knew tracking and the feeling of being tracked took over, telling the detective,

Three, no . . . four. At least four. Men? Four men. Four men and one woman. Big? No, heavy. Weighed down with power, heavy with strength and arrogance. Leader is cautious, however. Searching, careful. The others are a distraction, though. Younger, confident. Foolishly confident. Eager. Looking for trouble.

Well, thought London to all his father's fathers, let's give them some.

Above the detective, on the stairs leading down from the fourth floor, one of the invading vampires whispered to the one in front of him,

"Does it seem cold in here? I mean, colder than when we first came in?"

"Yeah," answered his companion, noticing for the first time that he could almost see his breath. "So what?"

"Quiet, you two," snarled the leader in a growling whis-

per. Placing his hand against the door to the third floor, he
felt out the area beyond it, looking to see what he could
feel on the other side. He didn't like the quiet he felt coming from the rest of the house. The front-door attack was
supposed to have been loud and long. The noise was supposed to give him and his troops—as well as those invading from below—time to enter the house unnoticed.

They were expendable, cannon fodder cheaply thrown
away in the elimination of London and his crew. But the
shooting had ended too soon, meaning that the leader's foe
had somehow eliminated them far quicker than had been
anticipated. The man leading the quartet down through the
house was not stupid. He understood that London was not
a man to be trifled with.

But, then again, he thought, neither am I.

His fingertips gently gliding across the upper panel of
the door, he let them circle the knob and then turn it. As
he pushed the door open, he slid his foot out gently and
felt it sink into the carpet without making a sound. Looking out into the hallway through the crack he had made,
the lead vampire saw nothing that worried him. He wondered at the tall, thin table against the wall and the empty
alcove before him, but he paid them no mind. After all, he
was not there to give London decorating tips, he was there
to kill him. Swinging the door open, he decided it was
about time to stop being so cautious and to start doing the
job he had come to do.

London felt the shift in the wind, as if some barrier had
suddenly been removed. He felt something beyond his line
of vision stirring the air currents, almost as if bodies were
moving toward him. He looked up the mountain trail
stretching away to his left, but he saw nothing out of
place. As he continued to sit, listening, barely breathing,
he suddenly heard voices whispering to each other. Instantly he knew something was wrong. Keeping himself
from panicking, he searched through his mind for any recent memories that might explain what he was sensing,
surprised to find that he had none at all.

Or, he thought, I've been denied them.

Asking his ancestors for any clues they might provide, he found them as cut off as he was.

All right, he told himself, get with the program, pal. Just what the hell have you gotten us into now?

This is not real.

He stirred at the unbidden thought, at the voice in his head that spoke to him only rarely, the one that out of all the hundreds he heard, he could not identify.

Well, if it's not, then what's going on? What could be happening? What am I doing on a mountain ... in my shirtsleeves, no less ... in the ...

And then it hit him.

I've Zenned out. I've made myself invisible. I'm hiding from someone.

As each new thought occurred to him, bits and pieces of the reality London had woven around him began to break up, blurring at the edges of his vision.

Who? he asked. Or is it what? Why am I hiding?

And then he heard a faraway voice he did not recognize, ordering,

"By my dancing feet, I smell trouble. Something is wrong here."

And then the detective thought,

Now I remember.

Reaching up, London grabbed the arms of the two closest vampires. Jerking them both into his reality, the detective gave both their wrists a savage twist and then pushed, flinging them forward off the narrow rock ledge. Their screams echoed throughout the mountains as they slammed against the cruel stone walls below.

"Murphy! Durando!" shouted the leader of the quintet as two of his people disappeared. Whipping around in the hallway, he suddenly felt a chill in the air, his mind seizing on what the man named Durando had said back on the steps.

"Cold?" he asked, feeling the temperature dropping all around him. "Cold? What the devil is happening here? Where are you, London?"

"My home too cold for you folks?" came the detective's voice from all corners of the hallway. "Here. Let me warm things up for you."

On both sides of the vampire leader, his two remaining companions suddenly burst into flame. The searing heat enveloped them from the inside out, burning through their chests and backs, spreading to their heads and feet in less than a second. Neither had time to even bleat before their lungs collapsed, their knees separated, their necks burned through. As the last vampire tried to take in what he was seeing, the two bodies charred away right in front of his eyes, disintegrating down into dust and then nothingness before a single speck could reach the floor.

Spinning around, searching for London, *knowing* the detective had to be nearby, he remembered the out-of-place table. His head snapped around, and everything fell into place as his eyes went immediately to the alcove.

"Bastard!" he snarled. Instantly he directed all of his will toward the alcove, throwing a blast of energy into the plastered curve that burned through the wall in a heartbeat. The torrent of force the vampire released represented a hundred stolen lives, its white-hot heat the energy of souls that had been saved for over three years.

Worth it, thought the vampire, his mind woozy, his body staggered from the rapid energy loss.

"Worth it," he repeated aloud.

But then, as the exhausted vampire reached out his hand to steady himself on the wall, his eyes bulged open as four spots of intense pain pierced his skin. Spinning around, he found London standing on the mountain trail behind him.

"Nice try," said the detective. "But I moved."

And then, looking down, the vampire saw the long thin legs of the alcove table protruding from his chest. London had used up his spare energy incinerating the second pair of vampires. He had been forced to find a more physical means of attacking the leader. As the vampire reached behind him, trying to extract the table from his back, he lost his footing on the slick floor beneath him.

"Snow?" blurted the vampire dumbly, shock and confusion slowing his reactions.

"My world," answered London, placing his foot against the vampire's side. "And welcome to it."

Pushing off with all his strength, the detective kicked out and sent the last of the five invaders over the edge of the mountain the Tibetans called Thumb to the Sky. Not bothering to listen to the man's screams, he sat back down in his spot against the rock wall, tired and exhausted. He closed his eyes, ready to work his way back home, but before he could concentrate, sudden applause broke out somewhere in front of him. Opening his eyes, he saw a man hanging in midair, clapping enthusiastically.

"Oh, bravo, bravo, Mr. London. How's it feel to be taking life without a second's thought again. Is it everything you remembered?"

"Tabor," said the detective.

"Yes. Poor, stupid, little, useless Martin Tabor. What was it your little helper called me? The CPA of the damned? His idea of a joke, if I remember correctly. Just before he murdered me in the arena."

"It was a fair fight," answered London, not able to comprehend how Tabor could have found his way into the dream-plane reality the detective had created.

"Interesting way of looking at it. But why not? After all, *all* is fair in love and war, I suppose."

"Then you won't mind if we kill you again, right?"

"Not to sound too ridiculous, but you've killed me for the last time, Mr. London. If I could reach you in a physical way right now, I'd rip your lungs out and slap you about the head and shoulders with them. But that grand moment will have to wait."

"For when?" asked the detective, goading the vampire on.

" 'For when,' he asks. Don't play me for a fool, London. I'm going to make the whole world pay for shunning me. Pay hard and pay dearly—you all shall. Don't think I'm stupid. I'm not about to try and take your children from you, or your little curly-headed breeding machine.

That would give you real incentive, real power to use against me."

London continued to sit in the snow, stunned but fascinated. As he did, the vampire began to float slowly backward toward the horizon. As he grew smaller, he said,

"I could have just nuked New York, you know. Killed the lot of you and not had to worry."

"Why didn't you? Frankly, I didn't think you were the one-on-one type, myself."

"No, Mr. London, I'm not fool enough to condemn myself to being tracked to the ends of the Earth by your vengeance. Your righteousness has proved itself nuisance enough. But I will explain it all to you. I attacked you personally instead of nuking the city because I did not want to harm the Confessor."

The detective's mouth fell open a slight way. Stunned, he could think of nothing to say. Tabor filled the silence as he continued to drift away, saying,

"I met the Confessor on the continent. Talking to him is an irresistible thing. Before I knew it, I had confessed all to him." London studied the distant vampire's face, probed his pained expression. He found he had no choice but to believe the vampire. Standing up out of the snow, he continued to listen as Tabor told him,

"People in my employ, thinking they were acting on my orders, killed him. They were not punished. I knew the Confessor was immortal. I knew he would not condemn me for their actions. But, I had the new Confessor watched. When it became clear that he was going to go to you—I had to act."

The vampire stopped his backward motion for a moment. Hanging in the air, his eyes closed, he whispered in a voice choked with regret,

"I tried to keep him out of all this. When I saw I couldn't, I tried to stop you before he could tell you anything." Then Tabor's eyes opened as he said,

"I will admit I didn't want to face you again. You worried me. And so, I did everything wrong. I accidentally killed the Confessor, and didn't kill you."

As London stood on the ledge he had created, too tired to reach the dream-plane image of Tabor disappearing in the distance, the vampire told him,

"But that's all over now. I've tested you this day, Mr. London, and I've found you wanting. You and your people did very well, but you've shown me your limits. I'm not afraid of you anymore, and so now you have a choice."

The vampire faded completely away then, not so much vanishing through distance but through dissipation. His voice stayed with the detective, however, still echoing throughout the mountains.

"You can either try and find me, which I would enjoy, because it would give me the opportunity to kill you with my own hands—close up." As London listened, suddenly his control of his environment slipped, sending him solidly back to the third floor of his home.

"Or," came Tabor's voice, gliding through the hallway, "you can sit back and wait to see what I do. And that, I must admit, would please me, too."

Shaking from the cold no longer around him, London leaned back against the wall. Stumbling into the ruined alcove, he was unable to stop himself from falling to the floor. Weak from his efforts, he tried to contain the violence of his shaking as Tabor's voice came to him there in his home, whispering,

"It's your move, Mr. London."

And then the detective was alone in the hallway, the smell of burning flesh hanging in the air and the sound of police sirens breaking the silence.

20

It had taken a long time to even begin straightening things out. The police had arrived too quickly. Some observant neighbor had spotted the invaders of London's home before they had quite begun their attack and had called 911. They had been on the phone, describing to an actual officer and not a recording machine, what looked to them like a lot of uniformed men with guns getting ready to rush the building across the street, when suddenly the violence started, loud enough for the police officer to hear over the phone. In seconds, radio dispatchers were sending every available squad car to the scene.

They did not like what they found. The building's front doors had been blown off their hinges . . . gallons of blood splattering the floor and all of the walls of the foyer . . . weapons and uniforms and dust were spread across the same room's floor, sounding suspiciously like the scene of a mass murder the day before. The officers became even more suspicious when it was discovered that the crime the day before had taken place at the office of the man whose building they were standing in.

They were made uncomfortable by the wide-eyed presence of one of their own, a lieutenant whose reputation for cold nerves did not match the screaming maniac they found already on the scene. They were also made uncomfortable by the six bodies lying in the back room of the basement that the coroner said had died from massive doses of poison, those that had not been blown apart by pistol fire. The investigating officers also had no love for finding his companion, a private detective, there in the basement with the lieutenant, with a bag of illegal weapons slung over his shoulder.

Nor were they extremely fond of discovering the shrapnel-riddled corpse of a Catholic cleric on the second floor. Or the monstrously incinerated pair of corpses on the third floor. Or the half-frozen private detective lying next to them. It was a mess beyond most patrol officers' wildest nightmares, and one that none of the eight policemen first to respond to the scene had any idea how to handle.

Nor did those that arrived after them, either. Before long, the entire block had been sealed to further traffic—excepting, of course, the stream of ambulances and police vehicles that continued to flood the area. News about the second massacre leaked quickly throughout the city, bringing a typical flocking of media people—print reporters, TV anchors, and the leg people who scouted out such tragedies for them—photographers, video jocks, and, as always, the producers and agents looking for witnesses whose rights could be tied up early on . . . in case there was as big a television movie in whatever was going on in New York as there seemed.

Arriving after the first wave of the curious, and the media ghouls who were always willing to exploit that curiosity, Captain William Hammonder was not happy with the carnival atmosphere he found. A solid policeman with twenty-three years' experience, he had been through enough similar scenes to dread having to deal with whatever was ahead of him before he even got to it. A medium-sized man with thinning red hair and perhaps thirty pounds too many for his frame, he had not been pleased with the news that there had been another mass killing in the city, nor with the way the scene had been allowed to deteriorate.

As soon as his car had managed to force its way through the milling throng that had slowed his approach to a crawl, the captain ordered his driver to stop. Getting out immediately, he started snapping orders to uniformed officers, sending for the scene coordinator, getting the crowd pushed back, and the ambulances moved forward, clearing the street and the sidewalks on both sides for a hundred feet to either side of London's home. As several of the news people began to make their usual objections, Hammonder stepped forward, barking,

"Some advice, people. Clam up, all of you. Now. Aside from the fact that you all are trampling a crime scene underfoot—which I assure you I will not tolerate—my advance reports tell me that poison gas was used on the inside. Now, since we have no way of knowing at this time whether or not there are any unexploded canisters still about, I will brook no opposition to this order on the grounds of public safety."

"We'll take our chances," shouted one newswoman, to whom the captain responded instantly, saying,

"Not on my watch, you won't." Turning to a much beleaguered unit sergeant, Hammonder ordered in a voice loud enough for all those protesting to hear,

"Have this street cleared in the manner I dictated—now. Anyone who gives you the slightest bit of trouble, take them in. They don't get their lawyer until after they've been booked, printed, mugged, and interrogated as for the reason they would want to hinder our investigation."

"Yes, sir," answered the sergeant smartly, a grin playing across his face as he moved toward the reporters and their fellows, eager to find the one determined to be made an example of.

In the meantime, without waiting to see how his orders would be implemented, the captain headed straight for the London residence, looking for the designated scene coordinator on the way. The officer chosen out of the initial eight on the scene to keep all their notes so as to update whoever took over the scene joined him halfway between the edge of the crowd and the London's front stoop. Pulling out her notebook, she saluted as Hammonder approached, saying,

"Where would you like me to start?"

"Wherever you feel it makes most sense to start, officer," the captain said, adding in a softer voice, "I hear this is even a bigger mess than yesterday's, and that they've got Swartz in there." When the woman nodded, Hammonder said,

"Great. Let's get to it. Give me everything you have in the fastest way you can. I want to know what the hell I'm talking about when I get in there."

"That may be a problem, Captain."

"How so?"

"Sir, it seems that several of the survivors we have interviewed so far—including Lieutenant Swartz—have said that . . ." The young woman stopped to clear her throat for a second, then continued, saying, "That it was *vampires* that were behind the attack."

Hammonder stopped in his tracks, turning to search the face of the woman at his side. After he had assured himself that she was not risking her career by making jokes for which he did not have time, the captain said,

"Let's walk slow."

Some fifteen minutes later, the captain was ushered into the Londons' dining room, where all the principal players had been gathered to await his arrival. He had been given as thorough a briefing as possible and, at that moment, knew everything the police did about what had happened. Looking over the cast of characters before him, he moved forward without hesitation. Centering on the person he correctly presumed to be London, he asked in a hostilely sweet voice,

"So, tell me, how is it that you were found suffering from what appeared to be near hypothermia in between two corpses that had been incinerated? And while you're at it, if you could explain how those bodies managed to burn, leaving a"—the captain referred to his notes—" 'a heavily charred aroma throughout the hallway,' but not setting anything else on fire—not even so much as scorching the carpeting—figure that I'd be most grateful for the information."

"Certainly, captain," answered London. Setting down the teacup he had been holding, the detective answered, "I incinerated the pair of vampires your people found with a concentrated burst of energy that I willed to excite the molecules of their bodies. When you can pull it off, it sets a chain reaction known as spontaneous combustion."

"Oh," said Hammonder, his voice skipping a small beat, "you did? And can I ask why?"

"Because I wanted to kill them. And I'll tell you why I wanted to do that, too."

"Please . . . please do," said the captain, an edge of anger creeping into his voice.

"They were here to murder me, my wife, and children . . . as well as my friends."

"And your proof?"

"Besides all the new bullet holes in my home?" asked the detective, picking up his teacup again.

"It's been a long day. Indulge me."

"My first guess that they weren't playing games came when they murdered Father Bain. I didn't even get to say . . . well, to say anything to him. When the first wave of attackers opened fire on me I thought that was a good sign, too. But then, when I was killing the five who came in over the roof—you won't find three of the corpses. I left them in another dimension—their leader appeared to me in a vision and pretty much confirmed my theory that they didn't mean us any good."

"You only killed five more people today? Were those some of the bodies found in the basement?"

"No, Captain," said Swartz, interrupting from across the room. "Mr. Morcey and I are responsible for all eight of those. Mr. London was never in the basement."

"And," asked Hammonder, turning back to the detective, "*where* are these other three people you say you killed?"

"Probably still at the bottom of the cliff I threw them off in the dream plane."

"Okay, goddamn it," blurted the captain, not willing to allow any sport to be made of himself, "nobody wants to get serious. . . . Fine . . . we can just leave these comfy surroundings and head uptown. You want to make wise cracks, London, you'll do it in handcuffs from behind bars."

"Shut up and sit down," said the detective in a soft tone that no one in the room took for anything but a command.

When Hammonder made to answer, London waved his hand in front of his face, snapping his fingers at the captain, rendering him mute. Taking another sip of his tea, he leaned his chair back on its hind legs, saying,

"I believe I told you to sit down." The captain stared, unable to speak, unable to turn away from London, unable to do anything except give in and sit down at the table, the feeling of hard, cold fingers that he could not see directing his every action. As the officer sat, the detective turned to Swartz and requested,

"Why don't you fill Captain Hammonder in on what's been happening for the past two days?"

"My pleasure, Mr. London." The lieutenant got up out of his chair and walked across the room with a curious bounce to his step. Turning toward the two policemen flanking the door, speaking to all the officers in the room, he said,

"The captain would like his briefing in private, wouldn't you, Captain?"

Hammonder screamed within his mind as he felt the urge to nod come over him. Straining himself to the utmost, cold fear curled around his spine as he felt all his efforts pushed aside, as he felt the invisible hands nodding his head for him. Most of the other officers in the room started to make for the door, but two held back. Old working partners of the captain's, they hesitated, one asking,

"Bill . . . you sure?"

Again Hammonder felt pain stabbing through his heart and lungs as he fought the suggestion in his brain, the one making his head bob up and down again. His two friends left reluctantly. Lacey closed the door behind them. Then London released the hold he had taken of the captain's will. With nothing holding him any longer, Hammonder fell backward in his chair from the suddenness of his release. Pulling himself up off the floor, he grabbed for his revolver, cursing,

"God damn you all." The captain stopped halfway to an upright position, thrown off by his inability to draw his weapon. As he stopped, dazed by the experience—half his

mind shouting at him to run, the other half still too terrified by having been touched by an outside consciousness
to react—London said,

"We can do this rough or we can do this easy, Captain.
Now, I'm not going to let you hurt anyone with that"—the
detective's eyes darted toward Hammonder's revolver, still
in its shoulder holster—"so why don't you just let go of it
and then sit down and listen to what we have to tell you?"

Swartz took a sip of coffee, then let a wide smile cross
his face. His eyes were still too wide and still a bit too
crazy to comfort Hammonder. Swartz set his cup down,
urging Hammonder,

"I'd do it, Captain. Honest. It goes down a lot easier if
you don't fight it."

The moment Hammonder decided to stop struggling, the
hard fingers he had felt holding him down disappeared. He
moved toward his overturned chair with nervous jerks, his
head darting from side to side. Righting his chair, he
moved it back toward the table and sat down in it again.
Almost afraid to try and speak, he finally got a grip on his
will and said,

"How? How can you do this? What are you?"

"I'm just a private detective who knows a few tricks.
That's all, Captain. The big secret here is that every once
in a while I get pulled into things I don't want to know
about . . . hell, things that no one wants to know about.
But, fate has sort of singled me out to be its right-hand
boy." London settled all four of his chair's legs back on
the floor. Leaning his elbows on the table, he stared in
Hammonder's eyes, telling him,

"There's a lot of stuff going on here, Captain. Things
you might not want to hear about." Then, looking deeper
into Hammonder's eyes, the detective noticed something
that he thought gave him some insight into the captain's
manner. Playing his hunch, he said,

"But then, it's too late for you, too, isn't it?" As
Hammonder blinked, London added, "You don't need us
to tell you about vampires, do you?" The captain struggled
within himself for a long moment, then finally said quietly,

"I've seen the voodoo files . . . some of them, anyway. It's the catch-all file for the department's weird cases—the unsolveds; hell, sometimes they're even solved . . . they just don't make any sense. City the size of New York, well over ten million people in its sphere of influence—lot of things happen here that no one can explain. At least, that no one can explain without using words like *vampire*."

"Well, Captain," said London, taking pity on the man across the table from him, "we've got a lot to tell you, and a lot of it is going to be filled with those kinds of words. After we're done, we're going to ask you to tell everyone that this building was attacked by the same people as yesterday, but that fewer people were killed this time. You will, of course, not be releasing any names today, just as you didn't yesterday. That's just routine procedure. Then, you're going to help my people and me get out of the city, and for that matter, the country, as soon as possible."

"Captain Hammonder," said Morcey, drawing all the room's attention to himself. "A few years ago I was a guy just like anybody else. I'd never thought of vampires bein' real, never thought I'd actually look into the face of the Devil, never thought I'd fight a werewolf, or see any of the shit I have. You, you're sweatin' just 'cause the boss threw a few suggestions in your head. Captain—you ain't felt nuthin'. Me, for the past few years, I've been seein' things beyond most people's comprehension every time I turn around." His hands at his sides, palms outward, the balding man took his most unassuming stance as he said,

"You look at the lieutenant, here. He was pretty spit and polish when he showed up yesterday. Just like you. I say you take a good long look at him today and then decide just how much you want us to prove to you."

Although he tried not to, the captain could not stop himself from looking again into Swartz's eyes. He had known the lieutenant only slightly before that morning, had heard many of the stories about him. The man sitting across from him with the wildly messed hair and the blood-drenched clothing, with the unnerving tick moving his left cheek up and down, and the demented look in his eyes, did not match Hammonder's recollections of the lieutenant. As if reading his fellow officer's mind, Swartz laughed a bit, then said,

"Like I said, Captain . . . I'd do it if I were you. It really does go down a lot easier if you don't fight it." Then, suddenly, an unexpected sob burst from Swartz, one lone note of grief that left him unchanged, except for the single tear running down the right side of his face. Readjusting his smile, the lieutenant added,

"A lot easier."

21

"Captain Hammonder turned out ta be a real cooperative kinda guy, didn't he, boss?"

"You could say that, Paul," answered London, throwing the second of his carry-on bags in the storage bin over his seat, raising his eyebrows suggestively.

"Oh, my . . . yeah," added Cat in a loud whisper, trying not to laugh. Her face sneering but happy, she stashed the bag with her special equipment under the seat in front of her as she said, "You could, you could indeed."

By the time Hammonder had arrived at London's home, the detective had already planned his next move. Before the first uniformed police response had arrived, London was five minutes finished with the phone call he had needed to make. When the captain had tried to take over the scene, the detective merely smiled and then told him everything that had happened.

While they had talked, London had kept Hammonder riveted with his eyes. He had filled his expression with a look that swore its owner could tell no lies. Then, going into Hammonder's mind while he talked to him, the detective whispered suggestions to the police captain's subconscious, forcing him to not only see the truth on London's terms, but to accept it as such. And when the detective had finished telling his tale, Swartz had backed him on every point, showing his superior that it was going to be very tough to cover up the incident in any way except whatever way London offered.

Before any offers could be made by either side, however, the detective's phone call paid off. One of the officers standing guard outside London's dining room knocked on the door, saying that they had a visitor. Hammonder had sent Morcey to see who was so important they could make their way upstairs past his men. When the

ex–maintenance man reached the hall he found Michael
Roth, an FBI agent that had gotten involved with London
and his people years earlier. The detective and Swartz
brought Roth up to speed, and then turned Hammonder's
education over to him. The FBI man told him,

"Captain, you have some real big decisions to make—
and very soon. There's a very curious world out there. The
CNN truck has just pulled up and there are a half dozen
others in front of it, prowling for space. And in case you
can't figure it out, they're all waiting for the chance to
start crawling down you throat."

"I've been around the block, Agent Roth. Get to the
point."

"Why, certainly, Captain," answered the FBI man.
"Happy to. Trust me when I say that Mr. London and one
of your own people have already told you more than you
need to know about what happened here. Take it from one
who found out the hard way—these things don't get any
easier to handle the longer you look at them. Best you get
down to cases."

"And what cases are we talking about?"

"What do you think?" snapped Roth. "The issue is
whether or not you believe them."

"Well, then," the captain answered, "I guess the issue
is all settled." The large man sat back in his chair and
scratched at his forehead. Thinking for just a moment, he
remembered all of the things he had seen in the detective's
eyes, and then shuddered as he said, "Oh, yes. I believe
them."

"Well, then, there's your problem. Aside, of course,
from the one you're going to have at night when you're
trying to sleep. . . ."

"Agent Roth," asked Hammonder in a curt tone, "are
you trying to scare me?"

"No, sir," answered the FBI man. "Believe me, you're
going to take care of that all by yourself. But, be all that
as it may, the real problem you have is that you can't go
outside and announce that there're vampires running

around town. Bad for business. Bad for tourism. Bad for careers. But I'll tell you what you can do . . ."

And that had been all there was to it. Hammonder knew he was in a tight spot—both politically and public relations wise. The captain had already cursed himself for grabbing the case. A group of mass murderers—one the grapevine said had already sent one senior officer over the line—that was the kind of stuff careers were made of. For a man who had aspirations beyond the department, it had sounded made to order. When that had backfired, like any good politician, Hammonder had become more than ready to cut a deal.

Officially, everyone was told of the plentiful deaths inside. *Officially*, the story was that the London Agency—which had also been hit the day before—had now been hit at home as well. Many were dead, and details would be released pending an FBI investigation. The warheads gave Roth as good an excuse as any to bring the case under federal jurisdiction . . . and out of Hammonder's . . . which was exactly where the captain had been happy to be led.

And so, to the world at large, the London Agency had been destroyed—all its members killed by parties who could not be named at present—and that was all anyone was telling the press. In the meantime, the agency went underground. While the police had dispersed the crowd, the detective and the others had begun to prepare for the trip to Hong Kong. Lacey and Lisa were going to watch over the children, the four of them moving to Mama Joan's during the interim.

London, Morcey, Lai Wan, Cat, and Swartz, on the other hand, had taken the first flight to Shanghai that could be arranged. They had all agreed that their enemies would be watching the incoming flights from the States to Hong Kong, maybe even those from Europe. However, as Roth had put it, how likely was it they would be watching the incoming trains from China? The FBI man had suggested the circuitous route, and all had agreed.

Roth stayed in New York, supposedly to head up the investigation into what had happened at the detective's, but more important, to coordinate communications between London, the FBI, and the NYPD, as well as between the detective and his family. As the agent had put it,

"What the hell—you know? One, it keeps the eye of the FBI on your wife and kids. When it comes to this stuff, you chase it, I'll handle the rear echelon. You'll do a better job over there if you're not so worried about over here. And two, if you're chasing the vampires, I'm not. And like Hammonder, maybe I like it that way."

And so, only eleven hours after they had been fighting for their lives, the five had found themselves boarding a jet that would take them to San Francisco, where they would make their connection to the East. As Morcey stored Lai Wan's larger carry-on bag along with his own above their seats, Swartz said,

"So, think this will get by this genius vampire bad guy of yours?"

"We'll find out, won't we?"

After London had told the lieutenant about his encounter with Martin Tabor on the dream plane, the two had decided that the vampire was not one to be underestimated. Both of them were sure that if Tabor knew what jet London and his people were on, he would have it destroyed. As Swartz had said,

"This guy is a classic. He'll just kill you. No fancy traps, no luring you into his lair. I don't see this clown playing any games. No, no way. He hates you from way back and thinks you're the only thing in the world that can stop him from whatever the hell it is that he's up to." The policeman brushed at his mustache, saying,

"You wanted my opinion, and since I seem to be part of this little jamboree now, I'm happy to give it. This guy is definitely out there. If he thought he had it narrowed down to ten planes—ten planes and two boats—he'd send them all to the bottom of the ocean."

"I agree," London had said. "That's why we'll take a hundred fifty planes and thirty ships."

The detective had then set everyone to work. While Roth made their real travel arrangements via San

Francisco and Shanghai, the others had used all the phones in the house to call every airline and travel agent they could, looking for flights from every available airport and boats from every possible port. London knew Tabor would see through the detective's ruse of getting himself and his people declared dead. What was supposed to throw him would be the sheer mass of trails to follow if he was actually determined to stop the detective before he could get to Hong Kong. London used the agency's bank account to pick up the staggering tab, leaving instructions with his wife on when to start cashing in the unused tickets.

After that, there had been nothing left for the detective to do but take the bags Lisa had packed for him, kiss his children, and head for the airport. As London settled into his seat on the plane, watching the other passengers file back and forth—fussing with their bags, looking for blankets and pillows and a magazine that suited their mood—he closed his eyes and relaxed, drifting back to the moment at his front door when he had stopped for one last moment to look at his family. Trying to be reassuring, he had told his wife,

"Don't worry too much. Tabor'll have to be awfully determined, or awfully lucky, to be able to take us out before we get to Hong Kong."

"I'm not all that worried about him getting you before you get to Hong Kong," she had said. "After you get there is when I plan to start worrying."

"Well," he had said, not able to keep how much he really did agree with her out of his voice, "I guess if you're determined to worry, that would be the time."

And then she had thrown her arms around him and hugged him as fiercely as she ever had. Her eyes suddenly brimming with tears, she told him,

"I don't want a hero anymore—do you hear me? I don't want the world saved if I have to lose you."

"Sweetheart," he had whispered, not wanting to worry Kevin or Kate, "if I don't pull this one off, I don't think you're going to have to worry about facing retirement alone."

"Good," she said quietly into his ear. "Good. If you can't stop this without dying . . . then let it happen. I mean it. Let the whole world die. Let it go up once and for all." She kissed his ear and then his neck, still holding on to him tightly as she said,

"You come back to me—all in one piece. Do you hear me?"

"Yes, Maw," he whispered, kissing her back, hugging her back—keeping her locked within his arms, absorbing the essence of her as if for the last time. Then he smiled, kissed her again, and finally released her, saying,

"I heard you."

Sitting in his seat, eyes still closed, he pushed himself away from the passengers around him, away from the flight attendants and their mundane concerns, away from the reality of the plane completely. Taking a deep breath, he slowed his heart rate dramatically, sinking into what a casual observer might mistake for a sound sleep—but what a medical examination would take for a coma. And once there within the recesses of his own mind, he called up all of his ancestors who had ever dealt with vampires, or even those who had ever even heard of them.

With half of his consciousness listening to their advice and stories and warnings, he set the other half to reviewing all of his own memories on the subject, up until and including the battle earlier in his own home. He set his mind to looking for corollaries between the two factions, looking for whatever the past might teach him about what was happening in the present. And as part of him listened to tales from Asia, Europe, and the Mediterranean, the other half reviewed his own past, taking him through everything he knew, bringing him full circle.

Once again he saw Father Bain lying glass-eyed dead in his dining room. He saw the heavily armed killers that had come to spray the bodies of his children and his wife with bullets. He saw the blood covering the walls of his office and his home, saw the five monsters that had crawled down out of his ceiling to kill him, saw the littered dead that had been piled all around him, saw his wife pleading with him to come back in one piece.

Nodding to himself unconsciously, he whispered to her one last time,

"I heard you, sweetheart. I heard you."

And then he began to piece his plan together.

22

"Vas is das?"

Morcey nudged London, pointing to a mobile billboard set on wheels, sitting in the middle of the train platform before them. Hiding a tired smile, the detective read,

"It says, 'Typhoon Signal Number One.'"

"I can read, boss," answered the balding man, dropping his TV Nazi accent. "I just ain't up to da interpretation. I mean, what're they tellin' us? That one is on its way right now, or is it, like, earthquakes—an' a 'one' is, like, okay—you know? I mean . . . a typhoonie might slow down our huntin' for vampires and nukes and the such."

"Well, I'll be happy to wait here for everyone else while you find someone who can explain it to us."

"You got it, boss. I think I'll dig up a cuppa coffee while I'm at it. You want anything?"

London answered that he did not need anything at the moment and sent his partner on his way. He watched the ex–maintenance man thread his way through the stacks of luggage and the crowds of people. In his path, the detective could see a soccer team, obviously waiting to be on their way to somewhere else. The high-spirited players were practicing in between the piles of crates and suitcases, sending their ball flying within inches of their fellow travelers, laughing at each one they made jump.

For some reason London could not discern, they did not notice Morcey's approach. The detective was amazed to see that his partner was not only limber enough to catch them off guard, but fast enough to interrupt their sport by stealing their ball away and then keeping it for nearly a full minute with footwork alone before one of the team managed to steal it back. The players all laughed, shouting "bravos" in heavy southern Italian accents while Morcey bowed and then continued on his way to the Maxim's Express fast-food restaurant he had spotted before. As he did, however, he merely shook his head, not able to believe how stiff he was.

It had been a longer trip than London had imagined. Standing on the rail platform of the train depot, he put the palms of his hands against the pit of his back and pushed. Forgetting about the others, knowing they would all meet where they had agreed as soon as their various errands had been run, the detective put them out of his mind as he pressed against the back of his belt, digging at the pain there.

Shutting his eyes, he turned his hands around and dug his knuckles into his back. As London felt his efforts starting to have some effect, he doubled his attack, letting his mind drift back over the torturously long trip he had just completed. They had first been delayed on the runway for almost two and a half hours by rain in New York, then kept from landing for almost as long by fog in San Francisco.

Can't get out of one town, the detective had thought, can't get into the next.

When their circling had finally come to an end, the group had had to rush from one end of the terminal to the other to catch their flight from California to Shanghai. Exhausted when they piled on board with the rest of their helpless fellow travelers, they were then treated to another eighteen hours in the air just to get to Shanghai, followed by the flight from there to Canton, and then the underground train ride from Canton to Hong Kong.

Working out the layers of knotted kinks that had made a nest in his back, London thought,

Well, that's one way to get a little time to think. Too bad I didn't use it to think of anything useful.

The aching in the detective's spine had become second nature to him while sitting in moving vehicles. Like all travelers, he had found a way to curl up that allowed him to ignore the knots growing in his back. By the time he finally found himself standing on solid ground with no ex-

ternal forward motion to help compensate for his aches, he
found the pain to be almost more than he could bear.

Closing his eyes again, he sent fingers from his mind
deep into the muscles of his back. Taking a long moment,
he spent it straightening out those connected to his vertebrae, half of his mind wondering all the while what took
him so long to think of doing this in the first place.

Just distracted, I guess, he told himself. Just too busy
looking for a next move.

As if, one of his ancestors said, it were likely you were
going to find one before you actually got here.

Why not? he reminded the long-dead shade. It's worked
before.

True enough, the voice conceded. But those were sim-
pler menaces, ones that—so far, anyway—had the decency
to stay dead when they were killed.

Oh well, thought London with a grin. You can't have
everything.

"No, you cannot," said Lai Wan, suddenly at the detective's side. "Where would you put it?"

London opened his eyes, a bit shocked at having been
taken off guard, at having missed the touch of someone
reading his thoughts without his being aware, even if it
had been a member of his own team. Giving the psychometrist a squint and a sour smile, he said,

"Was that a joke?"

"Someone else's, but yes it was. A good one, too, I
thought. Very reflective."

"Yeah. Something I wish I'd been on the trip."

"As the man said, Theodore, one can only stay ahead of
their time for so long."

The detective turned and looked at the woman in black,
eyeing her in a way which revealed that out of all the
things she might have said to him, what she had chosen
had been the least expected. As he stared into her face, she
chose not to look back. From the angle of her head he
could tell she was looking at Maxim's, searching for a
glimpse of her husband. London chided himself,

That's why she was in your head—just looking for Paul. Really, you're getting a little slow.

Maybe we're just getting old, he thought to the first voice within his brain to speak up, only to be answered,

Paul's got more than ten years on us and he can out-soccer a pro. Slow's not what we're getting.

Yeah? Well, you're so smart, then spill it—just what is our goddamned problem all of a sudden? Filled with a rage that boiled up out of nowhere, the detective thundered at all the voices in his head, demanding,

Let's hear it, damn it! Come on, give it up, big mouth. What the hell's happened to us? The last time something like this came down you didn't think anything of opening a hole in the dream plane and walking through it from one country to another—of leading whole parades of people around. Now out of nowhere we're playing Mission Impossible—why? What's going on? What are we afraid of?

And then everything suddenly cleared from London's head. His mouth opened in shock, then closed in a grim, straight line. He was surprised at the level of tension that ran through his shoulders, only to bleed off into the air just as quickly. He was not surprised to see the people around him on the train platform unconsciously moving away from him, some staring at him as if they somehow under-stood that the cold raging blast of nerves and fear that had just washed over the platform had come from him.

"What is it, Theodore?"

"I finally put some of the puzzle together," answered the detective. "The last time we got mixed up in this kind of stuff, I was a lot younger. It was only a few years, yeah—but I wasn't married. I wasn't a dad. Now . . . now everything's different. I can't stop thinking about Lisa and the kids, wondering if they're all right, if they're going to be all right . . . if I'm going to make it back to them." As the psychometrist took a step closer to London, he told her,

"It all fell in place when you skimmed me to find out where Paul was. Your being concerned like that finally woke me up—showed me what I'd been missing. All through this thing I've been walking around like I'm in slow motion. The Confessor showing up, the attack on the office, then on the house ..." Taking Lai Wan's arms above the elbows, he said,

"I wasn't concentrating—not once. Not totally. Over the years, its just become second nature to wonder what the kids are doing, where they are, who's with them—that kind of thing. My mind has split itself into two parts: the one that takes care of everything I have to take care of, and the one that worries about my family and plans for the future. I couldn't shut it down because I couldn't admit to myself that there was anything to shut down."

"Theodore," answered the woman, "not only do I understand, but you are beginning to bruise me."

The detective let go his hold at once, instantly apologetic. But before either of them could say anything further one of the many one-man mobile hand trucks that had been racing about the platform came speeding toward them, beep-beep-beeping for them to move. The two stepped to one side, letting the baggage handler move by. Then London stuck his hands into his pockets and said,

"There. You'll be safe now."

"I could be no place safer."

"Kind of you to say so, anyway," answered the detective. "But I haven't been doing a very good job so far. Just ask Father Bain."

"I was not hoping to swell your comfortably sized ego. But neither will I allow you to tear yourself apart when we do not have the time for it." Feeling both Cat and Swartz's presences moving across the platform, both heading for London and her position, she stared the detective in the eye and then spoke to him quickly in a sharp but quiet voice.

"If there is going to be safety in this thing at all, it will be wherever you are. If you have allowed yourself to become distracted with thoughts of Lisa and Kevin and Kate, then put them aside now, before more of us and perhaps the entire world joins Father Bain. I have cheated death

once. I think once is all they give you. Pull yourself together and leave their defense to the ones you charged
with it. You have your own work to do."

London pursed his lips on one side of his mouth, showing his displeasure with the way things had been going,
but nodded his head at the same time, indicating that he
understood. As he did so, Lai Wan turned away from him,
feeling Morcey coming back through the crowd.

So involved with looking for him was she, however,
that the psychometrist failed to notice the approach of two
other figures moving through the crowd. Suddenly realizing that someone's eyes were on his back, however, London spun around quickly, only to find,

"Jhong! What're you doing here?"

"Looking for you," answered the elder Chinese warrior
who had joined the ranks of the London Agency the first
time it had encountered the vampires. "There was little
doubt that you were in need of my assistance once again.
Thus, I am here."

Several years earlier, when the old man had reappeared
in the detective's life without warning, he claimed fate had
whispered to him that he had to be someplace else, and
that he had traveled until he had found himself at London's side once more. That time, the detective had been
surprised. This time, however, it was his traveling companion that shocked London.

Behind the martial warrior, a much larger man stood,
wide shouldered, thick as a couch and as hard as stone.
His wavy black hair lay in heaps upon his head and the
back of his neck, his eyes shone with the intensity of a
child at Christmas. However, it was not his size that
shocked the detective—it was the fact that he was alive.

The man was a vampire, one that had walked the Earth
for thousands of years. He had gone by human names
throughout the centuries, but the most enduring had been
Hercules. The first time he and London had met, the detective had been forced to kill him. The second time they had
met, it had been Jhong that had killed him.

"Interesting company you're keeping these days," said

London to the elder warrior with a trace of surprise still in his voice. The large man looked down, neither smiling nor frowning, saying simply,

"It's good to see you, too, Mr. London."

"You know, you're a harder man to kill than I thought."

"So are you, Mr. London," answered the vampire good-naturedly. "So are you. But if you don't mind, I have been waiting for this moment for some time."

The massive vampire stuck out his hand, waiting for the detective to fill it. Before London could ask, the vampire told him,

"I believe you have something that is rightfully mine."

Another full second passed before London realized what the vampire meant. And then, as he looked into the face of Hercules, into the eyes of the man who had toppled entire countries on his own, defeated whole armies by himself, the detective reached down to the bag next to him. Slipping open its lock, he dug his hand down in between his socks and shorts, finding the small lump he had hidden away there. Then, pulling it out, he dropped it onto the vampire's palm.

Reaching for the small wad of paper in his hand, the vampire unwrapped that which was at its core and then pulled forth the ring of the Confessor. Slipping it onto his finger, he felt the flow of fifty thousand years of human history and emotion flowing into him. The surge of it and all it implied almost overwhelmed the massive figure, but he shrugged it off. Ten minutes earlier, like Jhong, he had had little idea as to what had brought London to Hong Kong. That changed the moment he put on the ring, however. Turning to the others, already completely conversant with a past far beyond his own—already beginning to see the patterns leading into the future—he said,

"I don't know how to say this, but things are worse than you think."

{23}

"*You're* the new Confessor?" blurted London in surprise. The detective's face betrayed him, not holding any degree of his shock in reserve. When the vampire agreed simply that he was, London demanded,

"Then give out with it. What's the big secret? What was it the last Confessor was trying to tell us before he got taken over by the rest of the collective consciousness stored up in that goddamned thing?"

"Don't worry yourself, Destroyer," the vampire answered in a casual whisper. The detective stared up into the larger man's face. He could see in the vampire's eyes that he was already feeling the pull of the other Confessors—that they had begun to flood his brain with their collected millennia of information. Bending over slightly, bringing his large head closer to the detective's, the vampire added,

"I can ... *feel* in my head what you're talking about. But I can also feel that my predecessor was able to hold them off for several weeks. From what I can tell about him, he was what you would call a 'decent' man, but perhaps not that strong a one. Without being immodest, I think I can manage to at least match him until we round all of your belongings up and get ourselves to some place"—he spread his arms to both sides, indicating the press and confusion all about them—"a bit more, shall we say, private?" When the detective hesitated, the vampire added,

"Tabor is a clown, but he is not a stupid one."

"Jeez-it. I hate to say it, boss," said Morcey, "but it does add up. We did go to a lot of trouble to slip into this place without anyone gettin' wise. Maybe we shouldn't go and blow it now."

London agreed. It was foolish to think that Tabor didn't

have every access to the islands covered that he possibly could. As Cat and Swartz came up with the last of their bags, the detective split the bunch into two groups, hoping to make them less conspicuous. He sent Lai Wan, Swartz, and Cat with the vampire, giving the three of them a concerned signal as he did so. Raising his eyebrow in as suspicious a manner as he could, London tried to set the other three on their guard. Tabor knew the former Hercules by sight, but he had never seen any of the others or Jhong before.

The detective considered the possibility of the vampire trying something in the terminal but dismissed it. It was too convoluted a plan for the ancient slayer. Whatever he was up to, London decided they were safe for the moment and thus allowed the group to be split for its own safety, with he and Morcey going with the elder warrior. Their plan was to meet again in the parking lot where Jhong had left his bus and the vampire had left his car. If his three companions were not safe for the amount of time it would take to cross the train station, then it did not seem that any of them could be safe at all.

As they moved off through the milling crowd, across the vast stretches of platforms, across the different levels and down the long, packed escalators leading outside, the detective stared at the density of the crowd. It seemed as if every square inch of floor space were taken up either by someone's bags or their feet. It was a crushing press, bodies thick against bodies at every turn. Easily a hundred thousand people surrounded them—men and women with standard luggage, with cardboard boxes done up with string, plastic bags stuffed with who knew what.

One woman carried a large stuffed alligator under one arm and ten boxes of dry macaroni under the other. Another stood with her arms filled with ornately carved wooden poles tied together with heavy pink ribbon. The man behind her had a green nylon net slung over his back, stretched taut by a staggering load of bottles of various sizes, all filled with different-colored liquids. As the trio moved on, they were forced to thread their way through various lines of people, each one winding away from ticket windows and entrance ways, twisting around each other in hopelessly snaking trails impossible to separate from each other from any distance.

God, thought London, pushing his way along with the others, this is actually worse than New York.

As the three finally came within sight of the front entrance, the detective realized he only had a few more minutes in private with Jhong. Drawing up alongside the older man, London asked him,

"So, what's with Hercules? How come he's back from the dead again, and how come we're all pals now?"

Without breaking his stride, the elder warrior answered,

"We are not all 'pals' now. Not that I am aware of, at any rate. I came here today to find you. In my dreams as of late I have been told to prepare myself—to put my affairs in order, that my mind should be clear to do whatever you might need of me. Hercules and I found each other on the platform—both of us waiting for you."

"So what you're saying is that really, we don't know anything more about him than before."

"Essentially. He professes to not be working with your enemies," Jhong paused and then smiled, saying, "which is to say, *our* enemies of the moment. But then, of course, that does not actually mean that he desires to work with you—us—himself." As the detective nodded, starting part of his brain working on the question of what the large vampire might actually want, the older man continued, saying,

"As to exactly what agency it was that has brought him back from the dead, I do not know—he did not say. However, if I had to venture a guess, I would imagine that it would have been much the same kind of ceremony we witnessed the last time he was brought back from the dead."

Suddenly the detective's mind flashed back, giving him an instantaneous picture of that moment. Within his head he relived the scene from years earlier when he had peered over the edge of a forgotten balcony to witness the slaughter of a score of innocent people. The men and women had been put to the sword, their blood spilled with purposeful cruelty so that their pain would combine with their escaping life energy to reanimate the vampire Hercules.

"Another twenty people killed, you think?"

"It is the only way we know of to bring the dead back to life," answered the older man.

Twenty people, thought London, snuffed out to give a mass murderer just another handful of minutes of life. He had crawled off the table, ready to start killing again, but had been killed by Jhong instead. One life spilled for every thirty seconds that he got out of it. And now we're on the same team? I wonder.

"Well," answered the detective slowly as they neared the parking lot, "all in all, I have to admit that I didn't, what can I say? 'Feel' anything negative coming off him. As much as I wanted to just size things up at face value . . . don't know. He just *feels* all right. Just because he's alive doesn't mean he's up to his old tricks again." Turning to look at his elder companion as they passed through the doors, London asked,

"Do you know what I mean?"

"Yes, actually I do. And although I cannot put a logical reasoning behind it, I agree with you. We have both killed the man, and yet I did not sense any hostility in him toward either of us . . . nor did I feel that anything was being masked away—hidden—from us."

As the two passed through the last set of doors between themselves and the parking lot, Jhong added,

"My entire life—when I was a businessman, when I gave up riches to become a warrior, after I completed my training and had transformed myself completely from head to toe, still—I thought the same way I had throughout my life . . . until I met you." When the detective gave the older man a sideways glance, he smiled thinly, adding,

"Perhaps you just have an effect on people."

"That I do," said London, thinking back over the years, counting all the friends and acquaintances he had watched die—all the way up to Father Bain—wondering within himself who would be next.

"Oh, yeah ... that I do."

"So," asked London, throwing a small pile of vegetables on the burner before him, "you never did tell us what that typhoon watch sign was all about." Flipping his own pile of mixed beef and pork strips, Morcey answered,

"Oh, that was nothin'. They keep those things in all the airports and boatyards an' all. They just let people know how bad the storm watch is. They go from one to nine and what we saw, a one, that's like the 'all clear' sign. No big deal."

"Yes, most true, Paul," said Jhong. "One *is* the lowest watch number. But did anyone tell you what the next number on the scale is?" When the balding man admitted that he had already told all he knew the elder warrior said,

"Eight." As everyone at the table stared at Jhong, Hercules confirmed what he had told them.

"Hong Kong is in the middle of a storm lane that leads out into the open sea. Typhoons come through here all the time. Whenever there's any chance of a storm, they list it as a one. But as soon as that changes to a definite storm coming in, it goes from one to eight immediately."

"But," said Swartz slowly, wondering if he was somehow missing the point, "that only leaves two degrees of storms: eights and nines."

"They only have two kinds of storms here, Lieutenant," answered Jhong. "Bad, and very bad."

"Then," said Cat, raising her wineglass, "here's to number one."

Everyone raised their glasses and toasted everyone else, taking sips or gulps and then either replacing or refilling their glasses. After that, everyone at the table turned their attention back to their meals. As London moved his vegetables around to make sure they weren't burning, one level of his mind passed over the trip to the restaurant.

Many things had caught his eye on the way from the train station.

Most impressive—and most obvious—were the hundreds of forty- to sixty-story billboards that were everywhere throughout the city. Advertisements for Kent, Marlboro, Gulf, TDK, JVC, Salem, and scores of others dominated the cityscape, covering entire buildings. Some side streets had so many store signs overhanging the roadway that they actually blotted out the sky. More subtly, the detective also noticed that the city seemed broken into segments. Certain blocks appeared to be set aside for hardware sellers and makers. Other areas looked to be dominated by computer stores, electronic appliances, shoe and clothing sellers, antiquaries, et cetera. Even the restaurant they had ended up at had been on Food Street.

Everyone had been tired and out of sorts after their long journey. They had all had very little fitful sleep during the plane and train rides, and none of them was feeling really rested—not even London, who could usually shut his brain off and let his ancestor voices watch over things for him. Something was wrong this time, however, something he had not been able to put his finger on.

Ever since this case began, the detective thought, I haven't been up to the game. I've been ... I don't know, what should I call it?

Holding back? suggested one of the voices in his head.

A good enough name for it, he agreed, flipping his vegetables again absently. But why? If I'm holding back, what have I been holding back about, or over, or from or whatever? What's so different this time from every other time I've been caught up in one of these nightmares?

None of his voices had any answers for him—none that added up to anything, anyway. He looked at the way his life had been years ago, when Lisa had first come to him with her problems, drawing him into the world of the supernatural. Over the years, things had happened time and again. He and others had faced the most horrifying menaces the world had to offer. Many of his companions had died, but in the end the world had been saved a half dozen times over. Even the dead, when they had been given the chance, had said that it had all been worth it.

So what's got me so worried or whatever this time?

Unable to come up with an answer yet again, the detective turned back to his meal. The Mongolian Beef House, the place Jhong had brought them all, was one of the most interesting places London had ever eaten at. All of the tables were circular, each with its own grill in the center. After they had ordered, the waiter had lit the gas and then slipped a large iron disk over the grill. Then a large funnel had been pulled down out of the ceiling over the grill to pull away any smoke or smells or grease.

Then, once the grill was good and hot, platters of beef and lamb and chicken, all sliced razor-thin, were brought out along with bowls of minced garlic, chopped scallions, bean sprouts, peppers, and a dozen other vegetables and sauces. After that, the diners were on their own, taking what they wanted and cooking it right there on the iron disk in front of them. And for some reason, the simple act of cooking began to revive all their spirits. Lai Wan fussed over how much meat Morcey took, insisting he take more vegetables. That brought amused looks from all the men, and even Cat, all of them heaping abuse on their helpless companion.

While they all joked with each other, London's near silence went unnoticed. He stayed within his head, thinking about their situation, still trying to untangle the mystery of why he had been so slow to react. On the other hand, he did not feel he had been doing a poor job—how many other guys would even still be alive, he asked himself.

Doesn't matter, came an old voice from the back of his brain. *How many others have your abilities? How many others have your history? How many others are the Destroyer?*

Well, thought London, *now that you mention it . . .*

He let the words trail away in his head, turning his attention back to his dinner. As he filled his plate with the vegetables he had already cooked, he threw a new batch on the grill and then started to work on the steaming pile in front of him. Allowing himself to get lost in the food, he wondered how people could ignore places like the beef house for the proliferation of the familiar fast food houses he had seen in the city.

As London thought about it, he realized that in just their short drive from the train station he had seen a Burger King, a Pizza Hut and a Häagen Dazs, two Kentucky Fried Chickens, and two McDonald's franchises.

Guess some people don't have any sense everywhere.

The detective, besides marveling at the abundance of American food, also found himself impressed by the degree of convenience the city's planners had built into Hong Kong's design. Much of the city seemed divided up into ten-, fifteen-, and twenty-block squares, people and traffic kept segregated by long fences running the length of each section. It gave the streets a freewaylike effect, eliminating the need for signal lights at every corner for pedestrians since, in effect, there was nowhere for them to go.

The whole place was built for speed, thought London, speed and convenience.

Convenient? asked another voice in his head. Whose convenience? Could you see them trying to put those things up in New York? People would be jumping them all day long.

And defending the point, he countered. Not everything has to be for the individual. Sometimes the greater good counts for something, too, you know.

And then, just that easily, he had it—the thing that was different from all the other times he had faced the supernatural . . . the thing that had changed. Tired as he was, he had forgotten again that since the time he had picked up the title of the Destroyer that he had picked up another one as well. Dad.

All right, he thought. So a part of me isn't as dedicated as the rest of me. Just like before.

London thought back to the first time he had faced the unknown. He had put aside the things he was seeing, not trying to make heads or tails of them, ignoring the horrors for the sake of his quest. He had taken up the protectorship of a woman in distress, and that goal had shielded him from the nightmares that tried to bleach his mind and burn his soul. After that, when love had tried to interfere, to tie him down, he had rejected it, kept his distance from Lisa—hurting her and punishing himself—until he could balance his feelings for her with his duties as the Destroyer.

It had taken the detective nearly a year to feel that he could share his life with someone. Somehow understanding, Lisa had waited, patiently—knowing that he would never be totally hers—that the world would always demand access to its protector. But several years back, that had started to change. It had transformed itself subtly, without London's even knowing it, with the birth of his first child. By the time the second came along, the change was complete. He was no longer the Destroyer, he was a father. Before their arrival, he had placed some impressive notches on his belt. Almost single-handedly, he had repulsed from our world an eater of dimensions, a cold, inhuman god-thing that would have emptied out the universe. He had turned back a plague of vampires, broken a cycle of destruction caused by an insane werewolf, shattered a runaway planet that had been on a collision course with the Earth and defeated the Devil itself.

But those had been warring, destructive, violent accomplishments. After that, he had taken a sideways step for a Destroyer and performed a miracle so simple that until that moment he had not noticed it. He had created life. He had surrendered his immortality and passed his spirit on, narrowing his responsibilities from that of the welfare of the entire world to that of just two small people. Lisa's last words came back to him there in the restaurant.

I don't want the world saved if I have to lose you.

Not very noble of her, said one of the voices within London's head. Was it?

If you can't stop this without dying ... then let it happen.

We have a job to do—just like the Confessor. Outside considerations don't matter for people like us.

Let the whole world die.

You know you can't do that. If it's our time, it's our time. You said it yourself . . .

Let it go up once and for all.

. . . not everything has to be for the individual. Sometimes the greater good counts for something, too, you know.

The detective closed his eyes and concentrated, shutting out all the voices in his head, including the memory of Lisa.

Such a simple thing, he thought. You have kids, and suddenly there's a part of you that you don't control anymore—like it doesn't exist anymore. Well, that's all well and good, but it doesn't get the job done.

Reaching out into the ether, London concentrated on his children and his wife, and then thought,

I can't protect you if I don't protect the entire world. If I lose this one, the world ends—you, me, everything. I know you love me, and I love you, but I've got to do this because . . . well, because nobody else can.

After that, with both his hands trembling, he wished one final blessing toward Lisa and each of his children. His eyes still closed, quietly, calmly, he cut the memory of each of them from the dominant positions they had taken in his brain and shoved them all back into a small, recessed pocket of his mind. Then, suddenly not upset about anything in the least, he opened his eyes, fixed his gaze on Hercules, and said,

"All right. We're all private-like and comfortable and there's no time like the present. So spill it. What in the name of God is Tabor up to?"

"He wants to bring about the end of the world," answered the vampire casually, as if he had been talking about new car designs or television listings. Lifting a great load of beef and lamb and spinach into the air between his chopsticks, Hercules held it several inches from his mouth while he said,

"Not the destruction of the whole planet, or anything foolish like that. He just wants to kill most of the people, steal their life force, and then subjugate whatever survives the following nuclear winter and their descendants down until the end of time."

Everyone at the table sat in silence, staring at the vampire. Hercules shoved the mass of steaming meat and vegetables into his mouth, almost not registering the others' shock. Chewing the wad in his mouth, the vampire reached out and snagged several more beef strips with his chopsticks. Arranging them on the hot iron before him, he dropped several large pieces of garlic on top of them, then folded the beef over on itself. Looking up, seeing everyone else staring at him, he asked,

"What?"

"What?" responded London, his eyes narrow slits. Trying to keep his voice low enough to avoid being overheard by any of the other patrons, he whispered in a steel-hard voice,

"What do you think? You just told us someone is ready to kill, I don't know . . . what? Four billion, five billion people? Maybe more? Kill them and turn the world into some kind of vampire fiefdom for himself. You don't think that's supposed to be shocking news?"

"Actually," replied the vampire, watching the sizzling beef and garlic before him more carefully than he was the others at the table, "I thought you would have had most of it figured out by now."

"Well, stop giving me so much credit and spill it—what's going on? What's going to happen and when?"

The vampire gave his beef one last flip, then added some onions to the mix. Grabbing up some chicken, he set it to sizzling next to his beef, mixing in some scallions and ginger while he answered London, saying,

"I didn't have all the story straight before, but—" he paused, holding up his hand to flash the ring of the Confessor at the detective. "I do now. Believe it or not, Tabor was a Catholic back before he joined us beyond the veil. He never quite took to *the life*, never really proved himself. Always wanted to hunt with others—never went out and killed on his own. Not once that I can remember. That's why he was never very powerful, never much of a threat to anyone."

"That seems to have changed," said Swartz. The lieutenant stared at Hercules, as did the others at the table. All of them had stopped cooking, stopped eating, too absorbed in the sudden change in the conversation to worry about their meal. Taking note of the silence, the vampire told them,

"Please . . . eat. If for no other reason than we shouldn't draw any undue attention to ourselves." As the rest of the people at the table began to poke at the food on the hot iron circle in front of them, the new Confessor told them,

"Anyway, after meeting you, as the lieutenant has said, all of that changed. Mr. Morcey obviously did not kill Martin. Oh, you wounded him quite thoroughly. He was out of commission for several months I was told. But he did not die. Jorsha died, Karen died—most all of the circle died." The vampire paused again, then smiled, raising his head as he said,

"Even I died."

"I must admit to being curious about that," said Jhong.

"I guess you would be, old man," said Hercules, "since you were the last person to kill me. To answer your question, it was the ritual."

Only London, Cat, and Jhong knew what he was talking about. When the detective had gone against the vampires years earlier, a man named Jorsha had been their king, the woman Karen Tezzler his life mate. After London had slain Hercules, they had him brought back to life through a ceremony in which twenty humans were killed so their life forces could be diverted into the fallen vampire. He lived long enough to get off the table where his body lay before Jhong could reach him, challenge him, and then kill him once again.

In the battle that followed, the elder warrior, along with Cat and London's long-dead friend Pa'sha, had turned the tide, killing off most of the rank-and-file vampires. The detective had pursued their leaders. Tezzler was dispatched by her own greed for energy. Jorsha merely surrendered, tired out by the centuries of death he had witnessed and inflicted. Swallowing his beef and garlic, Hercules said,

"Martin had it performed. He knew he couldn't survive without me. I watched over him until he was healed, but my heart wasn't in creating another coven. I thanked him for reviving me, without telling him I wished he hadn't." Looking up from his meal, the new Confessor stared at both London and Jhong, telling them,

"Do you know that in the three thousand-odd years I've walked the Earth, you were the first person to kill me, Mr. London? The very first. Then I was revived and dead all over again—two times in two days. It was very depressing. Frankly, when Martin had me revived, I was just tired. It's one thing to follow a man like Jorsha, a sorcerer and a leader for thousands of years. But . . . Martin Tabor? I don't know if I can explain this well, but suddenly immortality didn't seem to be all we'd tricked ourselves into believing it was going to be."

"All right," said London, raging within himself to keep calm, to try and deal with the vampire as an ally, "so you decided to strike out on your own."

"In a sense, but not the one you mean. It wasn't that I didn't want to challenge Martin for the leadership rights of the circle, it was that I was tired of the life altogether. I just didn't want to kill anymore. I anointed Martin as leader, feeling I owed him something for bringing me back, giving me a chance to make restitution as it were, and then I left." Pulling his gingered chicken up from the grill before it could burn, the new Confessor said,

"I remember thinking, 'What could it hurt? How much trouble could Martin Tabor cause?' Of course, now we see that the answer is quite a lot. But I didn't know that then."

"And would you have done anything differently?" asked Lai Wan.

"No. I suppose not. Not then."

"But now's a different matter, right?" snapped Swartz. "Now everything's changed. You got religion and suddenly you're on our side."

Hercules held his chopsticks rigid, the food at the end of them forgotten. Staring at the lieutenant, he shifted his teeth back and forth, the motion showing through his cheeks. The vampire's lips pulled together as he thought over his reply. Finally, he set the chopsticks down and sat back from the table, crossing his arms at the wrists. Maintaining his low tone, the new Confessor said,

"I am not on your side, Mr. Swartz. Do you understand me? I am not on anyone's side anymore. Life has made me neutral. That is why I was chosen."

"Chosen?" answered the policeman. "Chosen for what?"

"Sweet bride of the night," muttered Morcey. Dropping his own chopsticks, the food he was holding falling into the small bowl of oyster sauce before him, he blurted,

"Boss, he's fallin' under. He's losin' it . . . goin' over to da Confessors." Understanding his partner instantly, London turned on the vampire, shouting,

"He's right. Enough stalling. Tell us what's going to happen—now. Do it!"

Hercules' face strained, the large man obviously fighting within himself. His eyes squeezed shut, his mouth turned into a broken line as his head descended toward the table. His fingers curling into fists, the vampire strove to hold on to his will as the force of the long line of Confessor spirits fought to bring him under their sway. London grabbed Hercules' arm, saying,

"Fight it! You're the guy that walked the streets of Greece telling the people that created civilization you were a god. If you can pull off that con you can pull this off. Tell us what's going on."

Straining against some inner force, the vampire hissed,

"After Martin took over, he . . . he figured out your secret, Mr. London. For centuries, we always thought victims had to be killed by hand—up close. We never thought the human will could suck in a life killed from afar."

The new Confessor's head shot bolt upright, startling both the people at his table, and at several others. As he struggled to regain control of himself, several waiters headed for the table. London snapped his fingers, indicating that Morcey should head them off and keep them back. Not bothering to turn in their direction, the detective relied on his partner to keep back the curious as he demanded,

"So Tabor learned that you can kill millions at one time and hold on to the energy. So what happened next?"

"I told you he was a Catholic . . . way back when. Fifteenth century. Things had changed, but still . . . the mindset stays. He wanted absolution. Began a quest for the Confessor. Found him. Told him everything, his whole life, all the blood and murder. Confessor listened. That's what we do. Listen and stay silent. No judgments passed—no right or wrong. Duty just to cleanse the spirit."

Swartz stood to help Morcey keep back those approaching the table. The vampire had become too hoarse, too noticeable. His rasping voice and his tortured struggle to keep talking despite the influence of the Confessor lineage was attracting too much attention. Desperate for information they could act on, London shouted,

"Keep talking, goddamn it. Tabor found the Confessor, got his sins off his chest. So what?"

"Having Confessor listen to him freed him—banished his guilt. Left him free to act on his plan. Started to gather his forces. Sent them out to kill for profit. Used the money

... to buy nuclear bombs from poor countries—Ukraine, India, China. They thought they had a sucker. Sold him unstable weapons, old ... falling apart. He didn't care. Didn't need delivery systems. Didn't care where they went off. Just needs to know *when* they go off to be ready to receive death energy."

London tried to give Hercules the power to resist, feeding the vampire as much energy as he could spare. Gripping the larger man by the arm, the detective said,

"But Tabor said he didn't want to kill the Confessor. Blowing everyone up is bound to take him out with the rest of us. Right?"

"Of course," spat Hercules. "Martin lied."

Sweat running down his face, slicking his hair to the sides of his head, the big man felt his own self slipping, being pulled into the collective consciousness of the Confessors despite his efforts. London's voice began to sound faraway, his words unintelligible, little more than a thin anchor to focus on. Using it for what it was worth, the vampire focused all of his remaining will, centering himself for one last push.

In the meantime, the Mongolian Beef House's manager had been summoned by several of his nervous employees. Hercules' increasingly deteriorating condition had frightened all the waiters; he looked like a man about to have a stroke. And since people keeling over in restaurants has always been bad for business, the manager headed for the spot in question immediately. Jhong had joined Morcey and Swartz in trying to maintain crowd control, filling in with the Chinese the first two lacked. By then, however, the entire restaurant had become agitated, everyone wondering what was going on at the table full of foreigners.

Trying to get everything out of Hercules before he either did have a stroke or slipped over to the other side completely, London shouted over the growing voices,

"Why? Why did Tabor try to kill the Confessor?"

"Envy. Fear. He was afraid someone else would unburden himself ... become as free as he had become. Do what he was going to do. Or that the Confessor might ...

reveal his plan. Let the world . . . know what he was up to. Stupid. Weak, foolish. But then, Martin never did . . . have what it took . . . took to win through . . . in the end."

And with those words suddenly Hercules let out a powerful roar that turned every head not already focused on the team's table. It was not a scream—not the sound of pain, but of defiance. His eyes coming open as if blown apart with explosives, he reached forward for one of the small, mostly decorative cleavers that had been set out with the plates of meat. Then, without thought or hesitation, he slashed down at his own hand. Screams broke out on every side. Men and women rose up from their tables, some pressing forward to see what had happened, just as many racing out of the room.

Blood squirted out from the vampire's hand, spraying across the table and the iron disk in its center. Instantly black clouds of blood smoke rolled up into the vent above the table. Hercules lifted his hand, inspecting the damage. He had cut three of his fingers badly, almost severing the one wearing the Confessor's ring. The weight of the golden lump dragged the dangling finger downward, causing it to swing back and forth. Catching hold of it with his other hand, the vampire shouted,

"Begone, offense!"

And then he twisted and pulled the finger free, tearing a long ragged strip of flesh up his hand and past his wrist, throwing it, ring and all, onto the center of the hot iron before him. Instantly more screams came from all around the table as people reacted to what they had seen. Several women and one man simply passed out, falling into the crowd, against chairs, onto tables. Twice their number choked immediately, heaving their dinners on all in their way. Just as many grabbed for their cameras and camcorders. As flashbulbs went off all around them, London asked.

"Good Christ! Are you all right?"

Hercules nodded weakly, a thin smile crossing his face. Looking up at the detective, who was now standing over him, the vampire said,

"Yes. I believe so." Then, holding his ruined hand under his armpit to try and squelch the profuse bleeding, he grabbed up his water glass with his other hand, took a small sip, and said,

"You know, Mr. London, perhaps I have taken a side after all."

And then, before anyone could say or do anything further, the first wave of shots burst through the front window of the restaurant, killing at least twenty in the crowd.

26

"Down!"

Everyone that could responded to London's order instantly, shoving aside chairs, crawling under the table, trying to get a fix on what was happening. Sending his mind out into those that had been wounded, the detective felt through their bodies, looking to see how badly they were injured. Finding two people he could see were beyond all hope, he whispered a tiny phrase inside their brains:

Forgive me.

And then he took their souls. Sucking the power of their spirits into him, the detective charged himself with their life force, then rose to one knee, saying,

"All right. Now let's try this again."

Focusing through the distracting waves of screaming, mindlessly panicking people all around him, London sought out their attackers. Immediately he spotted two figures wearing the same paramilitary uniforms he had seen in New York. Locking his eyes on the closest figure, he put his hands together and squeezed. At once the man started to gasp, clawing at his throat. In seconds he was dead, his windpipe crushed.

The woman standing next to him began talking into her throat mike, reporting what she had just seen to some unseen agent. Before she could say more than a few words, however, she felt the same blockage within her throat that her partner had. The woman dropped her weapon, then clawed frantically at her sidearm, but she was too late to do anything to stop the force that had knotted her windpipe. Only a few seconds after she first felt the detective's touch, she fell to the ground, hands twitching, eyes vacant, the flap of her holster still securely snapped.

His face set in grim lines, London sucked down the life energy of the two fallen soldiers, then crawled forward,

looking for more. As further members of the crowd fell,
mortally wounded, he took their life force as well, adding
it to the ammunition he already had. Several of the voices
in his head demanded that he stop, warning him of dam-
nation, threatening him with collars of guilt. Before he
could argue with any of them, however, a voice rang out
against them in his head, one of the mortally injured,
somehow understanding enough of what was happening,
blessed the detective, shouting within his brain,

Don't listen to them. Get them. Stop them. Pay them
back!

Use me!

London's lips pulled themselves into a thin, evil smile
as his pious voices fell to the wayside.

At the same time, Jhong had moved through the crowd,
sliding between the panicking mob with practiced ease.
Coming up behind one pair of attackers, he did not hesitate in taking them out in the quickest way possible. His
left foot came up first, shot forward, and buried itself in
the side of the attacker farthest from him. Five ribs
snapped like twigs, one impaling a kidney, two piercing a
lung. As the man screamed, blood splashing out of his
mouth, filling his helmet, the elder warrior turned, meeting
the second soldier. Turning sideways, he avoided the
man's weapon, positioning himself behind his opponent.
With another kick he cleanly snapped the man's spine. The
attacker's eyes bulged, his tongue shooting forward. His
arms flapping, hands jerking wildly, his legs gave out and
his knees folded in one direction while his torso fell back-
wards, flopping painfully against the floor.

All eyes turned when Hercules stood, bellowing,

"Me, little fools! Try and stop . . . *me*!"

Five machine gunners moved forward, looking to blast
the massive vampire. The ancient warrior grabbed up the
iron cooking disk, wrenching it from the table. The terrible
heat of it burning into his remaining fingers, he screamed
with rage as he charged the quintet. All of them fired, several of them hitting their mark. It did them no good, however. Consumed by the passion of battle, the vampire

ignored his wounds, pushing forward until he had run right through the enemy ranks. One man went down instantly, a dozen bones shattered. Hercules called the man's life to him, healing his wounds, then turned on his teammates.

As the others coming against him tried to regroup, the vampire took the burning iron disk in one hand and used it to swat two of them. The single swipe knocked them both from their feet, breaking one's skull, shattering the other's arm, shoulder, and breastbone. Ignoring them for the moment, Hercules threw the disk into one of the remaining pair, knocking her over with it. The woman fell trapped beneath the disk, the hot iron burning her hands, knees, chest, and face, heating the ammunition remaining in her magazine until it exploded, blowing a hole through her and into the floor.

The last of the five sighted and aimed, getting off eight more rounds before Hercules closed on him, three of the rounds burying themselves in the vampire's chest. Catching the man by the hands, the ancient warrior squeezed, breaking all the soldier's fingers, molding the pulped flesh and shattered bones into the metal of the man's weapon. Then, staggered by his wounds, the vampire stopped long enough to feed on the dying he had just slaughtered.

He gobbled down the life force flowing from the four near death, letting it sluice through his body. Instantly the blood stopped flowing from his wounds, the muscles and flesh over his heart healing at once, everything regenerating to the point it had been moments earlier down to the hair on his chest. So arresting was the sight of Hercules' healing that the soldier still within his grasp was mesmerized by the sight, forgetting the horrible pain in his shattered hand.

The vampire, however, had not forgotten him. Before the healing process had even finished completely, he pulled the crippled soldier forward, ramming his now completely healed hand through the man's chest. Closing his fingers around the soldier's still-beating heart, he crushed it into bloody tatters. The man died, sliding backward off Hercules' scarlet fist. Lifting his dripping hand to his mouth, the vampire licked at the drops pooling between his fingers even as he craned his head around, looking for more of the enemy.

In the meantime, Morcey, unarmed and willing to admit he was outclassed, had found Lai Wan first, then Swartz and Cat. With only a few words, he convinced the three to leave the combat to London and the others and started them toward the kitchen. Cat cursed, the fact her equipment bag was still in Jhong's vehicle. By the time they managed to reach the back, however, a second wave of attackers came in through the rear doors. Whoever had planned the battle had sent in their first assault team to draw everyone's attention to the front of the restaurant. Then, after two minutes, they had sent their second team in from the opposite direction in the hopes of crippling their possibly unprotected flank.

"Criminy!" shouted the balding man, spotting the first of the gunners as they came through the door. "Down, back. Get down, stay down. There's more of them!"

Luckily, none of the soldiers coming through the kitchen could hear Morcey giving his orders over the noise of the battle. Nor did they notice him and the others. With London, Jhong, and Hercules out in plain view, none of those moving in thought to bother with anyone else. Morcey counted ten in their party, with what looked like an equal number behind them. Not able to do anything about them himself and fully expecting London to sense their presence, the ponytailed man continued to hustle Lai Wan and Cat off to the side, pushing them to follow the stream of customers clogging the only other exit—one newly created through a smashed-out panorama window.

But, unknown to Morcey, something was blocking both his partner's and Jhong's heightened senses, masking the arrival of the soldiers behind them. And as the attack's three main targets remained oblivious to the arrival of the new forces, a first rank of seven moved in and went down on one knee, followed quickly by a second rank, who began positioning themselves behind the first row, preparing to fire over their heads.

"They're setting up a lead wall," shouted Swartz through the constant din ringing inside the restaurant. Knowing Morcey was busy trying to get the women clear, the lieutenant took a deep breath and then reached under his bulky overcoat. Quickly he unholstered a .357 magnum he had wangled through the various customs checkpoints, hidden away in a concealment case specially designed for a drug dealer the policeman had brought down a few years earlier. The dealer had gone to prison, but not all his belongings had made it to the property room.

"Like Uncle Fester used to say," the lieutenant snarled, taking aim, *"shoot 'em in the back!"*

Swartz pulled the trigger once, instantly exploding the lower back of one target out through his abdomen and through the skull of the man kneeling in front of him. Knowing he had only seconds, he shifted his aim to another of the standing soldiers, cutting his spine in two with his second shot. The man's chest exploded, bone and blood spraying five of his companions. As the back door squad tried to target their unexpected attacker, the lieutenant fired again and again, knocking three more of the soldiers down with the two shots.

By this time, London, Jhong, and Hercules had all heard the tremendous reports of the .357. Instantly the detective realized the diversionary purpose of the frontal push and signaled his two companions to keep those few remaining busy while he turned his attention to the back. Swartz's weapon bellowed twice more before London could do anything, then fell silent. The detective took line-of-sight aim on those soldiers he could see and concentrated, boiling the blood in their heads. The men dropped their weapons in screaming pain, falling one by one, their brains and eyes melting, pouring out across the floor.

Unfortunately, London could not see all of the soldiers, nearly half a dozen of them escaping his fury. Not knowing what was killing their companions, they did what they had been trained to do—they eliminated the obvious threat first.

"No!"

The detective screamed, but he was too late. Swartz went down under a hail of automatic fire, shredded by the sheer number of bullets sent at him. London pulled up every free ounce of power he had within him and then sent it out in a concentrated beam from the palm of his left hand. It killed those it touched instantly, leaving their bodies burning with a supercharged, white-hot glow. As soldiers died, the detective pulled their life force to him, sending it back out immediately through his hand, killing those remaining.

And after a few more minutes it was all over. Every one of the attackers had been dispatched—completely. Each of their bodies was crumpled on the ground, empty and desiccated, devoid of even the slightest drop of moisture. Hercules and Jhong both disappeared out into the street, the pair wanting to make sure the attack was actually over as well as not wanting to get involved with the Hong Kong police. Morcey, Lai Wan, and Cat kept on going outside as well, not wanting to wait for the police any more than anyone else.

Inside the decimated restaurant, London turned from side to side, taking in the bloody carnage all about him. Almost thirty of the customers were dead, perhaps an equal amount had been wounded. The detective searched through himself, checking to see how much energy he had left, how many more of the enemy he could kill through willpower alone. Walking across the room, he scanned the floor one last time, looking for anyone else who might be near death. The only spirit still hovering in between the light and the dark was the one working its way out of the body toward which he was headed. Going down on one knee, London touched Swartz's face, saying,

"Guess you think this makes you some kind of hero now?"

The lieutenant opened his eyes a thin slit, barely able to focus on the detective's face. He could feel blood soaking into one of his lungs, could not feel his legs or back or arms. There was blood bubbling out of his body from a score of spots, painting his clothes scarlet. His hands were covered with blood, as were his face and head, large drops dripping out of his nose and into his mustache, sliding from there over his lips, down off his chin. Laughing softly, he said, "Yeah. Doesn't it?"

"I should have heard them coming. People aren't supposed to be able to sneak up on me."

"Some fucking . . ." Swartz paused, coughed a phlegm-filled load of blood out, then whispered, "super, superhero . . . you turned out to be."

"I'm sorry," said London, taking the man's hand. "I should've known. I should have felt it. I don't understand."

"They mapped you—figured out . . . your M.O. Lucky thing you had, had an old . . . old . . . ha, haha, old cop to throw into the mix."

"I guess the whole world was lucky. I don't know if everybody's luck is going to run out—but I have to admit we all got another roll of the dice, thanks to you. You were a pain in the ass, Swartz, but you came through."

"Don't . . . don't know much about killin' monsters, but, but . . . I guess I . . ." And then the officer coughed again, longer and more violently than before. Blood sluiced out of his mouth and nose; thick, black blood mixed with food and lung tissue. His fingers tightened around London's as he coughed, and then suddenly started to go limp. Fear filled his eyes—not fear of dying, but of dying uselessly. Knowing he had only seconds, the lieutenant looked up at the detective, clearing his eyes as best he could as he said,

"Don't let me die . . . for nothing. Don't leave . . . leave anything for the bastards."

Tightening his fingers with all his might, half of him ashamed of his weakness, the rest of him understanding it, accepting it, leading him off into the encroaching blackness, he croaked hoarsely,

"Take it. Take it." And then, as his fingers went limp, the last seconds of his life filtering away, he whispered one final time,

"Take it."

And then he was gone.

Understanding what the policeman wanted, London snatched Swartz's drifting spirit from the air, reeling in the officer's battered life force, adding it to his own. As the lieutenant's consciousness poured into the detective's, he heard Swartz's last thought.

Use me good, London. Shove me down their throats and let 'em choke on me.

I'll see what I can do, the detective told the momentarily distinct voice in his head, then shut it away with the rest, knowing he had no other choice.

Then, hearing the police already coming up from outside, knowing they would be inside soon, London walked back across the room to where he and the others had been sitting earlier. He found the spot—chairs overturned, table gone, discharge vent still hanging down from the ceiling, swinging back and forth gently. Closing his eyes, the detective felt about himself mentally for a moment, searching.

Then, suddenly, he opened his eyes and turned toward the left. Bending down, he picked up the ring of the Confessor, saying,

"All right, this started all our troubles. This is going to finish it."

Removing Hercules' old finger from its center, the detective pocketed the ring, closed his eyes, and then willed himself away from the scene and off onto the dream plane just a few seconds before the police entered the restaurant.

27

"Now whadda we do?"

Morcey had asked this question more of himself than of anyone else in the small group around him. After exiting the Mongolian Beef House, he had hurried Lai Wan and Cat off into the crowd and then around the corner, determined to keep them safe. He had seen Swartz get gunned down. And, whereas he knew that London and the others might be able to take care of themselves against such odds, he knew he could not.

Minutes later, Jhong and Hercules had joined the trio but none of them had seen London. The five waited and watched until one by one various police vehicles began to arrive, but the detective never came out of the restaurant. Pulling back into the crowd, the group continued to scan the area, waiting for some sign of London. They tried to maintain a low profile, not only from the police, but from the customers the officers were interviewing, any of whom might recognize them as the people who were at the table where all the trouble started.

All around the quintet, light green–garbed officers swarmed through the crowd. Morcey studied them as they moved about, comparing them to the type of police he was used to seeing and dealing with in New York City. The Hong Kong officers seemed much more in command, much better equipped to handle the crowd. The ex-maintenance man noted the radios they all wore on their shoulders, held in place by a self- retracting cable. He also watched as they took off their hats to pull out the small pads and pencils they all kept there.

Before long he decided that it would be best if Jhong and Hercules left the area. Arranging a meeting place for three hours later, the balding man wished them well and sent them on their way, telling the pair to take Cat with

hem. The two men were bound to be noticed by
omeone—they had been too conspicuous during the
arlier conflict, had killed too many of the enemy not to be
emembered. As for Cat, she had been at the table, and the
ewer of them that remained in the area, the better. As he
old the trio,

"Where the boss is, what he's doin' . . . I don't know.
But I do think that Lai Wan and I are the only ones who
ave any kind of a chance of findin' out what happened to
im. Which means that right now, anyone else hangin'
round is just a liability. So, I got a couple of ideas I'm
onna try out with her help. Whether they pan out or not,
ve'll meet you in three hours at the hotel. Okay?"

Everyone agreed with different degrees of reluctance.
While the three leaving moved off to retrieve their vehi-
les, Morcey and Lai Wan went back toward the shattered
ront of the restaurant. As they moved through the ever-
ghtening crowd, the psychometrist asked,

"So, tell me this handsome set of ideas you have for
inding our missing Theodore."

"To be perfectly honest, I really don't got much of
nythin' at the moment."

"Well," said the woman with a loving smirk, "what a
omplete surprise."

"Yeah," answered the balding man drolly. "I love you,
oo, sweetheart."

As the pair came up to the edge of the barrier the police
ad erected to keep the curious out and those they wished
o question in, Lai Wan said,

"I understand the sending away of the others. All of us
ould be recognized—we were the center of the attack.
Hercules and Jhong made such a showing, sooner or later
hey would have been noticed. But the sense in their leav-
ng does not show me the sense in our staying."

"I wantta see if I can figure what happened to the boss.
This is some bad situation we've got ourselves in, you
now."

Morcey walked along the edge of the barrier, Lai Wan
ollowing, both of them looking at the restaurant. They

watched as the black-bagged bodies of the invaders an
the slain customers were brought out and lined up on th
sidewalk. Neither of them had thought that so many peo
ple had died in the scant few minutes of the attack.

So many bags. So many bodies. How many of each
wondered the psychometrist. How many are the killers
and how many are the people who just wanted to hav
dinner? Who died because we just wanted to have dinner

Don't think like that, Morcey told her within his head
hearing her thoughts, sending her his. We didn't start i
We didn't start any of this.

And then, suddenly, Lai Wan could not stand any more
Catching Morcey's shoulder, the woman in black stoppe
him, turning him around with her urgency. As the baldin
man came around, she fixed his eyes with her own, lettin
what she was feeling—what she had kept bottled up insid
for more time than she could remember—pour out of he
soul and into his before he could put up any of the barrier
that people automatically erect without even knowing it.

Instantly he fell into the depth of her anxiety, tasting he
fears, feeling the rising horror that had plagued her no
only since their trip had begun, but since she had first me
him and London and all they represented.

"This is not a comic book, Paul ... and I am not
superhero," she blurted, more frightened than he had eve
seen her. Trembling as Morcey took her in his arms, sh
whispered, "This is not a movie, I have no assurance tha
when the show is over all of us will still be alive.
thought, years ago, that I would help a pair of detective
once, and that would be that. But it was not. It has gon
on and on and on ... the horrors keep coming at us, an
the people keep dying."

As he held her, not knowing what else to do, she sai
in the same, terrified voice,

"I did not think, after the last time, when you were o
one side of the world and I was on the other—you i
China and me in America—both of us fighting for ou
lives, that it would ever stop. I waited after that, waite
every day to see what would come next. I woke up ever

day for the first year, sweating and scared, wondering if that would be the day it would start again. Then, as the next two years passed, I thought maybe, the time of our trials had finally passed. I thought maybe it would end, and after having died once, I would not have to die again until I was old and ready for it. But it will never stop— these things will just keep coming and coming . . . until finally they have killed us all."

And then she started to cry. Large tears, unbidden and unwanted, forced their way past the woman's ability to stop them. They rolled over her cheeks, dripping down onto her shawl, soaking through it and through her dress beyond, chilling her with their touch. For once she could not contain herself, could not control the emotions she had always disdained. For some reason she could not discern, she had lost control of her ability to deny her feelings, and suddenly, all of the terrors and fears of the crowd around her had invaded her mind, translating themselves into her own fears, paralyzing her.

Not knowing what else to do, Morcey moved his hands tenderly up her sides to her shoulders, his rough hands sliding over the silken lace of her shawl. A hard edge of loose skin caught in the dark image of a lotus embroidered into the fabric, ruining the smoothness of his attempt to comfort the woman he loved. Sheepishly he smiled at her, one side of his mouth higher than the other.

"Sweet bride of the night. Guess I can't do much of anything right sometimes."

She made to argue with him, already feeling foolish for her moment's loss of control, but Morcey quieted her with a soft sound. His eyes boring into hers, telling her how he felt about her, he jerked his finger free from her shawl as he softly told her,

"I know you're scared. We're all scared. And we got a good right to be. But this . . . this is what we do. All of us have died once. You died on the operatin' table and then came back to life. Me, you remember how banged up I got. I shouldn'ta lived through that any more than the boss shoulda lived through what happened when Elizabeth,

New Jersey, blew up. But we did. And now, if we get a few years off in between rounds—hey, I didn't ever think we'd get that much myself."

He held the woman tighter, pulling her close despite the crowd around them, not caring that anything they did to attract attention to themselves might attract the police's attention as well. As he did so, the balding man put his finger to his mouth and bit through the bothersome sliver of flesh, spitting it to the sidewalk. Then, looking into Lai Wan's eyes once more, he said,

"I did do one thing right, though." As the psychometrist looked up, wonder filling her eyes as she waited to hear what he would say, forcing herself not to hear the words out of his mind before he said them.

"If I had to wait with the boss for each new horror to show up, I did pick you to wait with me."

"You did not pick me," she said in her haughtiest tone, teasing him in a way that made her feel much younger than someone who was trying to save the world. "You stole me."

"I stole you, huh?"

"Yes," she snapped with feigned outrage, hanging on to the ex–maintenance man with all her strength. "Barbarians have been stealing civilized women since the beginning of time."

"A barbarian, am I?"

"Yes," she answered in mock horror. "The most terrible one I have ever seen."

He wanted to make another joke, keep bringing her spirits up, but he could not. He had a comment in mind, but it froze on his lips. Sensing the change in him, the psychometrist asked,

"What is it, my love?"

"I'm sorry. I'm just nervous, I guess. Or worried, or somethin' . . . you know? I mean . . ." Morcey pulled away from the woman slightly, only enough to be able to look her in the eye once more, then told her,

"The boss is gone—just disappeared into thin air, as usual—which puts me in charge. I've never been worried about takin' over for him before, but this time it's different. It's so much . . . *bigger.* And Father Bain is dead, and Swartz is dead, and we ain't even begun to get near the other side. I mean, look at us . . . we're lost in Hong Kong, lookin' for vampires who have enough nukes to finish off the world, and we ain't got the first clue where they are."

And then, a voice just above the ex–maintenance man's head said,

"A clue? Why, if all you want is a clue . . . janitor . . . all you have to do is look up."

28

"Now where am I?"

London looked about him, wondering what had happened to the dream plane. Usually when the detective first arrived in the dimension of dreams, his landing zone appeared the same—a long, flat purple plane, covered over by a blowing layer of scarlet dust. Such was not the case this time, though.

Yeah, he thought, *usually* looks that way—sure. But not always. Not if someone else is here waiting for me. Now for a few $64,000 questions: Who else is here? And are they here waiting for me, or did they have some other kind of trouble in mind for someone else? And ... he asked himself, who would I be kidding if I tried to think they're here waiting for anyone but me?

Looking out and around him, London took in the bizarre twist someone had applied to the dream plane. The detective found himself surrounded by what reminded his twentieth-century mind of the architecture of the ancient Greeks. Several of his ancestral voices assured him that he was correct. As they began to point out the differences in the arches and columns that proved they were Greek, and not Roman or Assyrian, London silenced them with a growl, whispering to himself,

"Cut it. We've got more to worry about than who invented the cornerstone."

"Why don't you tell us about them?"

The voice, coming out of nowhere, shocked the detective. He had been taken unawares again, as in the restaurant—something he had not thought was possible. Concealing his surprise as best he could, he answered,

"Cornerstones? Well, they're stones that lie at the corner of two walls, uniting them. They're usually laid with some kind of formal ceremonies. . . ."

"No ... oh, no ...," interrupted the older of the two figures dressed in white robes that had appeared behind London. Paying neither of the berobed men any heed, however, the detective continued,

"Often they're hollow. People use them to store documents ..."

"No, not that ...," offered the second. London ignored him as well, saying,

"Or like time capsules ... you know, concealing things in them that no one will see again—until whenever the building is torn down."

"That, my friend, is not what they meant," came a new voice, more forceful than the others. "They were asking you to share your worries."

The detective turned to find another man dressed in white. Whereas the first two appeared somewhat confused or apologetic, the third seemed much more composed, more sure of himself. Although dressed in white like the others, he affected a different style. His ration of white cloth had been fashioned into a double-breasted business suit, one with a high-collared shirt, a Windsor-knotted tie, and large, sharp lapels. Satisfied to have captured London's attention, he smiled smugly, adding,

"But I do believe you knew that."

"Oh, hey," answered the detective, keeping up a hard front. Determined to make those around him work for every bit of information they got out of him and getting ready to dig for his own, he said,

"Score one for your side. Give yourself a big white cigar."

"So, great Theodore London has finally come to pay his respects."

"I don't think I'd put it quite that way," answered the detective. "But then, since I don't think there's going to be much of a meeting of the minds between any of us, you won't mind if I just jaunt along my merry way."

London turned away from the determined figure in the white business suit with as casual an air as he could. Then, picking a direction at random in the maze of Grecian stair-

ways and columns, he started off, not looking back. He
could feel the dark eyes of the third man digging into his
back, could hear the sharp ends of his mustache bristling
in the wind.

"Running away is not a good method of handling one's
problems, Mr. London," shouted the man angrily, to which
the detective answered,

"That's why I stroll, pal."

The determined man said nothing London could hear.
Not worried about what happened to any of the three men
behind him, the detective pushed on, looking to see what
he could learn before his next confrontation. He stared at
the walls and flooring as he moved past and over them,
studying them to see what they could tell him about the
mind of their creator.

Everything he passed was marble—white, of course—
with only the thinnest of pale pink and black strata lines
running through it. Whoever had altered the section of the
dream plane he was on had gone to great extremes to create a certain look. The stone appeared hand processed, not
machine cut. Every inch of the thousands of square feet he
had already passed held the same look, as if all of it had
been carved by the same hand, crafted to reflect one idea.

As he walked around a corner and under an arch that led
out into a wide white plaza with a lone obelisk at its center, London came to a halt as yet another voice called out
to him,

"There *is* an impressive consistency to the workman-
ship, isn't there?"

The detective shifted his eyes to take in the latest of
those wandering the dream-plane city to attempt to engage
him in conversation. This time the speaker was female,
one who appeared to be in her mid-forties to fifties. She
was seated at a bench, not so much looking at London as
she was studying the wall behind him. As the detective
studied her face, he could see that she had decided to pose,
making it appear as if it did not matter all that much to her
if London answered her or not. Understanding the tactic,

but deciding to see how far she would go to maintain it, he said,

"I guess ... it's not the kind of thing I notice all that much one way or the other to tell the truth."

"Oh, I think you do yourself an injustice, Mr. London. I think you notice a great deal. That's what detectives do, isn't it? Notice things?"

"Well, I guess I should say I don't tend to notice much about architecture when I'm worrying about what a bunch of lunatics are going to try and do to me."

As London walked away, the woman called out,

"And who would these lunatics be?"

"You and the rest of the too-much-bleach crowd."

The detective turned the first corner, only to find the woman on another bench in front of him, this one a few feet higher than the last and sitting at the top of a small set of stairs. She was looking away again, studying a wall much like the one she had been studying behind him. London skidded to a halt, annoyed to be trapped inside someone else's image of the dream plane—annoyed to not be controlling events. He stood frozen for a long second, debating in his mind what he could do next.

It was clear that a strong mind had taken over the dream plane, bending it to its will. From out of the air, he could sense that attempting to transform the landscape to his own liking would take a great deal of power and time, neither of which he had in any great abundance. If he were to jump back to the real world, he would end up at the restaurant, which would put him in the middle of the police.

You could jump to some other spot you are familiar with, suggested one voice in his head.

It would take more energy, admitted a second voice, and you would have to find everyone anew, but it would get us out of here.

"Are you in such a hurry to leave here?" asked the woman, turning from her new wall. "Do you have so little curiosity about who we are and what we want that you would just run away—from those who have offered you no harm?"

"You're good, lady," answered the detective, folding his arms across his chest. "I'll give you that much. In one breath you question my maturity and my manhood." Taking a single step forward, he continued, saying,

"You and yours—however many of you are here—you invade my brain as if it were nothing, walk the dream plane, shape it like I've never seen before, move across it in groups, bend spatial laws without batting an eye, and then act as if it's all just a walk in the park."

London went forward again, stepping up the first few stairs of the vast marble stage he had been maneuvered onto toward the woman at the top. She had chosen a Victorian dress, high collared with buttoned cuffs and a great deal of ruffles. All in the same reflective, shining white as the others he had seen. The detective also noted that she had forgone the pull-buttoned boots that would have matched her outfit, opting for a more sensible pair of modern loafers instead. As his eyes drifted back up toward hers, she wiggled her feet back and forth, showing off her shoes, saying,

"You see, you do notice things."

"Yeah, hip hip hooray for me. Now, are you going to tell me where I am and what's going on around here, or am I going to have to take matters into my own hands?"

"Oh, silly man," she answered, her voice a hair away from being annoyed. London knew the tone, it was one he'd used with his own children on those rare occasions that they came close to pushing him too far. Hearing it made him remember his earlier revelation, which made him say,

"You know, a while back it dawned on me why I wasn't getting anywhere. The last time anything like this happened to me, I was still single. Since then I got married, settled down, had a couple of kids . . . you know, I stopped being a stud on the prowl, and I turned into Daddy."

He took two more purposefully slow and heavy steps, filling his posture with menace. Letting his hands hang at his sides, fingers empty—twitching.

"And you know, it really threw me off. Not being self-

centered anymore ... this having people to worry about,
to care about, it changes you—gives other people a hold
on you. Even when they don't do anything consciously,
there's this invisible threat in the air that they *could* do
something—if they wanted."

With a force beyond his weight, London stepped upward and forward, moving onto the level of the woman's
bench. He stood at the edge of the dais, looming over her,
putting himself in between her and the sun, darkening the
white of her starched-stiff clothes with his shadow.

"Well, you know, I just asked myself—was there ever a
time when people couldn't read my mind—when they
couldn't sneak up on me and catch me off guard and throw
me off balance ... and guess what? It was back before all
that—all the kids and wife and home and all that crap."

The woman drew her legs closer together—only a frac-
tion of an inch, but closer, nonetheless. Forcing herself to
breathe regularly, she said,

"Don't insult me. You don't mean that. I know you,
Theodore London. I've walked the passages of your brain.
You could no more turn your back on Lisa and Kevin and
Kate than you could ... could ..."

"What's the matter?" asked the detective in a harsh, grat-
ing tone. Taking another long stride closer, he said, "Go on.
Tell me more about what I can and cannot do. Take another
stroll through the passages of my brain."

He stepped closer again, closing the gap between the
two of them. His hand snaking out from his side, he
caught the front of the woman's dress. Grabbing it cruelly,
he jerked her up off the bench, shouting in her face,

"Try it! Try and read my mind now, you fucking bitch!
Come on—tell me again what a silly little man I am. Do
it!"

The woman closed her eyes, shutting herself off from
London, suddenly terrified. The detective, knowing he had
proved all he needed to to the both of them, released his
hold on the woman, shoving her back down on her bench.

"I hope I've proved my point, lady."

"Indeed," came the voice of the determined man, coming in echoes as if from a distance. "You have."

And then, before London could do anything further, a lightning bolt came out of the cloudless sky and knocked him from his feet. His body shook from the unexpected discharge, his nerves screaming, the water of his brain filled with random energy he could neither control nor discharge. He fell backward, blown away from the dais by the power of the bolt, stumbling down step after step, unable to regain his balance, to control his legs or arms, helpless to do anything but topple and fall.

He lay on the ground, blinking and shaking uncontrollably, frozen in a repeating pattern of jerking motions. And as he looked out across the expanse of marble in front of him, he watched as scores, then hundreds of figures all dressed in white moved toward him. As they closed in on him, he heard the determined man's voice again.

"Let the Parliament of Confessors now be convened."

And before anyone else could speak, the detective heard the woman's voice coming as if from a distance, saying,

"Lord Zeus, must it be this way?"

"Yes, my dear Hera, it must."

Morcey pushed Lai Wan aside while throwing himself forward over the police barrier. A rocking blast of energy consumed the space they had been in, burning the air, cracking the cement. The ex–maintenance man fell atop the nearest body bags on the other side of the barrier. He felt bones cracking beneath him, cold flesh molding to his form, breaking his fall. His head turning skyward, the balding man blinked the sweat out of his eyes to see,

"Tabor!"

Floating in midair some thirty-five feet above the scene he had just created, the thin vampire clasped his hands together, holding them near his head in a vulgar impersonation of a schoolgirl. His face a twisted mask, one revealing nothing but hate, he crooned,

"Why, Paul ... you remembered. And here I was so sure that you would have forgotten all about me."

After the vampire had released his initial energy bolt, people all around had scattered wildly in a screaming panic. The police had immediately moved forward as far as they could, only to be pushed back, their way blocked by the retreating throng.

"Remember when we first met—you and I? And you called me that endearing little name. What was it now? I can't seem to remember."

Feigning ignorance of the crowd and its actions, the vampire put his left hand to his head, his right cradling his other elbow. As he scratched at his temple, pretending to be searching his memory, he watched the mayhem in the streets. All about him and Morcey, people were being knocked down, trampled by each other, screams of fear and cries of agony erupting from a hundred points.

"Wait. Oh, silly me. I remember now. You called me

'the C.P.A. of the Damned.' That was it. Oh, how that made everyone laugh."

The vampire chuckled dryly, his eyes burning with the hate of years—half his brain screaming for revenge then and there, the other half counseling patience, demanding the chance to see Morcey beg. While the two continued to stare at each other, the police fought their way through the crowd as men and women and children all trampled each other, blindly stampeding away from the man on the ground and the one floating above him.

"And then," said the vampire finally, all pretense dropping from his pose, "and then you killed me. And, oh, I'll just bet that made them laugh, too."

Tabor turned away from Morcey then, not daring to look into his eyes, afraid to see that indeed the crowds had laughed after the overweight, middle-aged ex–maintenance man had all but killed him without the vampire being able to land a single blow. Instead, he studied the crowd's terror. As Tabor licked his lips, contemplating the horrified throng, Morcey did his best to keep a watch on Lai Wan's retreating form, praying she could disappear unharmed, glad she had had the good sense to get away before Tabor could go after her as well. The ponytailed man made to get back to his feet, but the vampire swooped down out of the sky, bringing himself parallel above Morcey's body. Shaking a single finger in front of his nose, he cautioned,

"Now, now, now, little wink . . . I wouldn't try that if I were you."

Wink, remembered Morcey. Vampire talk for humans . . . a wink in time—yeah, that's us. Another voice added, No, that's you.

The balding man stared up into the eyes of the vampire, just inches from his own, cruel and blood-filled, every atom of them brimming over with hatred for the man lying on the black rubber bags on the sidewalk.

"Ohhh," said Morcey softly, tensing himself for whatever his next move might be. "I see. You want me to get my beauty rest. Right?"

"No, you odious little bastard, I want you to die. I just have to figure out how to do it."

All around the pair, the initial panic of the crowd had started to turn into cautious curiosity. Although they pulled back a considerable distance, people still thronged the streets, watching to see what was going to happen next. Floating back up a few feet away from Morcey, Tabor swept his hand about him to indicate the crowd, saying,

"Look at them. Look at them all, Paul. One second they're terrified, running in blind panic, pushing each other down, climbing over each other's backs, breaking each other's skulls—and for what? To preserve their precious few seconds of life on the clock of eternity. And now, their intelligent, life-preserving instincts forgotten, they draw close again. Close to . . . do what? *Feel* what? What is it, Paul? What is it that prompts such a foolhardy, idiot's return?"

"I don't know, Marty," answered Morcey in an even, quiet voice. "Maybe they're just bored. You know how bad the tube is these days."

"No," answered Tabor facetiously. "But what about the miracle of cable."

"Not really any better."

"No—not cable, too?"

" 'Fraid so, Marty."

"My, my . . . the poor babies. I guess then we'll have to give them a little entertainment of our own."

As Morcey kept his place, lying on the cold black bags, his peripheral vision caught glimpses of the crowd around him. He watched in horror as the people pointed at Tabor, gawking and taking pictures, encouraging their children to go closer.

Whatda'ya stupid assholes think is comin'? he thought, knowing that to scream a warning would only redirect the vampire's wrath at him. For Christ's sake, start runnin', you morons. Can't you feel it comin'? *Can't you?*

But his mental entreaties did no good. As Tabor smiled, people continued to edge closer, despite the warnings of the police. The majority of the officers had busied them-

202 *Robert Morgan*

selves with trying to keep people back, but five had broken away, working their way toward the floating figure. As they moved in slowly the highest ranking of them called out to Tabor, the trembling in his voice giving away how confused he was, how unreal the situation seemed to him.

"You . . . in the sky . . . identify yourself."

Looking down at Morcey, the vampire smiled, saying,

"Now, look at what a good friend I am. I've gotten you a front-row seat for tonight's extravaganza."

"This is the police . . ."

Pulling on imaginary gloves, Tabor spoke to Morcey in a breathless, excited whisper,

"I guess it's show time once more."

"I repeat . . ."

"Lights . . ."

"Identify yourself . . ."

"Cameras . . ."

"Now."

"Action."

Spinning around to face the policeman below, the vampire threw his hands wide, placing himself between the sun and the officers, throwing his shadow across the land. People screamed, the sounds of their nervous release a drugging music to Tabor. In a voice as loud as he could manage, the vampire shouted down to the people below,

"Identify myself? But of course. I am the soon coming death of you."

And then, without another thought, the vampire turned and faced the five policemen. Concentrating on the closest, he began sucking the life out of the man. The officer trembled, not knowing consciously what was happening to him. Without understanding why, he felt his joints tightening, his brain thickening, his blood freezing—drying in his veins. Listening to the fear screaming through him, he gave in to the demands of his unconscious mind and raised his weapon, firing.

The bullet found its intended target, passing completely

through Tabor's body. The vampire looked down at the officer, smiled sweetly, and then said,

"Ouch."

Not hearing the vampire's joke or caring what it might have been, the policeman fired again and again, discharging his weapon until it was empty. None of his subsequent bullets had any more effect than the first. The officer stared in amazement, wondering how such a thing could be. He had been a good man, a good husband, a good policeman.

"How?" he gasped, and then fell to the ground. His body, completely devoid of liquid by the time it hit the street, burst open on impact, the dust which had been his fluids—blood and bile and all the juices of life—swirling away in the wind. By this time the other policemen had opened fire as well. Their bullets tore through Tabor, blowing chunks of him away, shredding his clothing, spraying his blood in the air.

Laughing, the vampire sucked the life from them one by one. As other officers made their way forward, adding their firepower to that of their brothers, they also were murdered, their lives gobbled down by the blood-soaked maniac floating about the street. Uniformed bodies dropped one after another, their skin brown and cracked, eye sockets dry and empty, hair brittle and withered. And then, finally, when all the police had been destroyed, the vampire turned on the crowd.

Tabor targeted groups at random, calling their lives to him like show dogs, replenishing himself a dozen times over. This time the crowd ran and kept running, but it did no good for the unfortunate ones Tabor picked out. The vampire sucked in the energy of hundreds. The damage done to his physical form was repaired and forgotten. Indeed, he had summoned so much human power to himself so quickly that he found he had to release some to keep from burning himself out. Happy to do so, he shouted,

"Here you go, winks! Here's some fucking entertainment for you."

Releasing another energy bolt, he sheared away a large

section of the top of a nearby building, hitting it at an angle so that the debris would slide down into the street. Scores were crushed to death, the vampire instantly sucking in their force, using the new energy to kill even more people. Targeting several distant vehicles, he reached into their gas tanks, releasing sparks, exploding them at random spots. Dozens died horribly, burned to death in their cars, torn apart by flying pieces of fiery steel and glass, or simply trampled to death by the fear of those around them.

Tabor laughed, using their lives to keep himself suspended in midair, to kill more, to frighten even more. Shouting out to Morcey, he called,

"London taught us! We'd always believed you had to club a person down yourself—that long-range killing wasn't possible. Well, Mr. London taught us different— didn't he?! Didn't he, you miserable little wink?"

Tabor, suddenly enraged that the ex–maintenance man had not answered him, spun around, ignoring the crowd, returning his attention to the spot where he had left Morcey. The spot where Morcey no longer was. Outraged, the vampire incinerated the spot where he had left the balding man, screaming,

"I told you not . . . to . . . move!"

Yeah, thought the balding man, making his way through the restaurant, that you did, you humpin' sonofabitch. That you goddamned did.

Desperately, Morcey searched for a weapon, anything that he might use against the vampire. As he looked, a dazzling light filled the large glassless area that had been the restaurant's front windows. Tabor had released a series of bolts that had reached the gas lines under the sidewalk. The first explosion had rocked the street and all the buildings along both sides, almost knocking the ex–maintenance man off his feet.

Turning away toward the kitchen, forced back by the raging heat boiling into the restaurant, Morcey suddenly noticed Swartz's fallen body. Racing over to it, he found the police's interrupted evidence examination. The contents of Swartz's pockets—his keys, a roll of Life Savers, wallet, pens, spare change, half-moon quick loads—all of it had been piled neatly next to his .357.

"Sweet bride of the night, Swartz, you just may have saved the world."

Running across the restaurant for the gun and ammunition, a voice in Morcey's head sounded, reminding him of what use guns had already been against the vampire.

Yeah, thought the balding man, what else am I supposed to do—spit at him?

You don't have enough spit.

Thanks, he growled at himself. Good to know that even my own fucking brain isn't on my side.

We are on your side, answered the terrified voices in his head. We are you. We are all there is. That thing out there is coming for us. Everything it's done so far has just been the warm-up act. Killing us is the big event.

Grabbing up the gun, the ponytailed man told himself, "Then, we'll have to do our part to make it a sell-out performance."

You're fat and old and tired and you haven't got a chance, responded his need for self-preservation with a desperate scream that filled his head. Bullets don't kill him.

"Yes, they do," Morcey answered with a grin, loading the cold gun he had taken from the floor. "I've seen them do it."

And then, out of the rolling flames eating away at the front of the restaurant, Tabor stepped inside, his eyes locked on the ex–maintenance man. His clothes aflame, he raised his hands to release another energy bolt, screaming,

"Die, janitor!"

Morcey brought up the .357, shouting back,

"Fuck you, ya geek!"

And then, they both fired.

30

"Mommy! Mommy! Mommy!"

"What is it, child?" asked Mama Joan, concern filling her voice. The elderly black woman had raised more than one child in her time—those that were hers and those belonging to other women—and she knew the noises children made. She knew when they were teasing, when they were bored, and when they were frightened. Thus she knew which kind of sound little Kate was making, and the fear rose so high in her that she actually had to beat it back with force.

Be gone, she snapped at the building terror in her head. I got no time for you.

Then, bending down on one knee to intercept the child running toward her, she caught the little girl up and lifted her into the air, shushing her and stroking her hair all with one motion, asking,

"Hush your shouting, demon child. What for you be wakin' up ol' Mama Joan?"

"Mommy, Mommy, Mommy, Mommy . . ."

"Yes, child, I understand. Where's your mommy now, little darling?"

"On the floor, she fall, she fall, Mommy fall down in the green room. Green room, *green room*! Mommy on the floor. Mommy, mommy . . ."

Mama Joan kept on comforting the child, carrying her back through the maze of halls that made up the old woman's bunker home to the room she felt sure had to be the one Kate was referring to. Coming into the greenhouse that took up half the building's second floor, Mama Joan called out,

"Lisa, Lisa girl . . . I got a mighty frightened little girl here with me." When no answer came, the old woman called out again,

"Lisa?"

This time she was rewarded with an answer, not from Lisa, but from her son.

"Back here. Mommy's back here."

Following Kevin's voice, Mama Joan found Lisa lying on the floor in an awkward heap, her arms and legs jerking spastically. Several clay pots lay shattered on the ground near her, looking as if she had pulled them down with her when she had fallen. The old woman noticed absently that the dirt and plants had spilled out of them. The fact that they had been somehow charred caught her immediate attention, however. Sniffing at the air, Mama Joan found the regularly humid air of the greenhouse thick with singed ozone. Lisa's clothing was traced over with burn marks, as was her hair.

Bending down, the old woman reached out to touch her. Kevin, however, who had been keeping his distance, grabbed at Mama Joan's hand, telling her,

"No. Don't touch her."

"I'm not gonna be hurtin' your mama, sweet boy."

"No, it'll hurt." Kevin raised his hand, showing it to the old woman, saying,

"I touched her and I got a shock."

Mama Joan looked down at the boy, then at his mother. Kevin's face was a mask of serious concern. She wondered at his calm and self-possession, so detached from the scene at such a young age. She noted that Lisa, on the other hand, had begun to calm down, the shaking of her legs and arms having slowed noticeably. Pushing Kate gently toward her brother, the old woman said,

"I'm what they call elderly, boy—it means I've been around long enough to have had all kinds of shocks in my life . . . some I hope you don't never need to know about, neither." Giving him a smile that showed teeth and a quick wink, she said,

"Let's see if I can figure what kind of shock done been come to your poor mama."

And then, reaching out, the woman took Lisa's arm in her hard, old fingers. Instantly she felt the current still

passing through the young woman's body. It had dwindled
to only a mild tickle, but Mama Joan could tell that for
even a trace of it to remain, Lisa must have received a se-
vere shock of some kind. Bending over the young woman,
putting her ear to Lisa's chest, the older woman wondered,

What done happened here? What kind of damn darkness
be crawlin' 'round my house now?

Feeling but the slightest movement from within Lisa's
chest, Mama Joan took the younger woman by the shoulders and pulled her up from the floor, cradling her as
gently as she could. Instantly the children rushed forward
but the older woman put up her hand, ordering them to
stay back.

"You babies wait now. Let me get your mama on her
feet before you two go smotherin' her. She the one that
been hurt now—you two be fine. Worry about her for a
minute . . . not yourselves."

Mama Joan slid her old hands under Lisa's back, ignoring the electrical shocks still running through the young
woman. Then, just before she started to lift her, she turned
back to the children and said,

"I'm sorry, sweet ones, but that just the way the world
is some times. Just the way it is. You too little to be
worryin' 'bout things, though. You stop worryin' . . . you
let old grandmama take this thing now."

While Kevin and Kate stood back, nervous but calm for
the moment, Mama Joan gently pulled Lisa up off the
floor, resting the young woman's head on her shoulder.
Holding on to her, rocking her back and forth, she sang in
her native tongue into Lisa's ear. It was a soft, faraway
song, and its tone made the children feel better, although
they did not understand the words. When they questioned
Mama Joan as to what they were, she told them,

"Your mama had some bad shock. It hurt her soul . . .
made it fall out her body. I'm just callin' to her, to her
soul . . . tellin' it how to find its way back."

Suddenly Lisa's eyelids began to flutter. One eye
opened a hairline crack, then the other. Finally she opened
them both wide, only to have to close them again against

the bright lights of the greenhouse ceiling. Lacey came in at that moment, asking what the problem was. Mama Joan only told him that the lights were too bright, and to please lower them as he went back out to check their defenses and to put all the others in the building on the alert.

"If the only problem is de lights, ol' woman," asked Lacey as he snapped off the main growing arc lights, leaving on only two much smaller wall lamps, "den why be we need to check de defenses, and jump everyone around checkin' guns and lookin' under all de beds?"

"Because, you lazy tree monkey," answered Mama Joan, looking down at Lisa, smiling, trying to keep the younger woman calm with her expression alone, "guns need checkin' and beds needs looked under once in a while."

Then, looking up, the old woman turned her head away to stare at Lacey and let her face drop into a fierce, dour mask. In a thin growl laced with menace, she said,

"Don't be questionin' me—not now, not ever. Just be on with doin' what you tolt. Dat all you have to worry 'bout. I be to worry 'bout these babies. Now go and do as you been tolt . . . and send somebody up with some soup from the stove for dis poor girl."

As Lacey left, grumbling, Lisa's shallow breathing choked off for a second, then deepened. She sputtered and coughed for a moment, then calmed down again. And finally, after a few more seconds, she smiled up into Mama Joan's face and said weakly,

"Hi."

"Hello to you, too. What happened here you burn up all my pretty tings?" Speaking in the softest of whispers, her voice quiet and distant, Lisa said,

"It was Teddy. I could see him."

"You saw Daddy?" asked Kevin, excitement over his mother's news chasing away his fears.

"Where's Daddy, Mommy?"

"He wasn't here, darlings. He was still far away. Far away from everywhere."

"You mean he was on the dreamer plane?"

"Yes, Kevin," answered Lisa, just realizing herself that that was what she had meant. "Yes, it was the dream plane. But it was different. Some part of it Mommy's never seen before."

"Was it a vision?" asked Mama Joan. "Or was you there?"

"It was like a real dream, but I was there."

Lisa tried to make it to her feet, but found herself too weak to stand without assistance. Mama Joan gave her the boost she needed, then helped maneuver her to a chair. As one of the old woman's security crew came in with a tray holding a spoon and a bowl of thick broth, the younger woman said,

"I was awake, but there was suddenly just . . . a tunnel, sort of—I don't know how else to describe it—in the air right in front of me. I could see Teddy across from me, in what looked like an ancient city."

Mama Joan fed Lisa a spoonful of broth, and then another. Taking the spoon from her, the younger woman fed herself another mouthful, drinking down its warmth. Then, letting her next spoonful cool, she said,

"I saw a man all in white come up behind Ted and throw . . . throw . . . a lightning bolt at him. I reached into the tunnel without thinking, trying to stop it—to warn Teddy. I wasn't really thinking, I just acted." She swallowed the mouthful of soup, then said,

"That's when I got hit by the lightning."

Turning toward her children, she set the soup and tray aside and told them,

"Darlings, I think Daddy's hurt. And I have to go to help him."

Four large eyes stared up at her, wanting to know everything but not having the words to know how to ask for it. Holding her arms out to both of them, she waited as they ran forward and buried themselves in her embrace. As they held on tightly to her, she said,

"Now . . . I have to go right now. You stay here, and you listen to Grandmama Joan. Do you understand?"

Both children nodded their heads, fighting to be brave,

not knowing why they should, but doing it because they knew from their mother's tone that they had no choice. Still clutching her side, Kevin asked,

"Can't we go with you? Can't we help?"

"No," she said, smiling into his face. "And I've got no time to explain why. Mainly because I don't know what's happened to Daddy. I just know—deep inside—that if I don't go to him something bad's going to happen."

Kate and Kevin looked at their mother as she stood up, gently shoving them back toward Mama Joan. They were young and confused, and certainly frightened, but their parents had never lied to them, and they knew they had no choice other than to listen to their mother. Kissing them both on the forehead she said,

"You mind Grandmama, now, and you take care of each other." Then she closed her eyes, pulling the edges of her will together into a tight ball at the center of her being. Crushing it down into its smallest form, she told it what she wanted, and then put all of herself into making it happen. She had never before gone to the dream plane without first going to sleep.

No time for that now, she thought, adding, besides, if he can do it, I can do it.

Then she concentrated on her husband's face, and all he meant to her, and whispered to her children,

"I love you both."

And then, before their eyes, she disappeared.

London lay where he had fallen. All around him white blobs danced in the distance, refusing to come into focus. In his mind he understood that they were people, but the lightning bolt that hit him had dilated his eyes too severely for him to see anything clearly.

All right, he told himself, so you can't see—big deal. You've got other senses—start using them.

Just grazing the surface of the polished marble beneath him with his fingertips, the detective tapped into the currents running through the ground. Feeling his way around, he was able to pinpoint the positions of all the people closest to him. In the meantime, his sense of smell brought him indications that something was not quite right with those around him, even for residents of the dream plane.

This bunch doesn't sweat. And their clothes don't collect dirt, either.

The smell of his battle in the restaurant still with him, the detective kept himself from smiling as he thought,

Well, I do. And I have before. And I get dirty, too. But not this bunch. Which means that there's something phony about this setup.

As London ran through his options, the part of his mind that kept a watch on the crowd let him know that one of the surrounding forms was moving toward him. His hearing, measuring the length of the strides being taken, combining the information with the weight of each footfall, let him know that it was the determined man in the business suit.

Yeah, he thought, the one the woman called "Zeus."

Several of his ancestors urged him to struggle to his feet while he still had the chance. An elder Germanic tribesman, however, a voice the detective had grown to respect, told him in flat tones,

Stay flat. Let him come to us. Crawling back up one knee at a time loses the crowd. He has the numbers and the power on us. Surprise is all we have.

Certainly, snapped the voice of a seventeenth-century cleric. That is, of course, *if* we can surprise him.

I lived to be eighty-seven years by never giving in. You surrendered at all turns, gave no offense, turned every cheek, and still died at thirty-two. The Germanic voice chuckled softly, then added,

On your knees, I believe.

Crossing the marble expanse, Zeus called out to the gathering Parliament of Confessors,

"So, this is the powerful and mighty Theodore London who has had everyone tied up in knots. The one you thought we could not bring low without some great master plan. Look at him, stretched out like a worm after the rain."

Let him yammer, advised the ancient German. He's coming right for us. So he can stand close and look like some great heroic champion for having shot us in the back.

Zeus strode across the stone plane with a steady pace, turning often to put himself within the line of sight of his fellows. Moving his arms exaggeratedly, making expansive gestures, he continued to berate those around him, shaming them relentlessly.

"Are you all not feeling just the least bit foolish now? Fretting and moaning like old washerwomen . . . terrified of *that*." Pointing at the detective lying still in the distance, he said,

"Mortal. Nothing more." Coming up alongside London, the ancient king of the gods nudged the detective with his foot, saying,

"They haven't changed much over the centuries."

"Neither have you, pal."

Shifting his legs to either side of Zeus's, London locked his ankles and then jerked his legs forward, pulling the god's legs out from under him and knocking him onto his back. Springing to his feet, the detective came up along-

side Zeus and kicked him in the head—twice—catching
him squarely in the ear with the toe of his boot both times.
Then, before Zeus could orient himself, London jumped
up and came down on one foot, planting his heel directly
on the god's Adam's apple.

The detective stepped off the godling, but only let one
foot touch the ground. Spinning himself around with the
momentum from his dismount, he came around to face
Zeus again, slamming his heel across the godling's chin as
he began to rise. The massive figure snapped back violently, then fell hard, not moving again once he hit the
ground.

Taking a step back, his sight almost returned to normal,
London surveyed his handiwork. Little over a yard away
from him—if he could believe what he had been told—lay
Zeus, the king of the gods, arms outstretched, legs akimbo,
his eyes closed and his breathing staggered.

Yeah, thought the detective, Zeus. Sure.

Why not? asked one of the voices in his head, swiftly
followed by another, which asked,

Why not indeed? After all, if you're willing to believe
that just a short time ago you were breaking bread with
Hercules . . .

All right, London offered, fine. That's the one and only
Zeus over there with the broken nose and I'm the one that
laid him out for the count. You'd think they'd build gods
out of sterner stuff.

Then, deciding to go with what he had been told, the
detective turned to face the crowd of white-clad men and
women around him, crying out,

"All right, which one of you Good Humor peddlers
wants a piece of me next?"

London could sense growing indecision in those surrounding him. Playing on that, he snarled,

"What? All it takes to back you flatheads into a corner
is knocking down loudmouth here? This gasbag throws
around a little electricity and you're all kowtowing? You
do know that this is the dream plane, for Christ's sake.
Anyone can throw around lightning here."

And then London snapped his fingers. Instantly the heavens darkened, the sky filling over with thick black clouds. Then, just as quickly, the dark blanket split open, showering the marble towers all around the detective with a forest of lightning, lighting the sudden night with a violent strobe effect until he finally allowed the discharge to die away.

Surveying the crowd as the last of the lightning faded from sight, he searched for those giving off the kinds of vibrations that would indicate that they might stand up to him. The lack of those capable of resistance relieved him. It also filled him with more questions.

Just what gives here? I'm beginning to think these bozos didn't have any kind of plan when they suckered me inside their little playground here.

"Very astute observation, Mr. London."

The detective turned toward the voice to find a thin, elderly man, one shorter than he by almost a head, coming toward him. The man walked with the help of a stick and wore a sort of half-toga, half-poncho affair, which London could not identify. Sensing no hostility from the approaching figure, the detective moved a few paces away from Zeus, who was still sputtering on the ground, trying to regain his composure, and then asked the newcomer,

"And who might you be?"

Raising his head, the old man showed London a brow covered with thinning gray hair which surrounded a solid face centered on a hawklike nose. Smiling at the detective, the old man told him,

"I was once called Abram. But if you know your Old Testament at all, then the name Abraham should be all the introduction I need." Not allowing his face to betray his amazement, London answered,

"I've heard of you. How's your nephew's wife?"

The ancient holy man, the personage agreed to be the first worshiper of a single God, bit at his lower lip gently, nodding his head.

"Is that all of the story you know, Mr. London? Is that all they remember in this day? Were the five cities of the

vale of Siddim so completely rent asunder that no one re-
members what happened there anymore?"

"Sure they remember," answered the detective. "But the
thought of people getting turned into pillars of salt is still
a pretty scary one."

A sad look crossed the patriarch's face. As London
checked on Zeus out of the corner of his eye, Abraham
spoke in a faraway voice, saying,

"I was always sorry I did that. But at the time I didn't
understand, you see."

"Didn't understand what?"

"This," answered the old man. Turning around with his
arms stretched out to either side, he gestured to the wide
expanse around the two of them, saying, "All of this . . .
what you call the dream plane."

As London stared at Abraham, not knowing what to say,
the ancient holy man began to move off toward the crowd.
Sensing a change in the mood all about him, the detective
decided to go along with him. As they walked, the elder
told him,

"The story you know, I assume, is that the voice of God
spoke to me. Told me that Sodom would be destroyed. I
begged God not to do it . . . to spare the city if there were
but fifty righteous people within its walls. And God told
me he would do this for me."

"That's the story I know, all right," agreed the detective.
Barely hearing London, however, the patriarch continued,
saying,

"And then I beseeched God further, asking, 'but, Lord,
what if I can find but forty-five righteous?' And he told
me that forty-five would be enough. And I pleaded again,
begging that would he not spare the city for the lives of
forty, and again God said that this would be enough to turn
his wrath."

As the two moved, the throng of white-clothed men and
women parted, backing away to allow them to pass. The
detective noted the fact, wondering if it were a courtesy, or
if they just did not want to be in the line of fire when the
next attack started. Hera had been distracting him when

Zeus attacked. Who, London wondered, might be waiting to strike while he listened to Abraham?

"And so we bartered down—forty to thirty-five, thirty-five to thirty, thirty to twenty-five, to twenty, to fifteen, to ten . . . to five and down to one." The ancient holy man turned to the detective, shaking his head, smiling sadly.

"Down to one. Who did I think I was?" he asked. "That I would argue with God so? I was so humble, I didn't even stop to think of what a great person I must have been—to bargain in human lives with the Supreme Being as if we were haggling over the price of fish. I went into Sodom—ran as fast as I could—looking for any whom God might choose as properly righteous. And of course, as you know, there were none I could find that measured up to my opinion of a worthy disciple of the one, true God."

The two had reached a long wall, which forced them to either turn or stop. Pausing for the moment, Abraham said,

"So I destroyed Sodom for not measuring up to my standards. And when Lot's wife didn't follow my dictates, I destroyed her as well."

London said nothing, his mind trying to digest what the patriarch was telling him. As the pair stood near the massive marble wall, the elder said,

"Do you not understand? The voice of *God* in my ear? It was *my* voice. *I* did it. I destroyed the largest cities of my world. In my pride as 'the friend of God' I chose to believe that my morality was the highest."

London stared, not knowing what to say. Years earlier a professor the detective had known had theorized that the dream plane was the essence of both God and Satan, that whenever people's souls died, that was where their souls migrated to, to become part of a great well of energy to be tapped into by any who could find their way there. As if reading his mind again, Abraham looked off toward the now-distant crowd of his white-garbed fellows and said,

"Do you not see it yet? All the gods and angels and demons and saints and miracle workers you have ever heard of . . . this is where it comes from. This is the source of their power. The voices in our heads—they are not the commandments of God or the temptations of devils . . they are our own minds, telling us whatever it is we want to hear, giving us leave to clear our conscience and do whatever it is we feel we must."

Then, turning back toward London, the patriarch stared deeply into the detective's eyes, telling him,

"We have gathered here throughout history—those of us who have found the ability to manipulate this world. We have sat here, watching . . . trying to guide the world, trying to keep the same mistakes from occurring over and over . . . calling ourselves the Confessors."

Not certain he was following the elder's story, London asked,

"But I thought the Confessor was a figure who listened to people's sins, going around dispensing absolution."

And then, Abraham laughed. It was not a chuckle or any kind of polite tittering. It was full-bodied, raucous laughter which shook the stones of the wall behind them. Leaning against the cold marble, the elder said,

"No, my friend, we call ourselves the Confessors not because of the sinners we have listened to, but because of all the sins we have to *confess*. All of us . . . every single one, all of us have arrived here covered in blood. Blood sometimes meanly wrought, sometimes from the best of intentions . . . sometimes, when achieved by fools like myself, through pride." Abraham brought his head up to again stare into London's eyes. Reaching out, the patriarch touched the detective on the sleeve, telling him,

"And now you."

"Me?" asked London, truly startled. "What in hell do I have to do with your little circus?"

"Through the centuries, we have named each new Confessor. Did you not think we named the Destroyers as well?" As the detective stared, momentarily shocked beyond his capacity to deal with what he was hearing, Abraham told him,

"Yes . . . you. It is your time to join us. You have tarried on the plane below long enough."

Struggling to regain control of his senses, London stammered,

"Now, now, now, wait a minute. Suppose I don't feel like joining you just yet? I like that plane below. And I've got a little unfinished business down there. Suppose I want to tarry a while longer?"

"You cannot."

"And why not?" asked the detective with a hostile tone. His eyes narrowing into slits, his fingers flexing, preparing for trouble, he asked again,

"Why not?"

"Because . . . soon there will be no plane there to tarry on." As London stared, waiting for an explanation, the ancient holy man said,

"Soon there will be a great conflagration, and all life below will cease."

"Yeah," responded the detective, "I know all about it. Tabor and his nukes. That's why I'm going back."

"We cannot allow that," said Abraham simply.

"You can't allow it?" answered London in a shocked tone. "And why the hell not?"

"My friend," said the elder, sorrow in his eyes, "who do you think gave Tabor the idea in the first place?"

And, even as the detective absorbed the patriarch's last words, all the white figures began to move forward toward him.

Morcey rolled across the floor, smothering the flames of his burning jacket. He had spun after firing his first shot, seeking to stay clear of the burst of flame coming for him. He managed to duck all but the narrowest plume of it, but that was still enough to ignite the ex–maintenance man's coat, burning him up the left side and across both his shoulders before he could snuff the fire out completely. His onetime foot-long ponytail suffered the worst damage, almost all of it burned away.

The balding man felt at the ruined end, telling himself under his breath ruefully,

"Oh well, at least Mom'll be happy."

Then, dragging himself to his feet, black smolder rising from his back, he searched through the growing smoke in the burning restaurant, looking for Tabor. He spotted the vampire standing casually in the center of a burning table.

"Not dead yet, janitor?"

"Naaahhhhhh . . . no way," replied Morcey, forcing a dark smile across his face. "I leave that walkin'-dead shit to assholes like you."

Tabor's mouth curled down into a hard line. His head shook as he spat in the ex–maintenance man's direction.

"That for you and your tough-guy pose," snarled the vampire. "This is the end of the show, little man. You and all the other winks are going to be my dinner. Tonight."

Morcey took a short breath, trying to avoid the smoke that was growing ever denser in the burning room. Fingering the .357 in his hand, he hefted it up to where Tabor could see it, telling him,

"You never know, chuckles. I took you down with one of these before. I might not miss with my next shot."

"I have news for you," responded the vampire. Putting his hand over his heart, Tabor pushed his fingers into his breast, down under the skin. Fishing around inside his chest, he suddenly extracted his hand, holding up a wad of lead.

"You didn't miss with the first one."

Then, throwing the bullet across the room, the vampire shouted,

"You lose this time. Do you understand? *You lose!* This time God is on my side. It's the end of *your* world and the start of *mine!*"

"The start of what, you dickhead? You're talkin' about blowin' up the whole planet. Where the hell do you think you're gonna live if there's nothin' left at all?"

Jumping down from the flaming table, the vampire moved through the restaurant, coming straight for Morcey. As he did he threw the chairs and tables in his way to the left and right with the force of his will alone. Drawing to within a few feet of the balding man, he said,

"Do you think I care if the grass is green or the sky is blue? I've had centuries of both, and centuries of abuse from your type and my own. But that all ends now."

Morcey listened to the vampire, looking for an opening, trying to resist the rising heat and condensing smoke in the restaurant. He had been waiting for the sprinklers to start working, but then noticed the system's nozzles had all been warped and twisted. Assuming it to be more of Tabor's handiwork, he looked for his next move while the vampire raged.

"This will be my world now—and if it has a population of one, I don't care."

"I noticed," the ex–maintenance man said, "that you didn't have too many vampires workin' for you. Mostly just winks with guns."

"Human greed, janitor. Proof you and your kind are not even fit to live. A handful of dollars and you'll help the enemy exterminate your own. No, London broke the power of the council, slaughtered most every high 'blessed' one there was. When the fools who were left brought Hercules back to life, he turned his back on them.

So, they finally turned to me, hoping I would teach them the council's secrets."

"And did you?" asked Morcey through gritted teeth, not knowing how much longer he could bear the smoke, which did not seem to bother Tabor.

"No. I killed them one by one and left them dead forever until those that were left came to me for safety. They came to me because they couldn't imagine who the killer was. But" —the vampire threw his head back, his eyes closed. With hate in his voice, he growled,

"They knew . . . *knew* that whoever it was, it couldn't be innocent little Martin Tabor."

And in the moment when the vampire's attention was turned inward, Morcey raised his weapon and fired, pumping one round after another into the monster. The first bullet exploded inside the vampire's head, shattering out the back of his skull. The next two ripped into his chest, hurling great quantities of blood into the air, staggering his body backward, spinning it around. The last two tore into his lurching body's abdomen, knocking Tabor completely over, flinging him backward into a stand of scattered, burning furniture.

Not waiting to see what effect his shots had, Morcey retreated immediately to the kitchen. Breaking through the doors to the back, he sucked in large lungfuls of the room's far cleaner air, then headed for the sink. Pulling a large pot of dark, soapy water up, he doused himself with it from head to toe, gagging with relief as he swallowed some.

Good move, hero, the back of his mind chided him. Bullets don't work on this one anymore. All you did was make him mad.

Fine, swell, good, he growled back at himself, tired of the taunting side of his brain that never gave him a moment's peace, that makes us even.

Coughing and hacking on the soapy water, which had at least soothed the burning in his smoke-filled throat, Morcey looked around the kitchen, searching for anything that might help him destroy the vampire. Knowing he had only seconds, his eyes darted from the cutting boards to the refrigerators, from the crates of vegetables and the hanging racks of meat to the massive flames of the Chinese pit stoves. Staring at the unattended fires, he thought,

Just what I need now . . . more fire.

And then his eyes lit up. Jerking a second pot of water up out of the sink, he immediately headed for the stoves.

In the meantime, out in the restaurant, Tabor clawed his way back to his feet, screaming in mindless rage. He cursed the ex–maintenance man for daring to shoot him, and his own foolishness for giving him the chance. Throughout the entire conflict he had stayed in the background, using others, playing his rivals in the council against each other, sending humans to kill humans, protecting himself at all costs.

But, he told himself, you just had to get the little, fat bald man yourself, didn't you?

Yes, he answered, willing his body to mend itself, forcing his bones to knit, his head to reassemble. While the flesh of his face boiled, soothing and shifting, his spilled blood slid across the floor toward him. Curling up his leg, sliding across his chest and over his neck, it poured down his throat, filling him anew. Then, still not completely re-formed, but able to begin moving again, the vampire walked through the surrounding wall of flames, screaming,

"You wanted to know where it is I'll live after I've destroyed this planet . . . after I've sucked the life out of it and you and every other drop-in-the-bucket wink there is or ever will be? Did you?!"

Throwing open the door to the kitchen, Tabor stepped into its frame just as Morcey opened the door to the outside. They stood, staring at each other, one framed in sunlight, the other in darkness and flames, staring at each other. Then the vampire pointed and howled,

"I'll tell you where I'll live, you miserable piece of nothing. I'll live in a castle made from the bones of my tormentors. I'll spend the rest of eternity building it, living on your energy, harvesting your rib cages to build the walls of it. I'll gather up wagons full of arms and legs and I'll craft it over a million years. And when I'm done I'll sit on a throne of skulls . . . and yours, janitor, will be at its crown."

Spitting again, Tabor released a massive burst of flame from his hand, one twice as large as the first. But before it could travel across half the kitchen, the entire room exploded. All four walls of the kitchen blew outward, the ceiling rising away from them some fifteen feet before it crashed back down into the blazing ruin beneath it.

Morcey was thrown backward out into the street, flying across and over the length of the sidewalk, an eighty-foot plume of fire screaming through the air behind him. The balding man hit the ground on his shoulder, flopping immediately onto his face, then over completely, and then over again. His legs tangled with each other, dragging across the concrete, pants tearing, skin tearing, blood flowing freely. Two of his fingers bent backward against the street, snapping instantly. He lay where he fell, unable to move, one eye swelling shut from the force of his impact with the street.

When he had doused the flames from the restaurant's giant pit stoves, letting the room fill with gas while hoping Tabor would try to kill the same way he had the last time, he had not actually expected to live. Now, lying in the street, the pain within him screaming that if he did not have broken ribs, he certainly had bruised some, he whispered to himself,

"Not bad for an old fat man." He coughed, smoke-blackened, bloody phlegm bursting from his torn lips, dripping from his nose. The action alone doubled the pain in his body, but he did not care. Lying on the ground, listening to the screams behind him, he whispered,

"Nawww. Not bad at all."

"No, I have to admit that it wasn't," came a voice from the direction of the restaurant. "But . . . ," said Tabor as he moved across the sidewalk,

"Neither was it all that good."

London stared out across the marble plane, half watching the advancing Confessors, half scanning the field past them. Not looking at Abraham, he casually asked,

"So, now I get to dress up in a white outfit and leave the cares of the physical world behind and, and . . . what? Sit around and play cards with you and the rest of the anointed for all eternity—is that it?"

Suspicious of the detective's nonchalant manner and tone, the ancient holy man replied warily,

"Yes, that would be about . . . ah, correct."

"That starts right after we let Martin Tabor blow up the world with his little arsenal, right?"

London moved closer to Abraham, leaning in toward him menacingly, bearing down on him with such a sudden burst of intensity that the elder was sent stumbling backward.

"So let me get this straight . . . getting to live here in NeverNeverLand . . . this is my big reward for all my good service, I suppose. For all my good deeds, right? For being hero enough to let my wife and children, let alone everyone else I know, die in a nuclear holocaust."

Moving forward, following the back pedaling Abraham, the detective reached out and caught the ancient holy man's robes, then dragged them together, shouting,

"I just let them all die—their flesh stripped from their bones and then their bones vaporized in radioactive fire. And that's the final bit of nobility attached to being the Destroyer, right?"

"Let me go," answered the old man in a trembling voice. "You cannot lay hands on me this way. I am one of the only to have taken your side. I protected you."

"You protected me? From what?"

"From Zeus—who would have destroyed you if he had had his way."

"Yeah, I know," drawled the detective. "I might point out that you didn't do much side taking when he was throwing lightning bolts at my back."

"Unhand the patriarch," came Zeus's voice echoing across the vast sheets of marble.

"Or what?" sneered London, whipping around to face the godling, dragging a stumbling Abraham along behind him. "You and your boys will take care of me?"

"You know not what you are doing, nor whom you are defying, young one."

"Then stop playing the sanctimonious shmuck and start cluing me in." Pulling himself up to his full height, the detective threw the force of his spirit across the expanse separating himself and Zeus like a physical challenge slapping the onetime king of the gods with his presence alone. Enraged at London's effrontery, the godling roared

"We have tried to teach . . . but you have learned nothing!"

As scores of white-robed figures crowded the marble plane, turning it into an arena, the detective kept a tight grip on his hostage. Despite the old man's struggles, he could not worm his way out of London's grasp. But knowing such an advantage could only work for so long the detective shouted back,

"I know nothing about *what*? Try teaching me a little less subtly. Like, just come out and say what it is you've got on your mind."

Zeus moved forward, his left hand held up next to his head, palm forward, indicating that the others should hold back. Moving forward slowly, his feet cracked the marble flooring of the plane as he walked, steam rising from in between the shattered chips left behind.

"I will say what is on my mind, dog. The thought on the very top of my mind is that you are not worthy to stand here amongst us. You are a pretender to the powers of this realm, and you are a thief who steals the title of Destroyer a reckless whelp who understands nothing of the cosmic forces with which you have been dealing."

"Bullshit, flathead," roared London. Realizing that he could only lose ground by hanging on to Abraham at that point, the detective pushed the elder away from him, moving forward to meet Zeus once more. Rolling the sleeves of his jacket up as he walked, London continued, saying,

"There's something going on here, and as my pal Paul might say, there's not a kosher label in sight. I've been to the dream plane before, and you yokels have never been a part of it, before. Why's that, Smilin' Jack?"

"We have seen your movements here," answered Zeus. "Pitiful struggles—easily dismissed. You are a child with a sword . . . possibly just as poised to injure yourself as you are others."

"I've done pretty good so far," he answered, spitting into his left palm, rubbing his hands together. "Think back to the little dance I just did on your face."

"You are arrogant and lucky—attributes that can carry a determined individual far. But no matter that I am willing to grant that you are a determined man, this is the end of your journey. The power you steal is ours, and you shall not be permitted to squander it further."

The two figures slowed to a stop several yards from each other. The motion set the boundary of an invisible circle, a broad circumference that the pair began to pace, keeping each other in sight as they prowled.

"You're either full of shit or just plain lying, flathead, and I'm just steamed enough to wonder which it is. I didn't ask for this. I didn't ask to be the Destroyer—to have my life twisted out of shape by fate or destiny or whatever moves things around here."

"You reached into the dream plane and tapped into our essence—and now you must answer for that crime."

"Fuck you, Jack," snarled London. His anger beginning to cloud his reason, he silenced the voices in his head begging him to be calm. Instead he continued to stalk the outer edge of the ring Zeus and he had created, screaming,

"I was pulled into this nuthouse by whatever, and I

barely got out with my life. I've done nothing by coming here except almost get myself killed a half dozen times. Where you get off calling me a thief, I'll never . . ."

And then, pieces began to fall together for the detective. He stopped moving suddenly, looking at his opponent, not just eyeing Zeus, but actually scrutinizing him for the first time. Smiling to himself, he whispered,

"Well, I'll hand it to you. You almost got me."

Standing still directly across from London, the godling sucked down a long breath, puffing himself up, swelling to his full size. Staring back at the detective with his chin thrust out, the onetime king of the gods spat,

"*Almost?* Nay, you are 'got,' dog. By now, you have been here too long. You are ours, and the world below is ours, once more."

Taking a step into the invisible circle that had been separating the pair, London pointed at Zeus, demanding,

"What is this crap you keep jabbering about? Because whatever it is, do you really think I'm going to throw in with you asinine bozos—that I'm going to let you destroy the world without a fight?"

And then Zeus put his hands to his hips and laughed. As London stopped short, thrown by the godling's reaction, his opponent reached up and loosened the knot in his white tie. Then, pulling it completely free, he folded it and stuffed it into one of his white pockets, saying,

"Your world has destroyed itself, whelp. We were pushed out when men first began to think for themselves. Not to think of trade and power and gold—a greedy heart is easily deceived, and even more easily controlled. But, once men actually began to truly think for themselves, their need for us faded."

"So what's your beef now?" asked London, wary of the sudden feeling of confidence he was picking up, not only from Zeus but from the crowd around them as well. As the detective continued to uneasily face off Zeus, the godling answered him, saying,

"Because now, for the first time in two thousand years, the tide has begun to turn. Men are no longer thinking for themselves. For centuries, the ranks of those who counted themselves responsible for their own lives have grown like rust on the wheat—but now, now . . ."

Zeus rubbed his hands together, then began to draw his suit coat off. Throwing it to one of his seconds, he unbuttoned his shirtsleeves, saying,

"Now men are falling back into the wombing sleep of tribalism—collectives of human life are becoming the norm of your world, and individual thought is drowning in a sea of fear and greed. Those who cannot find a place for God in their hearts will soon find they have nothing within themselves at all."

Stepping forward, coming to within only a yard of the detective, Zeus's smile widened as he said,

"It is about to be our time again, puppy. When men lose sight of the single force that rules the universe, they will gladly substitute anything in its place. Martin Tabor will destroy all of your civilizations in one stroke. And then we will return, and put everything anew. And the Earth will flourish under our strong hand once more."

But then, before the detective could answer . . . indeed before any present could react at all, a new voice spoke from behind the onetime king of the gods. It was a voice that parted the crowd surrounding Zeus and London, one that said,

"Well, well, well, Father. I see you're up to your old tricks, again."

And then, Hercules came forward and entered the circle.

34

When Lisa had first vanished from the sight of her children and Mama Joan, she had no real idea of where she was going. Her first thought had been to get herself to London's side, to face together whatever it was that had struck the two of them down. She had never dared to step through the dream plane on her own before. Indeed, she had only done it once in the company of her husband, and he himself had dared to do it only a few times more than that.

While she concentrated, however, thinking of London and how determined she was not to lose him to whatever it was that was threatening the world anew, a sudden thought had come to her. One of the voices in the back of her mind whispered to her,

If you fly to his side, will you not only end up running into whatever has already attacked him?

The thought flummoxed her, almost leaving her lost and adrift in the nether vapors of the astral plane. As part of her tried to hug to her original course out of desperation, the same voice asked,

What kind of help do you think you can be? If Teddy's getting knocked down, what do you think you can do . . . that he cannot?

Quickly her mind turned over other possibilities, and just as quickly rejected them all. Morcey and Swartz, she thought, would mostly likely be with her husband.

But, her mind asked her, what's the first thing Teddy and Paul do whenever there's trouble?

Of course, she thought, they hide the women in the nearest closet.

And with that thought in her head, she immediately turned her concentration from her husband to Lai Wan, knowing that if there was a safe place anywhere in Hong

Kong from which she could try to help her husband, that that was where the psychometrist would be.

Thus it was that Lisa faded into view in broad daylight on the same crowded street that Lai Wan was trying to fight her way down when first she had fled after Tabor's arrival at the restaurant. So frenzied was the terrified mob in which she had appeared that no one noticed her. They were all pushing, clawing, slamming their way forward, desperate to escape the flying monster behind them. The vampire had just begun exploding random cars seconds before Lisa's appearance. Another body to push out of the way scarcely made any impression on those around the young mother.

Unfortunately, push they did. Not expecting such a reception, Lisa went down instantly. The feet of men and women stepped on her, kicked her, tripped over her and fell on top of and beyond her. As the panic of the near mindless crowd worsened, Lisa called out from within her head,

Lai!

Instantly the psychometrist stopped, jamming herself firm against the pressing crowd, refusing to be budged by them. As some tried to push her out of the way, she released deep-buried memories from within her mind, leaving them on the surface of her skin. Any who touched her instantly sucked in the horrific memories which she had picked. In a half dozen seconds, the group mind of the herd had sent a subconscious message through all the members nearby to avoid the woman in the black shawl.

Turning from left to right, Lai Wan searched for her friend. When her first instinct to use her eyes failed, she pushed her senses down into the pavement, feeling about for her friend. Unavoidably, the gibbering terror of the crowd crawled into her, biting at her resolve. Fearful, mindless voices screamed in her head, pushing, shrieking, demanding that she join in the same animal panic consuming everyone around her. Tears rolled down her face as she rejected the agonizing cowardice of the crowd, finally zeroing in on her friend.

Shutting herself off from the mob around her, the psychometrist made her way to Lisa's side, pushing people aside, helping her friend up off the street. Locking hands, the two knew better than to try and speak in the center of the nightmare the avenue had become. Instead, they headed for the nearest building, speaking inside their heads through the physical connection of their fingers.

Lisa, asked Lai Wan, what are you doing here? How did you get here? Kate? Kevin?

Lisa quickly explained what had prompted her journey, letting her friend know that the children were fine, but that London was not. The psychometrist told her story next. Flooding Lisa's mind with pictures, she let her friend know where everyone else was as well as showing her what had caused the crowd's panic. As the two reached the sidewalk and then forced their way up against the closest building, Lisa screamed over the mindlessly loud noise of the street,

"What can we do? We've got to help them both. Paul can't hold out against that vampire long, but Teddy . . . whatever he's facing, I don't even . . ."

Holding up her hand, Lai Wan lay two of her fingers against her friend's lips. Then, when their eyes met, the psychometrist told Lisa,

"There are others here, ready to fight. Fools we would be to not use them now."

Lisa gulped, forcing away the contagious terror of the crowd around her. Then the young woman nodded her head, saying,

"You concentrate on where they are. I'll get us there."

"Are you sure you can do this?" asked Lai Wan. She could see the dark rings under her friend's eyes, feel the shaking dread in her trembling hands. The psychometrist could tell that the trip from New York to Hong Kong—the strain of moving her physical form thousands of miles across the astral plane—had greatly taxed her, perhaps far more than she knew. She could see that Lisa's nerves were jangled, fractured. Feeding her friend as much positive energy as she could through her touch, she asked quietly,

"You have just spanned half the world . . . and you have not done this before."

"If I just spanned half the world," shouted Lisa, "then what's another few miles? It's the end of the world, for God's sake. Holy Mother of God, what choice do we have?"

Lai Wan did not consider her friend's words any further. She merely nodded her head and concentrated on the others. As two more cars exploded, their shrapnel cutting down eighteen people, no one noticed as two women next to a store wall disappeared from view.

The shadow of Martin Tabor slid over Morcey's prone body, chilling the balding man. The sarcastic voice within his head that had been pushing him relentlessly came into his mind laughing, sneering at him once more.

We told you that you were fat and old and that you weren't going to be able to handle this guy. And now, here comes the proof. But please, don't just lay there and sulk—and get us all killed . . . do something.

The voice made a critical *tsk-tsking* sound, and then added,

Of course, even if you don't—or can't—please don't forget . . . we told you so.

The ex–maintenance man growled fiercely at his internal voices, sick to death of their constant berating of his abilities. What did they expect of him, he wondered. What more could any man do? He had faced everything that fate had thrown at the London Agency.

As the new king of the vampires moved toward him, his mind raced through the list of hell-things he had helped bring low. What could be left on the planet that he had not faced? Together, he and London had brought down ghosts, werewolves, vampire hordes, monsters from outer space and the dark beyond. They had stood toe to toe with Satan and battled against all the forces of his realm . . . and they had won.

And, he thought, I'm gonna win again.

"Mr. Morcey, having troubles, I see?"

"Nothin' I can't handle, ya rat bastard." With a superhuman effort that defied all belief, the balding man got his left hand beneath him and began to push, struggling to make it to his feet. Standing a few feet distant, Tabor clapped his hands together, saying,

"Oh, yes, come on. Stand up. Oh, please, yes. Make it to your feet so I can look into your eyes when I spill your guts across the pavement."

Behind the pair, the fire of the restaurant and the buildings to either side of it blazed, darkening the sky with its roiling black smoke. Screams and cries could still be heard in the distance, but the crowd had long since fled. Now the only people in the street, the ones Morcey had noticed but Tabor had not, were moving far more quietly than those who had just left.

We've got to keep his attention, said the balding man to all the various voices in his head. Forcing himself to keep moving, he told them: they don't get set up, we don't get dinner.

As the word "dinner" rang questioningly through his head, the ex–maintenance man smiled to himself, thinking,

Yeah—only the winner goes to dinner.

And then, gritting his teeth, pulling on everything he had, Morcey continued his struggle, putting every last ounce of strength he had into standing up.

"Don't let me down now, little man," sneered Tabor, enjoying the balding man's difficulty. "You know you can do it . . . janitor."

"Goddamned right I can," spat Morcey through clenched teeth. Moving upward, pushing with all his might, forcing away his fatigue, he gasped as a rush of pain tore across his waistline. Not wasting energy trying to ignore it, however, he ground his teeth down tighter, thinking,

Hurts? Yeah, it hurts. But it don't hurt enough. Come on . . . that the best you can do? Hurt me some more. Come on . . . hurt me some more!

And then, the ex–maintenance man made it to his feet. Reeling his head up like a man bringing in a prize fish, he pulled himself erect, standing as tall as he could. His body shaking, hands trembling, he fixed his stare on the king of the vampires, asking him,

"You like the show?"

"Indeed. Do you do any more tricks, janitor?"

"Yeah," answered Morcey, choking back the bile he could taste rising in his throat. "I tell amusin' stories. I'll tell ya one right now if ya'd like."

Tabor folded his arms across his chest, smiling at his intended victim's useless courage. Drumming his fingers against his sides, he said,

"By all means . . . an 'amusin' ' story, if you please."

"Once upon a time, there was a little shit who thought he was a tough guy."

"And that would be me?" asked the vampire.

"Don't get ahead of me," answered Morcey, wincing as the pain in his side ground away at him. Steeling his nerve, he continued, saying,

"He wanted to be the boss'a everythin', but he was, like, afraid of his own kind. So he turned on'em, and then he turned on everyone else, too. And he caused a lotta trouble, mainly, 'cause he really didn't know what he wanted. Sometimes he thought he wanted revenge, sometimes he thought he wanted ta rule the world, sometimes he thought he wanted ta live forever. But ya know what he really wanted?"

"No," answered Tabor, half annoyed, half intrigued. "Tell me."

"What he really wanted, was a friend." Morcey looked straight ahead at the vampire, through him, watching for a signal from those behind him. And then, suddenly getting it, he slipped into his best Mister Rogers imitation saying,

"Will you be my friend?"

"No," answered Tabor smugly. "I don't think so."

"Okay, folks," said Morcey. "You heard him."

And before the king of the vampires could react, he suddenly found himself rolling on the ground, screaming in pain.

Cat kept the white noise machine playing on the vampire, coaxing all the power she could out of the hand-held unit. The invisible wall of ear-shattering decibels battered the latest king of the vampires to his knees. Blood poured from Tabor's ears, leaking through his fingers as he tried to block out the terrible vibrations ripping through his head. Turning the device up to the last setting, she shouted,

"Amazing the equipment you can bring through customs, huh?"

"I am impressed," answered Morcey with all the air he had left. Falling into Lisa's arms, he stumbled out of the combat area, leaning on her shoulder heavily.

On the ground in the middle of the street, Tabor rolled in circles, trying desperately to escape the range of Cat's device. The move was a subconscious one, for the vampire had given in completely to his pain, unable to think, to open his eyes, to do anything except scream in torment.

Then, suddenly feeling the compact motors reaching their burnout point, the short strawberry blonde cut the power to her machine, yelling to Jhong,

"Go, go, go."

Flying through the air before she had given her first command, the elder martial artist hit the vampire with both feet, smashing his head into the pavement. Pushing himself upward as Tabor hit, Jhong came back down hard, landing on the vampire's spine, cracking it in two places. Then, immediately, pushing himself up again, he came down at a half turn, driving his heels down into Tabor's ribs, shattering seven of them.

Leaping off, the elder warrior landed on the vampire's back. Instantly he reached down, his left hand drawing back Tabor's head while his right pulled a wicked dark knife from beneath his shirt. And then, without hesitation or pity, Jhong drew the tempered knife across the vampire's throat, cutting an inch deep with his first pass.

His hand moving faster than any could follow, faster than he himself could even think about it, the elder martial artist cut again across the same stroke, severing Tabor's jugular and windpipe. The stroke sent torrents of blood lashing into the air. Ignoring the flying scarlet plumes, Jhong threw his knife into the air, freeing his hands so he could crack Tabor's spine in two. Then, catching the knife as it fell, he slashed his way through the back of the vampire's neck, completely severing Tabor's head from his body.

Falling back and away from the pumping blood, the elder warrior dropped the now useless head several feet from its onetime body. The corpse, still suffering from the effects of the white noise, shuddered slightly, its nerves pumping their last messages. And then the last energy fled the vampire's body, the tatters of his soul fleeing for the ether beyond, leaving Martin Tabor dead . . . for the last time.

"You shall not do this, Father," said Hercules.

"You dare speak thus to me, halfling?"

London looked over to Hercules, grateful for the help, saying,

"Your dad just doesn't like anyone, does he?" Then, noting Lai Wan coming up behind Hercules, he said,

"What brings you here?"

Before the psychometrist could answer, however, Zeus bellowed,

"Silence! Silence, all. Only I will be heard now!"

"They can hear you in Kansas," answered London, his face daring the onetime king of the gods to react. Not rising to the bait, however, Zeus said,

"What do you come here for, son—to stand with those who would oppose my will? As I have told you before, ally yourself with mortals, and pay mortal prices."

"And what other price can I pay? You give me life but

deny me a place in your heaven—leaving me to murder my way to immortality. Now, I am here . . . not by your leave, but on my own, and against you and that which you wish."

While the crowd centered on Zeus and Hercules' stand-off, London drew in on himself, pulling away from the attention of the white-suited spectators all around him. Then, when he had disappeared from everyone's field of notice, he moved off toward where Lai Wan was waiting. Coming up alongside her, he moved her back through the crowd. When they had made it to the outer reaches of the mass, the detective asked,

"What's going on?"

The pyshcometrist quickly explained what had happened to his wife, and to her and Morcey. She told him how Lisa had shifted to Hong Kong, found her, and then split their forces to try and turn the two separate tides that were now in motion.

"She wished to be here with you, as I wished to go to Paul. But we both knew where we could serve better, and thus I accompanied Hercules here to aid you against whatever we might find."

"Sounds good to me," whispered London. "And I understand bringing Herc here—good idea. But how did you know I could use him here, and what made you think you'd be of more use here than back home?"

"Before everything that happened to us today," answered Lai Wan, "I was studying the planet. Everywhere we went, I have been searching for Tabor's bombs. I have stretched my powers to their utmost, trying to feel any small sign of them." The detective looked into her eyes, expecting a positive answer. His own eyes narrowed to slits as she said,

"But I could feel nothing—anywhere. Not a sign. So today, when I ran from Tabor, when I had gone far enough so I could look and study him without him noticing, I turned my full power on him, trying to discover the hiding place of the bombs."

"And . . . ?"

"The reason I could not find them anywhere on the Earth is because they are *not* anywhere on the Earth." Gripping his hand with her own, the woman in black told the detective,

"They are *here*, Theodore. Here on the dream plane."

But then, before either of them could say more, the argument that had been growing in the center beyond them exploded as Zeus screamed,

"You will not defy me in this! The gods *will* return to the earthly plane. Mortals will again bend to the harvest as we direct, make our wine, weave our linen, roast our sheep, and entertain us with their petty concerns, as they did during the golden dawn!"

"Fie on you, Father," spat Hercules. "You preen as if you were something special. But you are not. Do you think to deceive anyone here? Has it been so long that you have forgotten that you are a mortal yourself?"

"Liar!" stormed Zeus, tiny strands of lightning sparking along the ends of his fingers.

"Liar, am I? Are you so sadly constructed that you must hide the truth even from yourself? You, Father—and all of you here—you cannot deny it. You are but men and women who learned to use the power of the dream plane—to bend its power to your will."

"Of course," whispered London. Pulling Lai Wan even farther from the crowd, he moved her back toward the marble city as he said,

"Now I understand this crowd. That's why there's no Jesus here, or Mohammed, or Buddha . . . just the petty-ego types."

"I do not—"

"People who get control of their destiny, who know what their soul is and what it's for . . . the miracle workers . . . they've been becoming gods all throughout history." Moving the psychometrist into the confines of the city, he told her,

"The real prophets . . . Paul and John the Baptist, you don't see them here. You and me, we thought we were fighting Satan once, remember? Only it was just another guy like Zeus out there, pretending to be a god. But then, at the end, the real Satan, that cosmic sludge that came pouring down at us—its touch destroying everything—that was the *real* devil. Well, I'm willing to bet it's just another part of the dream plane that we can't reach."

Stunned, almost frightened by the detective's words, Lai Wan stammered,

"Wha-what, what do you mean?"

"I mean that you and me, we're pikers. We've only walked around the center of the dream plane—that purple plane with the red dust we're used to seeing . . . that's purgatory. Heaven, Hell, Nirvana, Eden . . . don't you get it? It's all *here*. This is the place. But when real guys like Mohammed and the like leave the earth, they just don't flop around like Zeus . . . they, they, what Professor Goward said . . . they surrender their egos to the godhead."

Behind the pair, out on the marble plane that stretched to the horizon, suddenly a massive explosion was heard. A fierce blast of energy tore through the crowd, setting the various white-garbed figures screaming. There was no doubt in Lai Wan's mind that the battle between father and son had started. Paying it no mind, however, the detective staggered away from the psychometrist, caught up in his revelations. Walking through the city as if in a daze, London shouted in the empty streets,

"Jesus, Mary, all the truly good people, they all incorporated with the dream plane itself—we all do when we die. We go to whatever level we are worthy of going to, and then we wait for someone to snatch our energy free and use it for this or that, or until we get a chance to come back, lead another life, and then trade up."

Pointing out at the crowd scattering on the plane, his face pale, his eyes wide, his hair plastered to his head with his own sweat, he said,

"All except these cowards. Too full of themselves, too afraid to see if they were worthy of eternity, they clung to life here the way Tabor and his kind did down below—stealing the power to do so from others."

Getting a hold of herself, Lai Wan ran after the wandering detective. Grabbing him by his shirtfront, she said,

"But, what does it matter? If we do not act soon, these lunatics will end everyone's chance at eternity forever. Everyone's—Lisa's, Paul's, Kate's, Kevin's . . . *everyone's*!"

And then, as the tears began to roll down the psychometrist's face, London caught hold of the side of him that had taken control and forced it back to its proper size. Taking Lai Wan's arm gently, he asked her,

"Do you know where the nukes are?" When she nodded her head weakly, her eyes red and frightened, he said,

"Then let's go."

But even as the two moved off deeper into the city, on the plane, the Parliament of Confessors began to break down into factions, all either taking one side or the other or running for what cover they could find. In the center of it all, Zeus and Hercules strove against each other, waging a battle to the death with all the powers at their command. Huge chunks of the marble flooring lay broken and shattered, pulled out of the ground by Hercules, sometimes used as shields, sometimes as projectiles. Zeus had relied on his most comfortable weapon, sending bolt after bolt of fierce lightning against his son.

The onetime king struck a fearsome blow dead center on Hercules' chest, but the godling shook it off, laughing at his father's efforts.

"Despite your best attempts to prevent it, it would appear you've grown old, Father."

The son pulled free a slab of marble weighing nearly half a ton. Hurling it forward with deadly accuracy, he struck his father square in the chest, almost making him take a backward step. The hulk broke and crumpled while still hanging in the air, falling into ten thousand shattered pieces at Zeus's feet.

"And you have not grown at all, whelp."

But even as the two gods fought on in the center of all the other struggling combatants, in the center of the marble city, the detective and the psychometrist came across a

massive bronze door, one kept sealed by a series of chains.
Each link in the chains was as big around as a bicycle
wheel, looking to weigh perhaps two or three hundred
pounds each. As the pair stared at the door, Lai Wan answered the question she could feel coming from London.

"Yes. They are behind this door. All of them."

"Great. Now what? How do we get to them? How do
we even set them off? What the hell did they bring them
here for?"

"Because, Mr. London," came the voice of Hera, "my
husband has always had a sense of the dramatic." As the
man and woman turned, the goddess told them,

"He inspired Tabor in his plan, fed him the power to
make it succeed, and hid these weapons here so none
could stop it. After all these centuries, he wants to rule the
world again." With a sad sound strangling her voice, she
said,

"Even his bastard son has learned the folly . . . but not
. . . not him."

As London moved forward, approaching the goddess, he
suddenly froze as she pulled her head up, fixing him with
her stare.

"If you could somehow reach them, you would set these
bombs off now, wouldn't you, mortal? You would kill
yourself and me, my son and your companion, leave your
children without a father . . . your woman with no man,
your best friend with no wife." Hera's lower lip began to
shake, but she caught herself and stopped it, asking again,

"Wouldn't you?"

"Yes . . : I guess so."

The goddess smiled sadly, biting at her lip, turning away
from the detective as she said,

"You, female. Can you feel the devices within?"

Lai Wan fought her way through her own anxiety, reached
out beyond the massive bronze door, then answered,

"Yes, I can."

"Can you feel what I have done?"

The psychometrist returned her attention to the nukes.
Her eyes closed, breathing going shallow, she stood stock

still for a moment, then suddenly opened her eyes wide, shouting,

"Theodore!"

"What? What'd she do?"

"The bombs ... they ..."

"You do not have much time."

Out on the ruined plane of marble another lightning blast pulled itself down out of the sky, splattering against Hercules, burning him worse than any of the others. And then, just as his father turned his eye toward the city, the air went white, and the dream plane exploded with the force of a dying sun.

Epilogue

London and Lisa moved forward through the darkness, neither saying a word. They had taken the Peak Tram from Garden Road behind the Hong Kong Hilton up to the top of Victoria Peak, the highest point in all of the Royal Crown colony. There were a number of paths around the top of the mountain, many of them quite strenuous. Not caring for a workout, only wanting to see the lights of the city before they left for home, they had chosen the circular route around Harlech and Lugard Roads, which their waiter had assured them took only an hour, and which was flat the entire way.

They ducked under branches growing across the path, stopped occasionally to look at this or that building, and basically acted like any other pair of tourists. An orange-and-black moth larger around than a dessert plate flew between the two, landing on Lisa's shoulder. The pair laughed, and then London blew at the insect, but it did not move, which made them laugh again.

"Nobody's afraid of my hot air anymore."

"I could have told you that," said Lisa, smiling.

The detective rolled his eyes, but he could not help smiling, either. All in all, he thought, things could have been a lot worse.

It had been two days since he and Lai Wan had narrowly escaped the dream plane before Hera had set off Tabor's nuclear warheads. What had actually happened there, they did not know. But they had come back to find Tabor dead, and had not heard from Zeus or any of his followers for forty-eight hours. As the detective had put it just before he and Lisa had left for their mountaintop dinner,

"If they are still functioning, I think we would have heard about it."

"Then," Morcey had asked from his place on the couch, "you think this one is over, boss?"

"I sure hope so, buddy. I sure hope so."

They had debated what effect the bombs might have on the dream plane, wondering if they had actually sited Heaven as ground zero, but as Jhong had said,

"What will be, will be. Every second of every day, every creature in existence does exactly as it pleases—even the gods. And after all, since it was the goddess who set off the warheads, not you, I would think it best to not worry about the beyond. You are a father now, are you not, Theodore?" When the detective answered in the positive, the elder warrior had smiled and said,

"Then you have more than enough to think about without the added burden of worrying over the continued existence of the heavenly firmament."

"Yeah, boss," Morcey had added, "leave that to us philosophers."

"And," said Lai Wan, "what makes you think you will have such time?"

"Whatda'ya mean, sweetheart?" the ex–maintenance man asked. "It's not like we've got any kids." As soon as the words were out of his mouth, however he said,

"Oh, sweet bride of the night . . . you ain't sayin' . . ."

But one look at the smile on the psychometrist's face was more than enough to tell the entire room all they needed to know. Cat immediately handed Morcey the second half of the sandwich she had been eating, telling him,

"Eat up. You're going to need all the energy you can get . . . Daddy."

And then they had all laughed again as the Londons took their exit, heading for the restaurant on the mountaintop. Their meal had been a quiet affair, neither having much to say then. London had the Buddhist dinner, a combination plate of rice and vegetables, some spicy, some plain. Lisa had the chef's special breaded steak surrounded with broccoli and seasoned in oyster sauce. Neither of them had left a bite—not of dinner, not of the orange slices and almond cookies that followed that, or the hot

plum soup that had followed that. Once they had gotten
outside, however, they found themselves grateful for the
clear night and the fresh air and the long walk ahead.

Moving around the mountaintop, they chattered about
what had happened to them over the past few days. They
talked about the senselessness of Father Bain's death, the
uselessness of his dying for no reason. They talked of
Swartz's sacrifice in the restaurant, and of Hercules' on
the dream plane. Before long they were talking about the
end of the gods, and then of all the things they had witnessed since they had first met. Then, after another quiet
spell, Lisa suddenly asked,

"Are you sorry?"

"About what?" the detective asked, knowing what she
meant.

"About meeting me?" she explained, knowing he understood.

"You mean about having to save you from all those
monsters from Hell that followed you to my office?"

"Ummm-hummmmmm."

"And about getting picked by fate or whatever to be the
Destroyer—so that every day since I met you has either
been some kind of nightmare, fighting against some other
crazy thing, or waiting for the next one to show up?"

"Ummm-hummmmmm."

"You mean," he said, his voice taking on a less and less
serious tone as he went on, "about having you take over
my home? And having you tie me down with a pair of
kids—who just must be the worst, too-cute and too-
intelligent little brats in the world?"

"Unnh-huhhh."

"You mean," he said again, stopping them on the trail,
his voice suddenly deadly serious, "about having fallen in
love with you to the point where I wouldn't know what to
do without you? About saving the world so that I could
spend the rest of my life with you?"

"Yes," she said, sliding her arms around his neck,
knowing the answer on his lips—desperate to hear it once
more. "All of that."

"No, I'm not sorry," he told her, crushing her to him, part of his mind filled with despair at the thought of having to live even a single day without the woman in his arms, the rest of it filling itself with joy at the storehouse of memories they had already created together.

"Never."

Teddy London bent to kiss his wife, their lips coming together with the practiced ease of lips that had found each other in kitchens and bathrooms and taxicabs, on stairways and in forests and before the gates of Hell, that would find each other for the rest of eternity with the same casual ease—that would greet each other the same way every time . . . with the desperate passion of two people who knew just what they meant to each other, just how deeply, and just how much.

A firefly flew past the detective's head, its green-yellow glow bobbing as it disappeared down the path in the direction the pair had been heading. His eyes opening just as it moved by, London pointed, showing his wife the gathering of bobbing lights just ahead of them.

"My gosh," she said, surprised by the great number of the shining insects, "they're beautiful."

The fireflies danced against the stark black rock of Victoria's Peak. As the couple tilted their heads back to see just how many there were, they suddenly realized that the swarm before them extended up the entire mountainside, until they were indistinguishable from the stars above. It was a breathtaking illusion, not knowing where the earth stopped and the heavens started, and the two stared in wonder, delighted by the sight.

And then they kissed, and all around them the stars danced and fireflies lit the sky.